Escaping from the Abyss

Book III in The Crossings Trilogy

by D.L.Koontz

When you look into the abyss, the abyss also looks into you.

—Friedrich Nietzsche

Brimstone
Fiction

ESCAPING FROM THE ABYSS BY DL KOONTZ
Published by Brimstone Fiction
1440 W. Taylor Street, Suite 449
Chicago, IL 60607

ISBN: 978-1-946758-05-7
Copyright © 2017 By DL Koontz
Cover design by Elaina Lee, www.forthemusedesign.com
Interior design by Karthick Srinivasan

Available in print from your local bookstore, online, or from the publisher at:
www.brimstonefiction.com.

For more information on this book and the author visit: www.dlkoontz.com.

Brought to you by the creative team at Lighthouse Publishing of the Carolinas and Brimstone Fiction: Rowena Kuo, Eddie Jones, Meaghan Burnett, Shonda Savage, Lucie Winborne, Luke A. Wildman, and Brian Cross.

Library of Congress Cataloging-in-Publication Data
Koontz, D.L.
Escaping from the Abyss / DL Koontz 1st ed.

Printed in the United States of America

PRAISE FOR *ESCAPING FROM THE ABYSS*

The best stories are the ones that refuse to leave you, long after you've turned the last page and the books have found a permanent home on your shelf. With this series, D. L. Koontz has crafted exactly that kind of story. Grace MacKenna, with her unique abilities, her bravery in the face of the unknown, and her determination to uncover the truth, has lingered in my thoughts since I met her in *Crossing into the Mystic*. When I reached the end of *Edging through the Darkness,* I found myself so concerned for Grace's wellbeing I had to remind myself that she is a fictional character. I've been anxiously awaiting the conclusion to the series, and *Escaping from the Abyss*, with the lush description, historic details, and powerful storytelling I've come to expect from D. L. Koontz, did not disappoint. I read it—inhaled it, really—on a day when I had a million other things to do, because I could not stop turning the pages. *Escaping from the Abyss* is a powerful conclusion to this enthralling series.

Lynn Huggins Blackburn
www.lynnhugginsblackburn.com
Author of *Covert Justice*

I confess I loved Grace MacKenna from the first page of *Crossing into the Mystic*. Her tragic history, her resilience and independence, and her curiosity and maturity created instant respect and empathy. DL Koontz's trilogy is one page-turning supernatural mystery after another with each scene building to the dramatic conclusion in *Escaping from the Abyss*. Her masterful description of the West Virginia region along the banks of the Potomac river inspire a longing to wander the hills and enjoy the beautiful vistas she has described, and her compelling storytelling made me feel like an eyewitness to the action.

Felicia Bridges
Author, *International Mission Force* series
Adventuresthatinspireaction.wordpress.com

D. L. Koontz has once again delivered an edge of your seat story. *Escaping from the Abyss* is a thrilling end to Grace McKenna's story. It's a little sad to let the story go, but what a great ride it has been through the Crossings Trilogy.

Tamara D. Fickas
Contributing author: *God's Provision in Tough Times*
Columnist: *Broken but Priceless* Magazine

Dedication

*To my sister-cousin, Darlene, for more reasons than
I have space here to explain.*

Acknowledgements

For helping to bring *Escaping from the Abyss* into the world, I want to thank:

My husband, Joe, for loving and believing in me, my son, Matthew, for his encouragement and listening ear, and Joie and Megan for their continued enthusiasm.

My sweet mother, Mary, who lives on in my heart and memories.

My Aunt Janice for being the first in our family to pen a story, making me realize it was possible, and Aunt Jean for sharing a love of words with me.

Danny, for his keen feedback and boundless energy in sharing these stories with others.

Mike Hargrove, for his willingness to share his investigative insights and crime scene expertise.

Leslie C., for her astute advice and friendship.

Cynthia P., for her boundless, fail-safe friendship and huge heart.

Brenda O., Todd B., and Shannon B. for cheering me on.

My sisters and friends in the Light Brigade, for prayers, encouragement, and love.

Meaghan Burnett and Rowena Kuo, for their zeal toward these books, and for beautifully blurring the lines between work and friendship.

The rest of the staff at Lighthouse Publishing of the Carolinas and Brimstone Fiction: Eddie Jones, Brian Cross, Shonda Savage, and Paige Boggs.

The many, many clever and open-minded readers who have read these books, resonated with the characters, shared their own personal stories, and offered reviews and ideas. Thank you!

Finally, to God who makes all things possible.

We at Brimstone Fiction are pleased to bring you *Escaping from the Abyss,* the third book in The Crossing Series. In case you missed Books #1 (*Crossing into the Mystic*) and #2 (*Edging through the Darkness*), we offer the following overview of the key characters for your reading pleasure.

Grace MacKenna – Main character. Now 17 years old. Escaped an overbearing aunt in Boston to move into a remote mountainous West Virginia estate, *Crossings,* she inherited from her step-father Jack who, along with her mother and sister, were killed in a freak accident four years earlier. Due to her fragile emotions and heightened sensitivity to death, Grace develops "subtle vision" and is able to see and talk to the ghost of a Civil War hero (William Kavanaugh).

William Kavanaugh – Ghost at *Crossings.* Convinces Grace to solve his murder from 150+ years ago. Of course, he's suave, dashing, charming and oh-so-mysterious.

Clay Baxter – Incredibly handsome guy from the local town of Williamsport. Four years older than Grace, good friend of Adriana, and former soldier in Afghanistan who suffered a war injury while saving others from an IED. Sparks fly between Grace and Clay, but —thanks to Grace's Aunt Tish—they may never be together.

Seth Rendale – Another handsome guy from Williamsport. Grace's age. He's adopted, a local sports star, and a diamond in the rough. He is almost killed by a maniacal ghost in Book #1 and matures quickly from hothead to humble human. He is determined to win Grace's heart away from Clay Baxter and finds himself succeeding in Book #2.

Adriana Barrone – Grace's friend in the local town of Williamsport. A music major in college, she dreams of becoming a concert flutist. Adriana is four years older than Grace. She wants nothing to do with ghosts. In Book #2 she and Michael date before he becomes possessed by a ghost.

Michael Rosenburg – Grace's fun and jovial cousin from Boston. Eight years her senior. Son of Phil and Tish Rosenburg. He works as an engineer. Loves travel. Moves in with Grace at the end of Book #1. Is smitten with Adriana the moment they meet, but, when a ghost possesses his body (Book #2), he changes. Drastically.

Braxton Hood, Asa Garrett, Jubal McClain and Fergus Lowe – Ghosts. All four were friends of William Kavanaugh during the 1860s and fought in the Civil War together. In Book #1, Grace promises Braxton's ghost to resolve his brutal murder but discovers that the villainous ghost of Fergus may still dwell in her home. In Book #2 Grace keeps her promise to Braxton. Meanwhile, Jubal— an ancestor to Grace's deceased step-father Jack—died a natural death years after the war. Asa helps Grace in her attempts to solve Willian's murder. But to do so, Grace had to spend a terrifying night on the Antietam Battlefield.

Cassie Baxter – Clay's mother and owner of the café, the *Time Out*. Cassie never quite got over the abandonment of her husband (Clay's father), Mason. Cassie also has a daughter Reaghan, married to Sydney, and they have twin boys. Cassie finds a new romance in Book #2 but is having difficulty getting over the memories of her first husband.

Jarrod Mason Baxter – Grace "meets" and befriends this ghost along the C&O Canal towpath long before she realizes he is Clay's father. Meanwhile, Clay and his family think Mason abandoned them. Mason solicits Grace's help in solving his murder. Distracted with other murders to solve, Grace fails to tell Clay the truth about his father.

Holland Greer – Local historian with whom Grace has some rather uncomfortable encounters. He harbors secrets and is a little too interested in Grace, *Crossings,* and a gold coin in Grace's possession. In Book #2, Grace discovers he is a thief and a secret ghost-hunter, and she wonders if he could be a murderer as well.

Gwendolyn Bealle – Local librarian and busybody. Has a brother, Benny, and an odd connection to shady character Holland Greer.

Nidhi Michelson – Local bank manager. Has been kind to Grace.

Sheriff Barnes – County sheriff. Left New Orleans to get away from the "voodoo weirdness."

Henry and Greasy Jim – Two nasty home invaders who break into Grace's home demanding to be shown where the gold allegedly is hidden.

Pastor Dale – Insightful religious advisor everyone wants. He's wise, kind, easy going, fun and very knowledgeable about Biblical teaching and mysteries.

Kate Fletcher – High school chum to Grace from back in Boston. Kate has been touring France. In Book #2, during a visit, Kate faces a horrific fate in the tunnels under *Crossings* in the midst of an explosion and fire.

Hilda Hilson – Owner of Hilson's Antique Emporium. She's feisty, regal, and no-nonsense.

Lemule Chasen – Grace "sees" this ghost in Book #2 but hasn't "met" him yet. This brooding ghost may be able to help Grace resolve some age-old mysteries surrounding her estate and the town.

Josiah Sawyer – Builder of the original *Crossings* in the 1700s. Rumored dabbler in dark arts and a nefarious ghost who haunts the grounds of Grace's estate.

Enoch Crinshaw and Thadeus Fleming Calhoun – Both dead now but collected a long, sordid history with Josiah Sawyer and the gold at *Crossings* before dying.

Prologue

My mother once told me the past can steal your future if you're not careful. It's true. I allowed it to rob me of my seventeenth year.

But what do you do when the past won't stay behind you? How do you move on when memories and even ghosts literally step into your present and demand attention?

Last year, I escaped Boston to move alone into *Crossings*, the estate I inherited from my stepfather in the remote mountains of West Virginia. As imparted in two previous memoirs, I encountered souls from the past haunting my house, and my "subtle vision" matured, enabling me to interact with them, too.

The second memoir proved hardest to pen because my cousin, Michael, suffered at the grip of a demonic soul, part of my estate burned in a fiery explosion, and worst of all, my friend, Kate Fletcher, died.

At first, I attributed her death to paranormal activity since ghosts were part of the backdrop of my life, and her body had been found at the time of the fire. However, the detective investigating her death called two days later and dispelled that concern.

"Uh, yeah," he said as though paying little attention to the conversation he initiated. The sounds of crinkling tinfoil came across the line. "We, uh, we got the coroner's report back on the deceased."

The back of my neck prickled at his word choice. "You mean Kate Fletcher."

"Umm, yar der—"

"Excuse me?"

The sounds of swallowing and a whoosh of liquid came over the line.

"Sorry … eating … ton o' calls to make. The deceased … that is, Ms. Fletcher died from a meningococcal infection."

"A what?"

"She died from meningitis."

Meningitis? How could that be? I wrapped my free arm across my front, suppressing a shiver as a whisper of shame unfurled in my stomach. I'd thought her death was all about me, but it was all about *her*. Why hadn't I detected she was ill? She had endured achiness, fatigue, chills, and headaches in the week leading to her death.

"Hello?" His voice roused me from my thoughts, but the queasy sensation in my stomach remained.

"I'm here."

"Thought I lost you. Coroner said meningitis is a bacterial infection. Attacks the brain and spinal cord. Acts like the flu but can kill within 24 hours. Talked to her mother already. Mrs. Fletcher will be picking up her things."

"Kate's things?"

"In the trunk of her car. At your house. Clothes, toiletries, passport, stuff like that. You said she talked about visiting her sister in Richmond. Her sister confirmed those plans. Figure she must have packed for a visit, but decided to explore the grounds before leaving. For whatever reason, probably pure curiosity, she went into the tunnels, but never made it out."

"And nothing prevented her from coming back out?" I cringed at my own question, but I needed to know.

"She didn't die of smoke inhalation if that's what you're wondering. No signs of force anywhere. She simply collapsed and died before anyone found her. Coroner said she'da been dead no matter where she dropped."

I gripped the phone in a vice grip and tried to remain calm at his callousness. "Thank you. I appreciate the call."

"Sure, sure. She's being laid to rest tomorrow, I understand. Now you can attend, relax, and enjoy yourself, knowing that no one intentionally harmed her."

Heat prickled along my cheekbones. "It's a funeral, not a party."

"Yeah, well, in my line of work you'd be surprised how often suspects don't separate the two."

"Suspect? Are you saying I'm suspected of something?" The fire chief had closed the case on the fire since there was no sign of arson and no insurance money involved. Why would I be suspected of anything?

"I'm saying things aren't resolved at the house, and I think you know it. I'm going to share my files with the local sheriff. But I'll be keeping my eyes on all this."

When I clicked off the call, I vowed to keep as low a profile as possible.

I should have been relieved that paranormal activity was not involved in Kate's death, but I was left desolate, hollowed out in ways I wondered if I'd ever settle, and thus began a year of mourning and self-imposed seclusion. For six months, September through March, I grieved and blamed myself for not recognizing her symptoms as dire. Guilt plagued me. I had been distracted during her visit by supernatural activity. I wandered through the tunnels after she went missing, but the labyrinth was so expansive and inky black, I passed her body without realizing she laid there.

After the fire, Michael and I fled *Crossings*. He recovered and relocated closer to work, forty-five minutes from me while I moved into my friend Cassie's garage apartment across the river in Williamsport, Maryland. The new locale soothed me like aloe on a burn as the diversions of town life wafted to my windows, reminding me that life moved on: the rich aroma of coffee brewing at the café next door, music pounding from passing vehicles, and the laughter of children passing as they scampered to school. Those reminders of life sustained me, even as my own life went stagnant.

I haven't much to report about my period of mourning. I spent little time with my friend, Adriana, and even less with Clay and Seth, both local young men I'd grown to love. My history and romantic feelings for them were sweet *and* bittersweet. And confusing.

I plodded through homeschool classes online but otherwise excused myself from social functions, avoided commitments, eschewed dates with Seth, and ignored my promise to Clay's dead father's ghost to resolve his murder.

After six months of this hermit-like life, on a cold day in March, Michael and my friends—Cassie, Adriana and her family, Seth, and Pastor Dale—staged an intervention and demanded I return to the pulse of life. In an attempt to appease them and keep them at bay, I made an effort (although, if pushed, I couldn't name much I did) and agreed to move back to *Crossings* when I turned eighteen, six long months away. It struck me as a safe pledge to make at the time.

These promises and half-hearted undertakings also resulted in me working part-time at Hilson's Antique Emporium. I first met Hilda Hilson the week before the fire when I discovered her shop in Williamsport, although I had bee-lined it out of there after she demonstrated an unusual interest in me.

Let me begin my story at this half-hearted step out of my seclusion, shortly after the intervention and when I returned to Hilda's shop. A chance encounter that day proved to stick with me, even brewed in me, for months until my eighteenth birthday when I finally was thrust back into life and endured my final showdown against certain souls—these rulers of darkness and spiritual forces of evil, plaguing my estate and my life.

CHAPTER 1

Late April

Hilda Hilson smiled and accepted the employment forms from me. She donned wire glasses to read the top line. "MacKenna? That's your last name?"

I nodded, not surprised at her question. Seven months ago, on my first and only visit to her antique shop before today, she said her sister's name was Lavidia Kavanaugh.

Yes, *Kavanaugh*, a relation to William Kavanaugh, the Civil War hero, ancestor to my late stepfather Jack, and resident ghost at *Crossings* when I moved in. I'd grown to love, then fear, Will before terminating his sovereignty over my house and life by transferring his hauntings to the cemetery behind my estate.

"Then my hunch was correct."

"Pardon?" I asked the question out of courtesy, not curiosity. She believed people were brought together for a reason. She'd said so last year. I waited for her to branch the family tree together, to explain our connection.

"You're Jack MacKenna's stepdaughter, aren't you?" She lifted her cane up then down, tapping it once in a perfunctory manner suggestive of habit, not rudeness. She didn't wait for an answer. "Bless his heart. Such a good man. So sad what happened. And your mother and sister, too. Terrible accident." She shook her gray-haired head in what looked to be genuine sadness. "His father, Sam MacKenna, married a McClain, a descendent of Jubal and Sarah McClain. Sarah was a Kavanaugh, the family who owned *Crossings* back during the Civil War."

Yep. That's how Will explained Jack's lineage one night while we chatted by a fire. As I recall, the conversation had occurred mere days before Will solicited my help in solving his 150-year-old murder.

She continued. "Your stepfather and I discussed his ancestry several times, dear."

"It's a small world," I said, attempting politeness. I began to worry excess conversation might be *de rigueur* for the job.

When I had headed to the shop, I kept telling myself I was pursuing the job Hilda posted months ago to prevent my friends from worrying. But the truth is, I was drawn to her shop for two reasons: (1) I assumed the name Kavanaugh meant a family tie, and I liked that. The significance of belonging somewhere, with someone. (2) After moving to the area, I discovered old things appealing. Their history, origins, roles in people's lives through the ages fascinated me. Even their stagnant, musty smells testified to their travels through time.

Now, here before me, stood a short, widowed, octogenarian shop owner who shared my passion for antiques. And to sweeten the deal, she shared a family tie of sorts: my something-or-other distant great-aunt once removed ... perhaps even twice removed since I was a stepchild to Jack. But in short, other than Michael, Hilda was my only relative in the area, however distant and convoluted the link. Lavidia lived an hour away, and Hilda had two grown sons in Texas and Florida.

"Jack met Lavidia, too. He appreciated the importance of family." Hilda flushed as though realizing to whom she spoke. "Well, you already know that. He came in the shop every other month or so to talk. Brought things from the old house for me to see."

I contemplated asking if he ever talked about the ghosts he met there, but I didn't care anymore. Instead, I inquired: "Really? Like what?"

"Papers, china, photographs. Things like that. Once, he brought in a gold coin, too ..." She pulled her brows together, assessing me. "Dear, are you alright? Did I say something wrong?"

I tried to hide a frown. "No, I'm familiar with the coin. I've sort of tucked it away … for safekeeping." If you can call leaving it beside a tombstone in a century-old graveyard tucking it away.

She tilted her head and offered one of those warm, pursed-lip smiles, the kind that say, "How sweet." She patted my arm twice before ambling toward a small side office, her cane thumping in tandem. "Keep it safe. It's worth a lot of money. I know a few people in this town who'd like to get their hands on it." She placed my paperwork on her desk and added in a hushed tone, "Starting with a busybody named Holland Greer."

I followed her, watching as she leaned into the cane with every other step. "I've met him." *I also called him a fraud as a historian, destroyed his reputation in front of a camera crew, and took a map from him.* "We've shared words."

"He's a piece of work, that one. Came in the shop when Jack had the coin with him. Greer couldn't keep his hands off it. Kept interrupting us with questions. So impertinent and such a rubbernecker. I finally told him to leave. If you ask me, this town has suffered—"

Bells tinkled, signaling someone entered the shop.

Hilda patted my arm. "I need to tend to this customer, dear. Why don't you store your things in the office and start dusting the shelves?" She pointed at a feather duster hanging from a nail on a sidewall. "As soon as I'm done with these ladies, I'll get you started on the spreadsheet. Later, I'll introduce you to the part-timers in the back who fill our Internet orders."

By late morning, I sat at Hilda's desk in the side office, logging figures and growing impressed with both the amount of foot traffic in the shop—the bell tinkled every few minutes!—and, especially, with the volume of Hilda's Internet traffic. She had told me her deceased husband, Arthur, had been the "blue blood sort," having funded the business initially, but that when she began selling online, "sales got quite good." Studying these numbers now, I decided sales were more like "exceptional."

A few minutes before noon, a bearded gentleman in a flawless gray jacket and tweed cap cantered through the door with a small wooden box tucked under his arm. I looked up to see him after he cleared the distance of a long row of shelves separating us. He continued to the front counter and disappeared from view. The shelves stood floor to ceiling, bulging with an uncategorized mishmash of items, from vintage hats to farm tools, making it impossible to see everything from one location.

I wanted to make a good impression on my first day, so I re-focused on my work as Hilda tended to the customer. As such, I didn't register much about him until I heard Hilda speak.

"I said no. Take it out of here!"

Her tone alarmed me. I stood, moved to peer around the corner, and froze. Behind the bearded man stood a soul, the first I'd encountered in six months. The latter was thin, gaunt, dressed like a hobo with loose, ratted clothing and weathered boots. His eyes flickered with a diabolical sparkle, and a scowl emphasized his pointy chin. The soul gazed around the shop. The disdain on his face said he found it lacking. Before I could break my stupor, our gazes met. I jerked my head toward Hilda, pretending to focus on her.

"Why not? You can see it is of good quality," the bearded man scoffed, his tone a trifle petulant. "You could make considerable profit with little effort."

"No," Hilda said, her voice low and husky.

"But it's mahogany—a rare wood, and the etching is gold leaf."

Hilda stiffened her back and folded her hands atop her cane, looking every bit an obstinate aristocrat from a bygone era. She repeated her answer, never taking her eyes off the bearded man. He countered. They volleyed back and forth two or three times, tension rising before she called my name.

"Grace. Come look at this." Her face was pale and her eyes, troubled.

I hurried toward them, doing my best to gaze beyond the soul. As I neared, he stepped closer, but I ignored him. He stepped into my path, forcing me to continue *through* him. Hilda would not have understood me skirting around what appeared to be open space. I wasn't sure if the bearded man would wonder too, but I doubted he was aware of the soul. Once beside the gentleman, I noticed his jacket and aftershave were both Burberry. *Not cheap.* This was not a bum trying to hawk a worthless item.

"Yes, ma'am?" I asked.

"What do you think of this?" Hilda pointed at the box. "Would you purchase it?"

The man rolled his eyes and shoved it toward me, but I didn't touch it. I made a show of glancing at it—at least long enough to see an odd symbol of a circle surrounding three hook-like swirls etched on the top. It didn't matter what the box looked like, not to me. It was the center for the angry soul standing in our midst, and I didn't want it in the shop.

"Well?" Hilda prodded. "It's a fine piece. Would you commission it?"

I swallowed and shook my head. "No, I wouldn't."

Hilda tried to hide a smile, but it lurked there. "Why not? Because you heard me say I wouldn't?"

True, as my new employer, I would side with her, but that wasn't my reasoning. "It doesn't belong here" ... *careful, Grace* ... "I mean, with the other things we offer."

Ugh. The emporium offered a mismatch of inventory, an eclectic collection. Couldn't I formulate a better explanation?

Hilda remained quiet, but I could tell she was pleased.

"Then what am I supposed to do with it?" the man snapped.

Hilda lifted her cane straight up and down, making a cracking sound as she said, "Burn it," with a finality startling the man.

"What? Well, I never!" The man whirled and left in a huff. With the box went the soul.

Silence descended, and I turned to go back to my work.

"You felt it, didn't you?"

Hilda's words stopped me cold, but I didn't turn to make eye contact. "Pardon?"

"The evil. You felt it."

In that instant a truth washed over me: *She* could feel the evil. That's why she turned it down. She had an ability similar to mine.

She urged again. "Didn't you?"

I turned and looked her straight in the eye. "No, ma'am. I didn't feel it." I saw it.

* * *

The next day when I reported to work, Hilda handed me more sales figures ... and an offer: "If you ever want to talk about your ability, dear, let me know."

I didn't. I wanted nothing to do with it.

After that day, I completed my home school study each morning before robotically reporting to work in the afternoons. Hilda and I kept so busy buying and selling, promoting the website, and tracking and organizing inventory, we never did discuss our abilities, Holland, or the supposed suffering of the town she had mentioned the day before.

Frankly, that was fine with me because I didn't care. Work and school filled my life. Other than that, I tried to establish a healthy routine during off hours, but I often found myself waking on the sofa at what I assumed was morning to discover dusk outside my door, or taking out the trash and arriving at the dumpster with nothing in my hands. Most of these instances prompted tears and me curling up in a corner chair or climbing in bed.

This continued for months, until my eighteenth birthday when it finally struck me: the ghosts in my world were more alive than I was.

CHAPTER 2

Early September

"If you're going to live like you're dead, you may as well be!" The voice oozed with encouragement, certainty … a ring of practicality. "Come on, Grace. Join me."

I turned to see Kate extend a hand. Her smile was radiant, eyes large with excitement, infusing her proclamation with little doubt that complete bliss resided a mere stretched handhold and one quick nod away.

The drape of her white, gauzy gown billowed and flowed in the swirling fog with gentle, rhythmic movements. I felt mesmerized, paying little attention to the others who stepped into the cocoon of mist encasing us—Braxton, Eva, Asa, Mason, Hilda's dead husband, Arthur (whom I identified thanks to a photograph on her desk), and a dark wolf-like man with pointed sleek features, a sharp protruding nose, and long talon-like fingernails. Around—but not on us—rain poured, creating a backdrop of gray and gloom.

"We'll have a blast," she continued, her gaze boring into me. "You can see your mom again. You'd like that, wouldn't you? She misses you. We can go where we want, do what we want."

"She's right, you know." I recognized the owner of the voice as Braxton Hood, and I wrenched my gaze from Kate to see him standing to her left, arm-in-arm with his wife, Eva, who nodded her head and offered a sweet smile equal to Kate's. Eva and Braxton wore formal period clothing, resembling models for a wedding cake topper in the 1860s. "You dwell in death. You speak with death. It is your calling." His voice rang with the pragmatism of a scientist and the authority of someone who brought a hundred and fifty years experience in mortality to the group. "You may as well get on with it then."

"Such nonsense," Mason said, a tone of impatience edging his voice.

"Indeed." Arthur nodded, holding one elbow and stroking his chin with his free hand.

The wolf man said nothing. He was dressed in darkness with a black hat pulled low across his face, so I couldn't see his eyes. I would have questioned if he even had eyes, but his stare pierced through his low-drawn hat brim and burned into me. I jerked my gaze away.

"She knows the truth," Mason continued, looking at Kate. "How you died." His tone rang with a dismissive authority.

"She's eighteen now," Kate blazed back, eyes narrowed, although her gaze remained on me. "Time to be held fully accountable. No more excuses or sob stories." Her tone grew harsh. "Come, Grace."

She was right. I'm not sure why I thought that, but I did. I *should* be accountable.

Kate died. I didn't.

I owed her.

But my hand wouldn't move, as if paralyzed. Or, something forbade me to reach back.

Mason spoke next, disgust evident in his tone. "Leave her alone. There is purpose to her life. You can't entice her to the darkness."

"Yes, yes," Arthur said, "let her be. My Hilda recently found her." He looked at Mason. "She must stay to carry on Hilda's work." They nodded together.

Kate laughed, a demented sound. It echoed through the earthy grotto and bounced off the sheets of drenching rain, reverberating through us again. "Gentlemen, why be so selfish? You're only using her. You," she pointed a finger at Mason, "want her to solve your murder. Admit it! You're furious she ignored you for a year. And you," she turned her focus on Arthur, "tell us what that crazy wife of yours does behind closed doors? You want Grace to get involved in *that*? Tell her the truth about what will happen once her work with you is done!"

"This is not—" Mason began, and his voice collided with Arthur who said, "You can't know—"

"Silence!" Kate bellowed, rage emanating from her eyes. She raised her arms in a dramatic sweep, and the others faded away. Even the wolf man left, but I caught the briefest glimpse of a satisfied, fang-filled grin as he parted.

I found myself alone with Kate, facing the source of the heartache I'd lived with for the past year. "You owe me," she said, drifting toward me as if floating on air. "I died under your watch."

I couldn't talk. Couldn't move. The murky mist wrapped around me in layers of thick drifts, weighing me down, rendering me incapable of flight. I could swear the wolf man chortled from the darkness beyond.

"Are you listening? Give me your hand and come with me."

As she inched closer, I sensed a different energy, a stronger life force invading the space, and Kate scowled.

"Grace! Get your lazy butt out of bed. You're *not* going to sleep through your eighteenth birthday."

I jerked my eyes open to reality and sat up, drenched in sweat.

CHAPTER 3

"**C**ome on. Get up," the newest voice continued.

I gulped air as my heartbeat steadied. Something moved on my left, and I turned to see my dear friend, Adriana Baronne, appear at the interior doorway of the above-garage apartment I'd borrowed from Cassie Baxter for the past year. A crack of thunder sounded, breaking the steady rhythm of the drenching rain that had lulled me to sleep and into my dream.

Wasn't it a dream?

... What will happen once her work with you is done ...

I rubbed my face and reached for my cell phone to check the time: four-fifty in the afternoon, although the gloom accompanying the pouring rain curtained the windows, creating the illusion of a much later hour. The drench had continued for five days and nights, a concerning development for a small, hilly hamlet like Williamsport, Maryland, back-dropped as it was by mountains shedding its rainwater into the Potomac River edging the little town.

I clicked on the bedside light. My cat, Chubbs, stretched flat on his side at the foot of the bed as though determined not to let anyone disturb him. My dog, Tramp, was nowhere in sight. At Cassie's insistence, I'd started leaving the interior door open, so he could wander down the connecting flight of stairs and into her house for a visit. The apartment's other exit led across a short deck and down a sturdy flight of stairs, all the while offering a view of most of Williamsport and the C&O Canal in the distance.

Sitting up, I feigned a yawn to explain my disorientation. "Didn't sleep well last night. Took a nap. No big deal."

Or was it? ... *what will happen ... her work with you ...*

Adriana moved closer. The aromatic smell of coffee clung to her clothes. "Get up. I'm on a schedule." She began swatting my feet. "I'm already late thanks to the rerouted traffic."

"Traffic?"

"From the bridge collapse."

"Bridge? Ouch! What are you doing?" I kicked at her hand. "Stop that! It's *my* birthday. I can celebrate it any way I want."

She stood straight, parked her hands on her waist, and scoffed. "That tributary bridge, down the hill from the bank. Indigo Street. Some guy saved a kid from drowning. Big mystery where the guy went. TV says he disappeared like a ghost. Honestly, don't you listen to the news? And no, you can't celebrate it any way you want. You have to celebrate it the way we want."

I'm not sure why, but my whole body reacted to the words *like a ghost*—jaw tightened, muscles tensed, arm hairs stood on end—but my mind fought back and refused to figure out to what my body had reacted.

Instead, I focused on the supposed celebration. "*We?* What's that supposed to mean?"

She exhaled a sound of frustration. "It means there's a surprise party for you tonight at the café. So, get out of bed and be there by seven o'clock. And act surprised." More swatting.

"What!" I scooted across the bed, away from her. "You know I hate stuff like that."

She frowned and plopped her butt onto the opposite side of the bed. "I know. But we—"

"Again with the we ..."

"Cassie and I. We want you outta this funk. So this is as much a coming-out party as a birthday celebration. You either be there, or it'll be another intervention and—"

"There's no need for another this-is-what's-wrong-with-Grace session," I said. "I've been much better these past few months." Sure, I had a weird dream a moment ago that wasn't conducive to healing, but I didn't need another intervention.

"Well, yes—" she began.

"In May, I attended your college graduation."

"True, but—"

"In June, I earned my high school diploma—"

"Yeah—"

"... and we celebrated with a Caribbean cruise."

"But, Grace—"

"In July, I showed up at the Independence Day festival."

"I know, but—"

"I even signed up for college classes, and—"

"Grace!" She thumped her hands on the bed, causing her long raven-black curls to flop forward. "Enough. The problem is that you show up for everything physically, but you're not there mentally. It's like your mind is always somewhere else."

"That's not true."

She twisted to look me straight in the eyes and folded her arms over her chest. "Name the islands we toured."

"I ... okay ... um, Antigua ... and ... one of them started with a c ..."

"Humph. I suppose one out of five ain't bad." She pulled her brows together, making her gaze downright penetrating. "Who spoke at my graduation?"

When I hesitated, she continued in rapid fire: "What did we see in New York City? Describe Michael's townhouse. What about Cassie and Whit—are you concerned? Do you like Cory's new dog?"

I'd never seen Michael's place. I meant to. And, Cassie and Whit? What was the concern? I exhaled, drew my knees close, and dropped my head into them. "I don't have those answers."

"See what I mean?"

"Come on, Ade. How would I know your brother got a dog?"

"You met Scrounger two days ago!"

That's right. I remembered it now. They'd been out walking

when I descended the exterior apartment steps to go to work.

"Never mind," she said, rising from the bed. "I must go decorate."

I reached across the divide and pulled her back. "You know," I said, watching her, "you two wouldn't plan a party for me without inviting Michael ... right? I mean, he is my cousin." Adriana and Michael had dated for a while last year, but suffered a terrible breakup when he became possessed by a demon ghost or *soul*, as Will—the ghost who had inhabited *Crossings*—had taught me to call them.

Without blinking an eye, she pulled her hand back, stood, and said, "Of course, he'll be there. He's the one assigned to make sure you come."

"He never said anything about being here." *Who else was coming?* My mind jumped from Michael to Clay Baxter—I couldn't help it. She would know; they were good friends. But I was sure the answer would be no. So why embarrass myself by asking?

"Just act surprised," she said, heading for the door. She stopped at the dresser, picked up an antique hourglass, and turned to look at me, an eyebrow heightened.

"From Hilda. For my birthday," I said, but flicking through my mind was: *Hilda ... behind closed doors ... the truth ... what will happen ...*

In a mingled tone of incredulity and bemusement, Ade said, "Still can't believe she's a distant relative to Jack."

I nodded. "Believe it."

"I like her. She reminds me of one of those old-time dowagers back in Victorian England with her perfect posture and braided hair, the way it coils around her head like a crown." Adriana giggled. "I always wish I had dressed better when I'm with her."

My phone began to ring.

I ignored it. "Ade, what about—"

"Aren't you going to get that?"

"I'll call them back." I wanted to talk about Michael ... and

Clay.

"It's your birthday for pity's sake. Someone probably wants to wish you well."

She wouldn't let this drop, so to appease her, I reached for the demanding gadget. "Okay, but do not leave! Please."

"We can talk later—"

"No! Wait. I'll make it quick."

She threw up her hands in surrender and paused her departure.

In haste, I clicked on without reading the caller ID.

"Ms. MacKenna?" a gruff voice asked. It sounded familiar, but I could not place it.

"This is she."

"Sheriff Barnes, Washington County PD. I'd like to ask you a few questions."

So far, this birthday wasn't so great.

CHAPTER 4

S heriff Barnes. What now? He had stood on my porch at *Crossings* with my Aunt Tish and Michael when Clay and I returned from a quick, harrowing trip to Georgia the year before.

"Ma'am, we're investigating the bridge collapse on the north side of town. Maybe you heard about it?"

"What does that have to do with me?"

"A man says he was saved by—"

"A man? I thought it was a little kid."

"Ah, no, ma'am, he's full grown. A Mister Jerome Knight. Black male. Age thirty-four. Wife. Two kids. Strong as an ox. Nice guy. Runs the Velocity gym in Clarksburg. Maybe you heard of it?"

"No, sorry."

"Ah, well, Mr. Knight said a stranger pulled him from the floodwater after the bridge collapsed. Which, of course, doesn't make much sense because he is a pretty large man. Popeye arms and such. But that's what he said."

I had no idea what this had to do with me, so I focused as much on Adriana as on what the sheriff said. She stepped to a tufted chair where I'd tossed the red, silky shirt I had worn the day before. Picking it up, she stroked its sheen before stretching it from neck to waist against her body and assessing her reflection in the dresser mirror. I smiled, liking her comfort with my things, but realized the sheriff was waiting, so I offered: "Maybe he's delirious."

"Nah, his wife saw the guy, too."

"I don't understand what this has to do with me."

"Ah, yes, ma'am, the hero disappeared. Like he never existed. He's not wanted for anything because he didn't have anything to do with the collapse. Act of God and all. And no one was hurt. But folks are in a tizzy about this and want some answers." He hesitated, and in a hushed tone, said, "Truth is, a dadgum reporter got whiff of this story, and it'll look bad for the force if we can't even identify the guy."

"And you think I can help? I wasn't there." I watched Adriana abandon the red shirt to step to my clothes closet and pull out a blue one.

"Well …" he took a breath, "your name keeps coming up for weird stuff like this."

Weird stuff?

I gripped the phone tighter, tasting dryness and dread in my mouth. Adriana could hear me, so I limited my response. "Stuff like what?"

"Look, I don't know. I left detective work in N'awlins over fifteen years ago because of all that voodoo and witchcraft stuff down there. Now here I am again surrounded by weirdness. Ms. MacKenna, I don't put credence in hocus-pocus, but I'm aware of other police forces keeping psychics on call … and … well, fact is, they've helped identify a few perps. The thing is … you know … what with your house and its reputation and that crazy fire last year … well, I thought you might be able to help us out."

I found it hard to breathe. The sheriff associated me with weirdness, voodoo, witchcraft, and psychics. A Bible verse Pastor Dale once shared blipped through my head: "Do not turn to mediums or spiritists; do not seek them out to be defiled by them."

How should I respond to this request?

"Hello?"

"I'm here," I answered with as even a tone as I could manage. "I don't know what good I—"

"I don't either. But my sketch artist did a rendering of the guy. I'd like you to look at it. That's all. Just look."

Agreeing to see the drawing seemed like an easier thing to do than try to argue my innocence of voodoo or weirdness, especially in proximity of Adriana. To argue would prompt him to build his case as to why I *should* take a look.

"Okay, I'll look, as long as my name is not involved—"

"Good," he said, relief evident in his tone. "There's a lot going on, what with that flood. Campers almost drowning. Roads washed out."

As he paused, I could hear thumping across the line, like he was more focused on plopping things around on his desk in a blind effort to prioritize or triage his many cases. Still, I wasn't sure why he voiced these tidbits out loud or why he sounded so frustrated until he spoke the next words in a hoarse voice, almost as if to himself. "Think we've got a missing person, too. Doesn't sit right with me ..." He cleared his throat and spoke louder. "Say, you ah ... have you seen Ms. Michelson today? Works at the bank?"

"Nidhi? You mean Nidhi Michelson? That's who's missing?"

"There've been no reports on her whereabouts since noon. So, have ya? Seen her, I mean?"

I hated to disappoint him. He sounded anxious, but I had to answer, "No, I haven't."

Through the line came a loud sigh and another thumping of papers being relocated. "Where will you be in about two hours?" Frustration laced his tone.

My heart dropped at the thought of my answer. Stifling a groan, I said, "At the *Time Out* café. Canal Street."

"I know the place. See you then." He clicked off.

I tossed the phone on the bed and feigned a smile.

"Everything okay?" Adriana asked, her gaze in the mirror as she assessed the shirt draped against her torso.

I shrugged. "Nidhi Michelson might be missing."

"What? How awful."

"But it's only been since noon."

"Well for goodness sake, she probably went shopping. I could easily kill eight hours in the mall. Like that." She snapped two fingers despite gripping the shirt.

"I didn't think police got involved until forty-eight hours went by."

Adriana smirked. "I guess exceptions are made when the cop is sweet on the missing person."

"Sweet?"

"Rumors are Sheriff Barnes and Nidhi are seeing one another."

"You mean romantically?"

"No, Grace, as chess partners." She rolled her eyes. "Of course, I mean romantically. She's been looking real happy lately. Haven't you noticed? No, of course you didn't. She's losing weight, too. He's single. She's single." She shrugged. "I could see it."

I considered that. I could see it too, I suppose, if I let my imagination run. But I couldn't imagine Nidhi missing or lost, so I decided she was probably fine. No doubt she wanted some time away from the sheriff and didn't tell him because she wasn't used to answering to someone, career woman that she projected herself to be. Besides, I wasn't about to let the mention of romance go by without addressing what Adriana once shared with my cousin. "So, back to what you were saying … were *you* the one who asked him?"

"Him who?" she replied with what I could tell was a false nonchalance as she studied the shirt front and back.

"Michael."

Despite the sheriff's call souring my mood, I found Adriana's pretense of indifference toward Michael to be comical. I bit my lip to keep from grinning.

"Oh. Umm, no, Cassie did." She lifted the shirt to her face. The shade of her skin always reminded me of coffee with cream, and her eyes were black, so she looked good in almost every color.

I blew a resigned breath. I had hoped she and Michael were friends again. "I see."

Adriana pulled back her shoulders and turned to look at me. "You see nothing. Anyway, Dad says good judgment comes from experience, and a lot of experience comes from bad judgment."

"What's that supposed to mean?" Her father often issued thought-provoking but quirky comments Adriana loved to repeat.

She shrugged. "I guess it means you can develop good judgment from bad experiences. But you have to be smart. To identify what was good and what was bad."

I hesitated, trying to determine her meaning, then plunged ahead. "So ... is Michael good or bad judgment?"

"It was good until he changed. What he got involved with was bad. But I believe he's a good person now ... after the accident and his coma and all. I do believe it won't happen again. Whatever it was."

Whatever it was? It was time to discuss Michael again, whether she liked it or not.

"You two started talking again?"

She raised a shoulder in a negligent gesture, but her lips betrayed that indifference by turning up at the edges. "We've talked." She whirled back to the mirror and raised the red shirt to her face again.

"And?" The way I said it, the word came out as one of those two-syllable inquiries.

"And nothing. We've talked; that's all. Honestly, Grace, don't go there. He's a friend, and that's it. I don't know if we're right for each other. Besides, I'm committed to a blind date tomorrow night, and I—"

"With whom?"

"With whom what?"

"Your date. With whom?"

She hesitated, smiling a private smile meant to be hers alone. "Never you mind. As I was saying, I have bigger things to think about. When can I borrow this? It'll go great with the necklace we found in SoHo."

I ignored her question. Of course, she could borrow the shirt anytime she wanted, but I wasn't about to encourage her. Even though I stood a few inches taller than her, height wasn't a concern as much as her weight. She'd gained at least ten pounds in the past year, and I doubted the shirt would fit. Adriana was always bubbly, enthusiastic, positive, but the breakup with Michael, followed by her senior year and concerns about finding work, prompted her to overeat.

"Like what?" I asked.

"What do you mean like what?"

"Why do you keep repeating my questions? You said you have bigger things to think about. Like what?"

"Doesn't matter," she mumbled and tossed both shirts back on the chair. "I'm too fat anyway." She hesitated and shook her head in admonishment of herself, as though she comprehended such self-talk was not part of her constitution.

In an exasperated voice, she said, "Bigger things like getting my career underway. I don't want to work in the *Perfect Rhythm* my whole life."

Four years older than me, Adriana had worked at the local music shop while pursuing her degree in flute performance from the Conservatory of Music in Brooklyn. From the moment I met her, she had her heart set on joining the National Symphony Orchestra in nearby Washington, DC.

"You applied in DC yet?"

"Of course," she said, frowning, "along with hundreds of other flutists. But an application isn't enough in the music world. You must audition. Plus, you need lots of experience."

"You have experience. You've performed at tons of concerts in college. And you belong to a string quartet. And—"

"I don't want to talk about it," she said, folding her arms over her chest and shifting her weight to one leg. "I'm anxious enough already, and until I get a break to audition, nothing will happen anyway. The thing is, I might be offered a position in Seattle. Don't get me wrong, it would be a fantastic opportunity but—"

"That's three thousand miles away! You can't go there."

"I might not have a choice. It's a dream job, although not where I—"

"But if you get a position in DC you could quit Seattle, right?"

"I can't do that. I'd have to stay at least two years. Professional courtesy. Besides, the performance industry is a small world. The venues learn quickly who has been hired where. Dad says I need to be flexible, that those who are least likely to bend are most likely to snap."

While she talked, she sauntered aimlessly around the room, her restlessness evident, and she studied each aspect of the studio apartment as if doing so for the first time. "You know, this really *is* a cute place. I will enjoy living here a lot."

I frowned at her change in topic. "Did I miss something?" Sure, I only borrowed the apartment, but I'd been living there for a year, and it felt like home. "Are you moving in with me?"

"No, silly, after you move out. And if I don't move to Seattle. We talked about that, remember?" She looked back and tilted her head, studying me. "No, clearly you don't. Honestly, Grace, it's time you joined life again and stopped living with the ghosts of the past."

Her words, with their bullet-like precision and unintended double meaning regarding ghosts, hit me like a fist. As healed as I thought I was, the truth hovered: I spent about 90 percent of my time dwelling on the past and only about 10 percent thinking about the future. No doubt the balance should be the exact opposite, but I wasn't about to confess it out loud. Adriana would pounce on the thought and use it to drag me into the present where I would have to be ... well ... *present*. What I wanted was to be left blissfully alone.

I shrugged. "I remember. You want to live here someday. I didn't think you meant so soon."

"Grace, you said you would move home when you turned eighteen."

The conversation flashed through my mind. I said I'd return to *Crossings* when I turned eighteen, but I remember it occurred during the intervention when my friends had ganged up on me.

So my pledge to move back had been a knee-jerk reaction and shouldn't count. *Right?*

Besides, Clay once lived here before leaving for law school in Lexington, Virginia; it was my puerile way of being close to him without defying the restraining order.

She scowled. "Never mind. We'll talk about this later. I need to get to the café. Cassie wants to close early so we can decorate."

I groaned. "Please, keep it simple. And no party hats."

"Be there in two hours." As she spoke, she returned to the door leading to the interior stairway. She looked back and frowned. "And act surprised. We need some joy around here."

CHAPTER 5

*J*oy. The word reverberated in my head as I changed into a green sundress Cassie once said resembled the shade of my eyes, brushed my wild mane of unruly autumn-colored hair, and braided it in a loose French twist.

We need some joy around here.

Then again, those words sounded more like they came from Cassie. No doubt she worried about both Ade and me. She would say I spent my time worrying about the past while Adriana dwelled too much on the future.

Joy through a party? I had my doubts, especially after the sheriff joined us.

Sure, it would be a gathering of friends, but my preference for social functions involved showing up when I wanted, leaving at my leisure, and in between, limiting participation to observation.

Hair finished, I meandered to the window and peered at the downpour. The walls of drench pressed in, so I turned to look at the expanse of the apartment.

Perhaps living here had worked against me. When I lived at *Crossings*, my friends had no idea what I was or *wasn't* doing. But living here, near Cassie, they witnessed me choosing to sit out much of life.

Now Adriana expected me to move back to the estate. For her sake, I should. She needed something to occupy her mind and setting up her own apartment could be the perfect outlet to help. Maybe even enough to forego any opportunities in Seattle?

However, I wasn't ready to move. This place brought me some measure of peace, although it had taken me a while to shed the vestiges of *Crossings* I'd brought with me: hearing footsteps that weren't there, seeing shadows that didn't move, tasting fear that defied interpretation. Sure, it had been a year, but I had more questions now than before I arrived in the area seeking answers.

And what about Clay? Did I stick close to the apartment in case he showed up? Per police orders, he was instructed not to come near me while I remained underage. I may not have registered much in the past year, but I did notice the few times he was in town, catching glimpses of his safari-green Land Rover parked at his mom's. I had never talked to him about what happened at the tunnels, although I'd pieced together his involvement from conversations with Cassie.

If Cassie remembered I turned eighteen today, then Clay surely knew too. Yet, there had been no call, card, or visit. All day I'd harbored a ridiculous hope he wouldn't let the day go by without contacting me.

Would he attend the party, or had he grown frustrated with me?

Was he weary of my ghost sleuthing? If the sheriff believed it, rumors would spread soon.

Another obstacle between Clay and me, and one he didn't even know about yet was the death of his father. He believed Mason abandoned the family years ago, but …

I plopped down on the red stripes of the bedspread and rolled onto my back. I could lead police to Mason's body, but how would I explain my knowledge? And, how awful for Clay and Cassie to learn about his death *after* a dead body had been found! The speculation as to how it happened—and by whom—would drive them crazy. No, it would be better if they *first* learned he was dead. That he'd been killed. Then they could mourn while the police quietly found his decomposed body. But I was the only one who could make that approach work by first resolving his murder.

And yet, I couldn't summon the energy or gumption to tackle such a daunting task.

Why bother anyway? They'd moved on, hadn't they?

My cell phone sounded, and the display registered Seth's name. I clicked on to hear him sing happy birthday. I hadn't talked to him for a while, so I startled again at the maturity and huskiness in his voice.

"Sorry I didn't call earlier," he said. "I worked today. The rain flooded the canal. We were busy with Labor Day vacationers. Then, traffic from the collapsed bridge—what a mess getting home."

Williamsport was a small town compared to Boston where I'd lived with my aunt and uncle, so I had a hard time imagining chaotic traffic, but I had no problem picturing Seth in his ranger uniform getting soaked at his part-time Canal job. He also volunteered at the hospital with the intent of studying medicine one day.

"No worries. Thanks for remembering." I meant it. His voice warmed me like a fond memory. Last year, he'd made it clear he wanted a relationship with me, but after Kate's death, I pulled away, preferring solitude. I hadn't anticipated how much I missed him.

"'Course I would. Besides, I couldn't wait to tell you my news." He sounded excited, his enthusiasm contagious.

"What is it?"

"Well," he paused as if embarrassed, "it's *your* birthday and all, but I'm the one who got the present."

"What are you talking about?"

"Got a letter. Today. From an attorney in Hagerstown. He said a private party—that's the words he used, has funded my college education. Can you believe that?"

"Is someone playing a trick on you?"

"That's what I said, too."

"Maybe it's your dad. He's probably too proud to admit he wants to pay."

"Dad? Not likely. You should have seen how angry he got when he read the letter. Besides, the attorney swears it's for real."

"But who?"

"That's the part he can't tell me. The party wants to remain anonymous."

"Why? What's the catch?"

"No catch. I'm not obligated in any way. No loans, no time commitments, no payback of any kind after I graduate. There are conditions for the schooling, but none are a problem for me."

"What kind of conditions?"

"I must attend the local community college my first two years. You're doing that, right? We could schedule classes together."

"That's it?"

"I have to finish my last two years of undergrad at a four-year institution within a three-hour drive. The same with medical school, if possible."

"Sounds like someone wants you to stay in Maryland."

"No, a three-hour drive can stretch into Pennsylvania, Virginia, or West Virginia, too. I get the impression staying local is the goal."

I considered this. "Why? I don't want to rain on your parade, but it sounds too good to be true. Are you sure there's no hidden obligation? Like you're required to work ten years for free, or you must join the Foreign Legion?" I laughed, but only to lighten the moment, not because I found any of this humorous, or even plausible. "Maybe you'll be required to doctor some grouchy old codger for the rest of his life."

"Ha, ha," he singsonged. "Very funny. I'm telling you, there is no obligation."

"Seth, if it sounds too good to be true, it generally is." Ugh, I sounded so different from Adriana. She would applaud right now, never doubting the legitimacy of the situation.

"The attorney assured me there are no hidden motives or agendas. I'm supposed to be in his office Wednesday. Want to go?"

"I'd like that."

"Great. If this proves legit, then I'll cancel the whopping school loan for West Virginia University. They'll let me delay attendance for two years. Meanwhile, I can attend community college to get my gen ed classes out of the way."

"If this works out," I said with as much enthusiasm as I could muster, "then I'm thrilled for you."

"Thanks. We'll find out Wednesday. What are you doing tonight?"

I assumed he was invited to the party, but Adriana had instructed me not to let on I knew about the gathering. "This and that. Probably nothing. Maybe I'll go for a walk."

"In this rain? No, you can't," he said. "Look, there's a surprise party for you in the café tonight. But don't tell anyone I told you."

"Really?" *Ugh. I wasn't much of an actress.* "How nice."

"Hey, you only turn eighteen once. I better go. Gotta let Mom's dog out. Are we still on for tomorrow?"

"Tomorrow?"

"Party in the Park. Labor Day festival, remember?"

No, I didn't remember. Maybe Adriana was right about me not being fully present. "Sure. I'm not sure where my mind was. But it looks like the festival might be rained out."

"We're supposed to get a break in the gloom tomorrow, so I imagine it will be on. Besides, I told Celeste I would—"

"Celeste?"

"Kicklighter. You remember, I escorted her to the prom."

Seth had asked me to his prom in the spring, but I'd said no, so he asked someone else. "You're still seeing her?"

I heard, "Down boy," on his end of the line. "Oops, gotta go. See you tonight. And, Grace? Remember to act surprised."

I clicked off, tossing the cell phone on the bed, then slumped my body down as well. I had wanted Seth to deny any inclinations toward this other girl. But he hadn't, and it bothered me more than it should that I could be disappointed by him.

What did that say about my feelings toward Clay?

CHAPTER 6

As I searched for my rain boots under the bed and attempted to stymie thoughts of the dream, the sheriff, and even Nidhi Michelson, I heard knocking at the exterior entrance. Michael opened the door and poked his head in. Thunder rumbled as he yelled, "Grace, you here?"

Dank odors from the outdoors drifted in with him.

"This is a surprise," I said in the best actress voice I could muster as I climbed off the floor.

After tossing his wet umbrella on a rug, Michael removed his wire-rimmed glasses and dried them on his shirt.

I hurried to the bathroom to get a towel. "Yesterday, you said I wouldn't see you until Saturday evening. What's up?" I was curious to find out how he planned to trick me into going to the café.

He brushed the towel over his head, tossed it on the bed, and pulled me into an embrace. "It's your birthday, Sis! We have to celebrate. You're finally a free woman!" He stepped back and raised his palm forward, eye-height.

I tapped his high-five and laughed, knowing full well what he meant. After my family was killed in a freak car accident when I was thirteen, I moved in with Michael's family. As it turned out, my mom's sister—Aunt Tish—had wanted me there solely for the trust fund I received from a large insurance payoff after my family's death. So Michael, although eight years older, had plotted with me on how I could escape his mother. As a result, we grew close and shared an unspoken awareness I now was of legal age and no longer beholden to her whims.

"Aunt Tish hasn't bothered me this past year. I haven't even talked to her for a month."

"Yeah, because she remembered you turn eighteen, and she'll lose access to your money. She's either in mourning or hiding, hoping you'll forget."

"Michael, she's not that bad." Even as the words came out of my mouth, I cringed knowing full well he spoke the truth.

"Oh, yeah? Did she call you today? Send a card? An email? A text message? A smoke signal?"

Of course not. She hadn't even visited Michael when he recovered in the hospital last year. "Doesn't matter. Didn't you work today?"

He shrugged. "A half day. Funny how no one wants to labor near Labor Day. Made myself scarce, too. Would have been here earlier, but that traffic! News said some guy saved a teenager and—"

"It was a grown man."

He tilted his head as though tracking back through a memory. "Dang reporters. They said a teenaged kid. Anyway, the hero disappeared. Like he didn't even exist. Weird, eh?"

Like he didn't even exist. A chill washed over me again, and I brushed my arms to shed it. Weird yes, but no, I would give this no more thought until I spoke with Sheriff Barnes. News is often wrong or confusing after such incidences. And, for the same reason, I refused to give any credibility to the notion Nidhi was missing.

"What about you?" He read his watch. "I thought you worked until five."

"Hilda sent me home early. I worked a lot earlier in the week shipping out Internet orders."

Michael shook his head and whistled an exhale. "Who'da thought that blue-haired fossil—who's older than the antiques she sells, I might add—operated a quiet Internet empire."

A wave of defensiveness washed through me, and I was surprised by how much Hilda and her business meant to me. But I shrugged it off and grinned. "Yeah, she's doing quite well, and don't call her a fossil. She is my relative, you know."

He rolled his eyes and held up an index finger. "Her sister

married a cousin of Jack's. I'd say that's rather distant. Remember, I'm number one. Me, the studly *first* cousin." He folded his thin, wiry body into a comical he-man pose to emphasize his point.

I laughed, glad to see him happy again. "You *are* a Dapper Dan. No hot date tonight?"

He shot a smile that spanned ear to ear. "Yes, in fact. With my beautiful sister-cousin. Look at you." He circled and eyed me like I was being auctioned to the highest bidder. "Looks like you already have plans."

I scoffed. "Nothing like that."

"Well then, you either knew I was coming or ..." he said and squinted his eyes, assessing me. "Look, I don't want to ruin the surprise, but there's a party for you tonight. At the *Time Out*. So whatever plans you already made, change 'em. I'm assigned to make sure you show up."

I turned away lest he see my underwhelming look of surprise, ambled to the dresser mirror, and applied mascara. "How nice! But you know I hate stuff like that."

Michael brushed aside the shirts Adriana earlier admired, dropped into the tufted chair, and settled his right foot on his left knee. "Which is why everyone is sure you will be surprised. So act like you are."

I set the mascara down, clicked my heels, and saluted. "Yes, sergeant major, sir."

"Okay, okay, smart-aleck. Look, party's at seven. We need to make a quick side trip before going there, so get your shoes."

I scurried into action, dropping to my knees again to search for those elusive rain boots. "Where're we going?"

When he didn't reply, I looked at him. His face flushed.

"Michael, where are we going?" I repeated, a suspicious tone in my voice.

"*Crossings*."

"No." I abandoned the search and stood. "I'm not going."

"Grace—"

"I'm not ready yet."

"It's been a year." He sat forward and clasped his hands between his knees as though posturing reasoning.

"No ... and besides, what's there anyway I haven't seen already? The grounds are still a charred mess."

He donned a sheepish grin. "Not anymore. I've been doing some things." He stretched his length to reach into his jeans without standing up, pulled out a key, and thrust it toward me. "Happy birthday, Sis. Today, you get true freedom from Mom, and you get to move back into the place you love."

I looked at the key in his hand, swallowed, and decided on a different tact. "You've been doing things? Why would you go back after everything that happened there? Are you crazy? You were in a coma for almost twenty-four hours, and it took a month for you to return to normal. You almost lost your job."

"When you're thrown from a horse, you gotta get right back on."

"That makes no sense," I said, stifling the thought that he sounded like Adriana. "Being tossed from a horse is child's play compared to what happened. Kate died, and we almost lost you."

"But you didn't. I'm fine. The evil is gone. Besides, Kate died of meningitis. Not one single bit of that had anything to do with *Crossings*."

I dropped down on the bed and pressed my fingertips to my eyes, swept anew with the intense longing to have her back. "I still miss her."

"I know." He moved to sit beside me. "Me too. Remember, I knew her almost as long as you did." He draped an arm around my shoulder. "You two were quite the duo. I watched you grow up."

"Did you know Mrs. Fletcher offered me a place to live after Mom and Jack died? I wish I'd done that. Or spent more time with them. Maybe Kate wouldn't have gone out of the country and contracted meningitis. Maybe she'd still be alive. Maybe—"

"Too many maybes, Sis." He clasped my hand. "What happened

was terrible, but you can't go back, and you can't place your life on hold anymore. Heck, even Mrs. Fletcher made changes, moved on."

"Like what?"

"She left Massachusetts. Moved to Bethesda, near Roxanne. She never remarried, you know, after Kate's dad passed away. And now with Kate gone, I guess she decided she wanted to live near her other daughter."

"How do you know?"

"I kept in touch with Roxanne after Kate's funeral."

"They don't blame me for any of that?" I already knew Mrs. Fletcher didn't blame me, but I needed reassurance.

"Of course not. Besides, they're not focused on blame. They're concentrating on healing. And so should you. We talked about this, at the intervention months ago, remember? You agreed when you turned eighteen to move home. Now come on, find your shoes, and let's go. We're running out of time."

It would do no good to argue. He wouldn't let it drop until I saw what he'd done. Besides, curiosity overcame me. It had been a year.

What *would* I find at *Crossings*?

CHAPTER 7

Clouds muscled across the dreary sky as though nature was hosting a boxing match. Fisted tufts collided, producing thunder and lightning. Water beaded on the windshield, and our wipers beat out a steady rhythm to combat the drench. I wondered if the weather foreshadowed what to expect at *Crossings*.

As we crossed the Cushwa Basin Bridge, I wiped the mist from the side window, shocked to see the height and width of the flooded Potomac River. Branches and other debris swirled and crashed together in the racing, muddy water. "It's so scary looking!"

"Yeah, be careful tomorrow."

Curious, I looked at him. "What's that supposed to mean?"

His eyes flicked larger, and he shrugged. "Nothing. I meant be careful … in general."

The congested traffic from the bridge collapse was the opposite direction of our destination, so we reached the estate in about eight quick minutes—a half mile down Canal Street, across the long expanse of the bridge, a sharp right onto Whistle Ridge Road, then left onto a crude lane that inclined about a quarter mile to *Crossings*. Days of pouring rain had rutted the dirt lane, and our car lurched and bounced. Through the curling mist and iridescent rain, trees, and bushes appeared and disappeared on both sides of the car.

The estate perched on a sloping hill across the river from Williamsport, but it may as well have sat a hundred miles away; that's how secluded and remote the house was, nestled in the ridges of the mountains making up the entry to the Shenandoah Valley in West Virginia and Virginia.

I'd driven between the estate and Williamsport dozens of times in the first couple months after moving from Boston, but I had not made the drive in the past year, so the trip once again unfolded like a new experience.

On my first visit to the estate, it had been almost dusk, and I was overwhelmed by its size and gloom factor. This trip wasn't much different.

The gray drench and foggy vapor made the estate look defeated, sad. Michael pulled to a stop in front of the house and turned off the car. As though he suspected I needed to take this trek slowly, he didn't move, letting me absorb everything in silence, as much as the roaring rain would allow.

I peered through the downpour and expected déjà vu to wash over me. Instead, I saw change: (1) construction equipment sat nearby—a hoist, a backhoe, a dump truck, and (2) shrubs bloomed green and lush, and frilled rows of mums and drifts of asters and blue sage edged the landscape fronting both the house and the apartment. Despite limited lighting from a dreary sky, the flora and fauna burst so succulent and colorful, it made *Crossings* look much more forlorn in comparison, and I was overcome with the annoying desire to get to work on restoring the house to fit its landscaping.

I inhaled a deep breath, climbed from the car, and popped up my umbrella. "I didn't know you had a green thumb."

"I don't," he confessed, exiting the car and fiddling with his umbrella. "They started blooming on their own."

I shot my gaze to him as he hurried around the car. Was he joking? Last year the vegetation was as dead as the ghost in the house.

"How?" I yelled to be heard against the rainfall.

He shrugged, dropping his umbrella closer to the top of his head. "I don't know. I wondered, too." He turned and made eye contact. "Maybe it's because …"

"What? What are you thinking?"

He dropped his shoulders. "I don't understand what happened last year, but my instincts say whatever it was is now gone. Right? Death, I mean. Death is gone. Don't you think?"

The question sounded rhetorical, so I treated it as such. In truth, despite my mind being on heightened alert, I didn't sense anything untoward. No presence, no heaviness, no hair standing up. I wondered if the interior would be the same.

He grasped my elbow and steered me toward the apartment. "Come on. We're gonna drown out here."

We climbed the stairway and stepped onto the refurbished porch. New fern-green chairs with black-and-white-swirled fabric pillows and a new rug greeted us, creating an enticing outdoor oasis. He pointed to a rectangular shape beside the door. "It's a doggie door, so Tramp can let himself in and out."

As Michael dug in his pocket for the apartment key he'd tried to give me earlier, my gaze wandered from the stained glass splash of framed color hanging from chains on the east side of the porch to the luxuriant green ferns in black-and-white ceramic pots, to the wind chimes that hurled my thoughts back to the moment when I'd sat on this same porch last year with Will. The only two pieces remaining from my former life were the chimes and the glider Clay brought me after I moved in.

I shook my head at the memory and forced my gaze toward Williamsport. Usually, the view encompassed the long, rolling lawn sloping down to the Potomac River, but today I couldn't see that distance due to the gloom and relentless downpour. That old sensation of being cut off from the rest of the world came back, bringing with it an odd mixture of pleasure and pain.

Michael must have thought me dismayed by the changes because he said, "Don't worry. The old stuff is stored in the house. Second floor. In case you want it back."

He cracked the apartment door open, reached in and flipped a switch. Hundreds of twinkling lights sparkled, making the porch look like an outdoor retreat from a home and garden magazine.

I threw a hand to my chest. "I love it," I declared, and meant it.

He grinned. "Wait, there's more." He pushed the door open with a dramatic flourish and gestured inside. "After you, Princess."

I stepped in and gasped. The apartment was transformed into an upscale, contemporary retreat. Gone were the dark, carved wood cabinets, flowered linoleum, visually heavy furniture, ornate details, and patterned fabrics. Instead, I took in the modern simplicity and geometry of polished metal—stainless steel, nickel and chrome, sleek hardwood floors, exposed lightwoods, frosted glass, and distressed leathers.

One corner featured a large built-in unit with a desk and floor-to-ceiling shelves that issued a library/study vibe to it, no doubt added to accommodate my college studies. Overall, the new backdrop of tans and grays provided a visual rest for the eyes, and the lines made the place look twice as big as before. The pleasing smell of progress filled my nostrils: new lumber, paint, varnish.

A startling amount of light poured into the rooms thanks to new oversized windows on the west and north sides. The house and apartment had been built facing north, probably to take advantage of the scenic river. The east and south tucked partially into the surrounding hill, and when I looked through the new floor-to-ceiling windows on the west, all I could see—when the mist cooperated—was gradual, inclining lawns and the sky beyond.

As I moved from window to window taking in the view, I delighted in seeing a slight northwest glimpse of the river as it snaked through the area. The grounds between the river and where I stood now contained the underground tunnel, where the explosion occurred last year. Instead of the straight expanse of lawn that once was there, the terrain rumpled and dropped where the support beams must have collapsed in the fire. To look at the stretch of land, covered in a sea of green grass, a visitor would never guess what occurred. But somewhere, under that wavering mess, sat a fortune in gold, still waiting to be recovered. Seth and I once calculated that more than ten million dollars in gold coins had been hidden there in the 1860s.

Now, yards of new turfgrass covered it, a reminder of yet another task left undone.

I turned away and circled through the living area and open kitchen—with its new granite counter top and silver metallic appliances, then stepped into the bedroom and en-suite bathroom to see they too had undergone a contemporary transformation. As I returned to the main room, the thought raced through my head: a ghost would not be comfortable in such a modern retreat.

I found Michael standing in the same spot where I'd left him, grinning.

I splayed my hands in the air, acknowledgment of his success. "It's incredible. How did you do all this so quickly?"

"Quickly? It's been a year, kiddo. A lot can happen in a year."

There was that reminder again. A year of change for everyone but me. I ignored it. "It's beautiful. So different. So refreshing."

He shrugged. "I figure the less it looks like the former place, the better. I had a woman on our design team at work select the decor. You like it?"

"Who wouldn't? It's a little contemporary for my taste, but it can be softened up. Toss pillows. Maybe a couple antiques from the Emporium."

"Whoa, not too much."

I shot him a questioning look. He shot back a grin.

"Did I forget to mention I want to move in here next year? And this is all mine?"

"Here? You want to move back?"

"Yes," he said, splaying both hands toward me, "and before you remind me the last time didn't go so well, let me point out how peaceful it is here."

I sighed. "I don't know …"

Michael continued: "Remember last year before all the weird things happened? We tried to start renovations, but the carpenters kept being spooked and left?"

I nodded. How could I forget?

"Well, I've had countless carpenters and architects and electricians and inspectors in the house. Not a single one of them sensed a thing. So, the place is clean, I'm telling ya." He continued, smiling, pacing, and gesturing more than I'd ever seen from him. "Here's the plan. I've started work on the old house, too. No, don't worry, not to make it contemporary. I'm using the designs you sketched last year. Just getting the wheels in motion. Foundation. Plumbing. Electricity. Bringing it up to code." He smirked. "Although, everyone who has looked at it so far is startled the place is as sound as it is. But you know that already."

I rolled my eyes and nodded. Will's ghostly presence and his unfinished business had kept the place intact.

"So you return to this apartment while the crew works next door. Then, in a year or so—"

"A year or so? Why would the house take so long if it's in good shape?"

"The crew can't return for a while. But when the work is mostly done, you can move into the house, and I'll move in here. This way, we can be near one another, but define our own spaces. You seem determined to live in this area indefinitely. Meanwhile, I'm not sure where work will take me. So it's best if I live small for now and rent from you rather than buy."

"What about your job?" I hedged. "And city life? You're going to have a long commute and boring evenings living so far outside D.C."

He sucked in air as though preparing to deliver bad news. "Yeah, about that ..."

My heart sank. "What?"

"I requested a transfer. To our foreign offices. Two weeks ago it was approved."

My shoulders slumped as if the joy left me in a tangible way. "When do you go and for how long?" I dropped onto the leather couch. I needed support for this conversation.

"Next month ... and how long? Pshh, probably three years. That's the way the program works. But it could change. It cycles. Six weeks gone, two weeks back. That's the rotation. So, there's no sense in paying sky-high rent in the District if I'll hardly ever be there."

"Where will you go?"

"Third-world countries. Mostly Africa. Maybe South America, too."

"Why? Wanderlust again?"

"It's not that."

"Then what?"

He moved his gaze around the room. "This. All this. Everything that happened here." He grew serious and dropped into a chair near me. "Between what little I remember and what you described in the hospital, I've pieced together enough to know I experienced evil on a large scale. Yet I was saved from it. I want to give back. That's all. Besides, if I get a few years of international experience under my belt, I'll move into upper management sooner."

"Does Adriana know?"

"I doubt it would matter to her." His tone was resigned, a man who had learned to live with something he didn't like.

Judging from Adriana's comments earlier that afternoon, I'd agree she wouldn't care. I slouched back in the seat and closed my eyes, trying to figure out how I would deliver a double blow, this second heartache to my beloved cousin that I wasn't moving back to *Crossings*.

Because as different as it looked and as *normal* as it felt, I had no intention of moving back.

CHAPTER 8

"Surprise!"
The group yelled in unison as I entered the café. I could tell from the smiles my reaction reflected the delight they aimed for.

Why delight? Because my gaze functioned like sonar honing in on Clay—that strong jaw, those blue-green eyes so much like Caribbean water. My concern about looking appreciative had been for naught because I simply mirrored what swelled in my heart.

In the spring, I'd overheard Cassie say Clay found a job as a legal assistant for the summer in Lexington, the Virginia town where he attended law school. I'd had trouble picturing this muscled, active guy sitting at a desk day by day, and I wondered what it would do to his physique and his psyche. Looking at him now, however, it was clear the man still worked out. His shoulders and abs revealed firm definition. He looked so comfortable in his own skin, my heart raced. Only his shirtsleeves fell short of perfect. He'd rolled them into messy cuffs at the elbows, but I liked the confidence and comfort it suggested.

I had no chance to talk with him before a dozen or so other people gathered around me—Cassie, her love interest and part-time employee, Whit, two other café waitpersons, Zebecca and Daniella, Adriana and her parents and brother, Cory, Pastor Dale and his wife, Clarisa, Hilda Hilson, Seth, and a tall black man of about twenty-eight or thirty years of age who couldn't keep his eyes off Adriana. Through quick introductions, I learned Jamaar Palmer was a friend of Clay's from law school.

I blushed as the group sang "Happy Birthday" and showered me with hugs, greetings, and gifts. I hurried through cutting the cake so people could eat and focus on something besides me. Then—*finally!*—people began to mingle, breaking into scattered groups to enjoy the spaciousness of the café.

When I found myself alone, I sat on one of the stools by the serving counter and sensed someone approach from my right. I didn't need to turn to see who it was. My inner core had tracked Clay's movements since I strolled through the door.

"May I join you?"

I turned to see him standing there in all his handsome splendor, a smile across his face that said, "I didn't think we'd ever make it, but here we are."

Or, perhaps that was *my* thought. The last time I had been in the café with him, the tables were shoved aside, the lights dimmed, and music poured from the rafters. The rendezvous was orchestrated by Adriana and Cassie to give Clay and me a last private—and quite clandestine—goodbye before he left for law school, an effort to honor the restraining order between us. We danced, and it was perfect and heart-wrenching all in one.

Now, as I looked at him, I tried to flatline my smile and rein in my hopes. I didn't want to look like my heart hammered excitedly in my chest. Which it did. But I failed miserably. I called defeat, allowing the full ear-to-ear grin to do its thing, and gestured to the next seat. "Please."

"This is nice, eh? Together in public. Finally." He emphasized the last word as he folded his body onto a stool. Scents of musk and fresh laundry reached my nostrils, reminding me again of our dance the year before. A large, handled brown paper bag dangled from his left hand, and he placed it on the floor. "I didn't think you'd ever turn eighteen," he mumbled, rolling his eyes. He looked around as though to ensure no one watched before bending forward, pulling from the bag a package the size of a coat box, and propping it on my lap. It was wrapped in silver foil and garnished with a glittery white bow.

"Another package!" Zebecca squealed and materialized out of

nowhere. There's something about a wrapped box that provokes a mystery everyone wants to solve. As a result, anyone standing within a few feet of us turned to watch.

Clay flinched and frowned. "Looks like we've got an audience," he whispered.

I tried to stifle my grin. Hesitating, I first soaked in his proximity. I wanted to touch his cheek where he'd cut himself shaving, to kiss my fingertip and place it at the nick. No, forget that, I wanted to kiss it directly. Instead, I pulled from my stupor, untied the bow, lifted the lid and pulled back the tissue paper to reveal an orange life vest.

Huh? I'm sure that's what my face registered because my brows pulled together as I looked at Clay for an explanation. Seth now stood a couple yards behind him.

"Figured you might want it tomorrow." Clay's voice was edged in hope.

An odd combination of excited curiosity and disappointment unfurled in my stomach. Hadn't I already promised the next day to Seth?

"Tomorrow?" I looked up to read his face, but simultaneously noticed Seth's expression sober.

"We're supposed to get a break in the rain, and I haven't been out on the river in a while. I was hoping you'd join me—"

"How romantic," Zebecca cooed. "Of course, she'll go. Won't you, Grace?"

Clay's eyes widened at her words, but he never broke his gaze with me. "Doc Henderson—an old family friend—has a large boat he lets me borrow. The only kind I'd trust on the river as high as it is from the rain. We'll start at the dock in Williamsport. Take it upriver a few miles. He owns property near Four Locks, right along the Potomac. I told him I'd check on it. Thought you might want to see how the river snakes through the countryside."

Tomorrow? Did he really say tomorrow? Heart sinking, I opened my mouth to explain I already had plans. "I … I don't—"

"Sounds like a good time," Seth offered, "especially with the river as wild as it is right now."

We locked gazes, and he offered me one of those "go-ahead" nods, reminding me yet again of what a good man he'd become, so different than when I first met him. Disappointment washed over me at his encouragement, a realization that I'd been looking forward to spending time with him, too. Further, this whole Celeste thing rubbed me the wrong way, but people were watching, so I figured I could make it up to him later.

I looked back at Clay. "I'd love to."

He must have caught the visual exchanges because his gaze cut to Seth before returning. He hesitated but settled on a smile. "Great. I'll call in the morning, and we'll work out the time."

"So, this beautiful lady is the reason you are abandoning me tomorrow?" The question came from my right, in the most perfect enunciation I ever heard. I turned to see Jamaar nod at me. "Hello again, Ms. Grace. Thank you for letting me crash your party."

Adriana stood beside him donning a huge grin and keeping her focus on this tall stranger. I said exactly what I felt: "I'm glad you did." I liked seeing Ade smile. I hoped Michael did, too. The two of them hadn't talked much that evening.

"Jamaar recently graduated," Clay said. "He starts work at a firm in Silver Spring next week. Mom said you planned to move home after you turned eighteen, so I told Jamaar he could stay in the apartment until he learns the area."

"Oh ..." My mind raced. I looked at Adriana, hoping she'd call first dibs on the apartment. She could rescue me from having to explain I wasn't moving. Later, I could argue with her for more time.

Instead, she beamed and said, "Isn't that a great idea? When Jamaar is done with the place, I'll move in. Works out for everyone."

Yes, everyone but me. I pulled my shoulders back. "The thing is—"

"Grace!"

I looked up to see Cassie approaching, a worried look on her face. "Sheriff Barnes wants to talk to you …?"

He sidled up behind her, and I caught a whiff of spicy aftershave mixed with tobacco.

"Larry," Clay said, standing to shake Sheriff Barnes' hand. "Long time, no see." Clay grinned. "You here to make sure she's eighteen?"

"What? Ahhh now you know I was only doin' my job. Nah, I'm here to see Ms. MacKenna on other business." As though he'd said, "Give us privacy" rather than "other business," most of the people within earshot ambled away. He carried a portfolio in his left hand. From it, he pulled a sheet of paper and shoved it at me.

I hoisted the vest and box onto the counter and received the drawing, all the while taking a deep breath and preparing to explain I didn't recognize the face sketched on the paper. But something about the eyes made me study closer. The sketch depicted a man of around twenty-eight or thirty with a square chin and no neck. His cropped hair was light in color.

I did recognize him! It was the soul I'd seen outside the barbershop last year, near the bank. And directly up the street from Indigo Street where the bridge collapsed! He had been a fireman and died in a blaze in 1962. He said he hadn't moved on yet because he wanted to save a life, and if seen in human form while doing so, it would be attributed to superhuman strength. My body tensed as the thought washed over me that he'd finally accomplished his unfinished business and moved on.

"What's this all about?" Clay asked, glancing at the sketch. "He wanted for something?"

Sheriff Barnes nodded. "Yeah, but for once it's nothing bad. The guy saved a Clarksburg man from drowning. After the bridge collapsed. Our hero here up and disappeared. Like he was some kind of ghost."

I looked up to see Clay's face sober and watched a muscle twitch in his jaw as he digested the sheriff's unintended implication of possible paranormal activity. He'd witnessed such phenomena firsthand last year when we took a quick trip to Georgia. Later he told me at least twice my ghost sleuthing must stop.

Clay opened his mouth as if to say more, but closed it again, and I could hear the strain of disapproval in his silence.

But how could I explain to the sheriff what I experienced last year? I couldn't tell him the man in the picture was already dead, and that I talked to him *after* he'd died.

Sheriff Barnes parked his portfolio under his elbow and stuffed his hands in his pockets. "Mr. Knight, the guy pulled from the river … he said this guy," the sheriff jerked his chin toward the sketch, "told him not to be afraid. That he'd get him outta the water in seconds without problem." The sheriff's gaze bore into me as he added, "Musta' been one cool cookie to be so sure of himself in that strong current."

A memory struck, and a rush of heat colored my face. The ghost who saved me from a speeding car in Lexington had told me not to be afraid, too. Pastor Dale once said angels in the Bible often declared, "Don't be afraid," when they appeared. Was it true then what some people believed? Were angels among us? Did they move in and out of our lives to help us? I'd spent the better part of this past year believing the souls I met were evil, Will included, such that I'd blocked myself from the possibility he had been a good guy.

"Well, what about it, ma'am? You know the guy?"

I bit my lip as silence fell, brief blips of time. *You know the guy?* That was the question put before me, and I could honestly say no. After all, I *didn't* know the guy. I knew his soul. And given that I felt confident the soul had resolved his unfinished business and moved on, there seemed to be no point in getting into the details and causing undue concern.

I shook my head. "No, I don't know this guy … sorry."

The sheriff continued to study me, and for a moment I thought he might pepper me with more questions. He dragged a hand down his cheek and over his lips. Shook his head in disappointment ... or doubt? I wasn't sure. But it sure looked like he wasn't satisfied.

Clay clapped a hand on the sheriff's shoulder. "I guess the guy doesn't want to be found. That it, Larry? We're trying to hold a little celebration here. Why don't you eat some cake before you go?"

"Yeah, yeah, sure," he mumbled. "I want to talk to your mom about Ms. Michelson anyway."

I handed the paper back to the sheriff and forced myself to keep quiet about Nidhi. I was concerned but didn't want him wondering if I could help with that, too.

Sheriff Barnes stuffed the drawing into his portfolio, handed me a business card, and muttered, "Thanks for your time, ma'am. Call if ya think of anything." He allowed Clay to lead him to the food table, Jamaar and Adriana following.

I shifted in my seat and looked up to see Hilda studying me from a distance. She nodded and winked as though casting approval for something I'd done. I wasn't sure what to say or how to respond, but she took the need away by turning to Seth and speaking to him.

I watched as they approached.

Seth said, "I'm going to see that Mrs. Hilson gets home safely. I'll call it a night after that." He leaned down and kissed me on the cheek. "Happy birthday."

I grabbed his arm. Despite Hilda standing there, I said, "Seth, about tomorrow—"

"It's okay." His gaze shot to Hilda and back. "We'll talk later. Make different plans."

I nodded and swallowed my disappointment. It didn't go down easy.

"Good night, dear," Hilda said. "You did right with the sheriff. Some things are better left unsaid."

They paid their respects to the others as they headed to the door. The woman moved at a startling pace despite being dependent on a cane, and I'd learned from four months of working with her that despite her physical limitations, she had the ability to appear at the least likely times.

But it wasn't her stealth that stymied me now; rather, it was what she'd said. Where had that come from?

Michael captured my attention as he plopped on the seat Clay abandoned, wearing a big smile and an expectant look.

"What?" I smiled back.

He picked up the life vest and looked it over. "Boating, eh?"

I remembered his comment about being careful tomorrow. "You knew."

His gaze darted to Adriana as her laughter reached us from where she and Jamaar stood, pouring punch. His smile sobered before looking back. "What? Yeah, I knew." The smile returned. "We've talked, played golf a few times."

"You and Clay?"

"Sure. Who do you think painted your new apartment? He's a good painter ... can draw a mean straight line."

Michael's words hit me like an arrow touching the target's center. I assumed he referred to Clay's physical skill of painting a straight line, but I thought about the unwavering line he'd drawn between us too, refusing to see me for a year so as not to jeopardize my ability to stay in the area. Then again, although he'd stayed on his side of the proverbial line when it came to interaction with me, he certainly reached across it when he could to become familiar with the whole prospect of my new apartment, to paint it, and spend time cozying up with my cousin. "Clay was a part of the renovation?"

"I think he wants my approval. To date you." He shrugged. "Either that or he wants to make sure he's not getting involved with a loony family. That's probably his greater concern."

"Stop it." I laughed, grabbed the vest, and jabbed him with it.

The next hour proved relaxing. I made the rounds, assured Pastor Dale and Clarisa I looked forward to starting college classes, swapped a few memories of birthdays past with Jamaar, and thanked the others for helping me celebrate the day.

Zebecca and Daniella attempted to draw me into a conversation of what my refurbished apartment looked like, each declaring the prospect exciting. I extricated myself from further discussion with the excuse of needing more punch. The mere thought of returning to *Crossings* made my pulse race. Yet, Adriana and Jamaar wanted the apartment, Michael had prepped a new home for me, and everyone expected me to move back. Besides, if I dated Clay now, it would be too awkward to live in his mom's house when he came home.

I looked around the crowd and suddenly felt heavy, weighed down. Like an iceberg. Only one-eighth of those frozen masses can be seen above water. The rest—the dark, threatening, precarious part—is hidden below the surface. These good people saw only the visible portion of me. The part that greets the sun. The other seven-eighths of me were weighed down by last year's events, confusion over the paranormal activity I experienced, and most of all, my friends' expectations and opinions about my secluded life and *Crossings*. But they were wrong. I hadn't missed out on this past year, or on life.

No, I'd made my plans. I would stay in the apartment as long as I wanted.

I would stick with my plan.

The door rattled, and I watched as Clay's sister, Reaghan, breezed in with her husband, Sidney, and their four children, muttering apologies for being late. Reaghan recently gave birth to their second set of twins—Kristin and Kylie—and each parent carried one of the girls. The boys, Ethan and Elias, raced ahead to the food counter as Reaghan and Sidney set the girls on the floor. I watched in stunned fascination as the girls tottered their way to Clay, who scooped them up in his arms and showered them with kisses.

"They're walking!"

I didn't realize I spoke aloud until Whit responded, "They've been walking for two months."

How could that be? Hadn't I thought a moment ago they were born *recently?* What happened to the rolling-over moments? The crawling stage? Their first steps?

My breath hitched as reality settled over me—I missed their whole year of growth.

An entire year!

These were Clay's nieces, Cassie's grandchildren, beloved to the people I loved. From a distance, I'd seen the girls with Reaghan from time to time, but they were in a stroller or carriers, and I exchanged little with them or her. Now, here they were, walking!

Adriana was right—I'd gone a complete trip around the sun and hadn't lived in the moment during the ride. These children had continued to develop, grow, and graduate through multiple rites of passage, but I had nothing to show for my entire seventeenth year.

I dropped into the nearest seat feeling the nature of my life rumbling, as though my body was its own earth, and deep in my core it experienced a tremor that shifted and restructured everything all the way to the surface, especially undermining my certainty that I'd been fully functioning these past twelve months.

I was right about the iceberg. So much of me resided below the surface, but it wasn't loss and expectation that weighed me down. *It was denial.*

Time to melt that frozen chunk and move back to *Crossings.*

CHAPTER 9

I tossed and turned and flipped my pillow many times that night. Thoughts of returning to *Crossings* energized my mind, but punching a cushion wouldn't make them go away.

Around one a.m., I recalled my dream and the memories it invoked—Kate's death, Michael's brush with possession, the horrific confrontation with Fergus. Each had occurred at the estate.

By two a.m. I thought of Jack's love for the place, my first encounters with Clay, and the many fireside chats I'd shared with Will.

So, in one hour's time, I progressed from worrying that some sinister part of the house wouldn't leave me, to admitting a part of me had never left it.

At three a.m. I decided worrying did no good. I already had made the decision to move back, so delaying the inevitable seemed senseless. It would be an easy move. I hadn't brought much with me—clothes, toiletries, laptop, pets. My only new purchases were college textbooks.

I had to return. People needed the garage apartment and wanted me to step back into the fabric of life. Besides, hadn't Michael convinced me *Crossings* was safe? The only place I experienced anxiety was in my own head anyway.

But first, I needed to settle something in me: I had to find out if Will moved on for eternity, or if he still remained. No, not to bring him back with me. I was done solving murders, chasing shadows, and talking with ghosts, including Mason, Clay's father. To solve his murder would merely swap one pain with another for Clay and his family. Which was worse? Assuming your father abandoned you, or learning he'd been murdered in cold blood? Neither choice sounded bearable, and I refused to do that to him.

Yet, how could I return to *Crossings* without Will? He was as much a part of the house as the wavy glass windows and dusty floorboards.

Then again, how could I return *with* him?

I'd been left with many questions about his behavior the year before. Why hadn't he protected Michael from Fergus? Why had he elevated gold over helping people? What had he meant when he said Josiah rejected Fergus? Did he mean Josiah Sawyer, the builder of *Crossings* and rumored dabbler in evil and black arts?

During the past year, I repeatedly concluded Will was a cunning, charming demon in disguise, hidden behind a facade of righteousness.

But, why then had he been so kind to us—me, Grandma Sadie when she passed away, and Clay when a deranged Naomi tossed him like a ragdoll in Georgia?

At six o'clock the next morning, I climbed out of bed, gulped some coffee, and drove to the cemetery where, at my request, Clay had placed the coin—Will's center—on the night the tunnels burned and Kate died. I hadn't meant for Will to remain in the cemetery, or to stay away from the estate myself for so long, but then I learned the full extent of the damage and discovered that living at Cassie's place allowed me to ignore it all.

The sun had not yet risen, so it was, by all logical arguments, not a pleasant time to visit a graveyard. However, I needed to talk with Will when he would command optimal use of his energy, which meant before a dawning light. I needed him at full capacity so I could gauge his reactions.

I parked in the lane beside *Crossings* and stepped onto the lawns, scanning the blackness in the direction of the cemetery. The rain had stopped, but the lawns remained saturated, and fog pooled near the ground like some evil miasma seeping out of the earth. As the near-full moon dropped, it cast a faint, white trail between the hazy silhouette of trees, oddly enough, a trail leading to the cemetery. A chill chased down my back as I experienced again that eerie sensation of being separated from time and space, and the rest of the world.

Ignoring my speeding heartbeat, I clicked on the flashlight and waded through the swirling mist straight to my destination, crossing the two rolling hills to the small graveyard on the northwest side of the property. Despite cumbersome rain boots, I moved as if sent there on a mission, albeit a self-imposed mission. I suppose, in some ways, I was spoiling for a fight.

Clay had been right about the break in the rain, but the fog was so thick that by the time I reached the site, I was drenched anyway. Despite dawn approaching, the air grew colder as I neared my destination.

I opened the rusted cemetery gate and froze as flashes of memory came: stumbling over Will's tombstone after moving here, realizing his body lay *in the ground*, learning to trust him again when Grandma Sadie died, trusting in his alleged departure, hearing Eva reveal Will never left and discovering him again in the tunnels.

An owl hooted nearby, snapping me back to reality. I stood at the gate breathing in the moist air and contemplating the darkness in the backdrop of woods creeping toward the cemetery. Although barely visible through the shifting fog, the contour of the trees made them look like they drooped and ogled me. The grounds loomed much scarier at night, and the sounds emitting from the murky darkness—frogs, cicadas, an owl, and the rush of the swift currents from the river—echoed as otherworldly, like they came out of nowhere. Clay had said the Potomac snaked around the region, and I now grasped that a considerable portion of my estate backed into it in several directions.

I took a deep breath and stepped forward, lifting the flashlight high and playing the narrowed beam of light over the grave markers, each weathered and more than a century and a half old.

I found his headstone without problem—"William Alan Kavanaugh, Born: August 16, 1844, Died: May 24, 1863," and scanned the light right and left, looking for any bright gleam amidst the groundcover.

Nothing.

Perhaps the weeds had grown over the coin in a year's time? I dropped to my knees, moving the flashlight and patting the soaked ground. I began to panic. I felt certain Clay carried out my request, but what if someone had found the coin and taken Will along with it? With a whimper, I began combing my fingers through the dirt.

Despite my dampened clothing and the roar of the river, my skin prickled as a chill swept over me. My breath hitched, and I jerked back.

"It's there. Behind the headstone." A directive from the dark.

I choked out an inane sound and shot to my feet, probing the beam in the direction of the voice.

A figure stepped from the fog and into the light.

Will!

For a heartbeat, I soaked in his familiarity—tattered pants, knee-high boots, Confederate jacket, mustache, and scraggly, shoulder-length hair. His machismo struck me anew. The rugged handsomeness from a bygone era. And those eyes! They always looked shadowed—mysterious and dark. I couldn't look into them for long without wanting to melt into his essence. Their attentiveness pulled me close, yet their ferocity repelled me.

He emitted a slight gauzy, transparent glow I remembered so well. Between his aura and the swift dawning light shifting from black to gray to pink, the flashlight proved redundant, so I clicked it off.

A thrill rushed through me, despite my apprehension about his intentions. I once trusted him, thought I loved him. He helped me grow, saved me from Greasy Jim and Henry when they held a knife to my throat. There always had been something about Will that pulled me like a magnet, an attracting force beyond my control. Perhaps I'd been wrong about him; he certainly didn't look demonic, standing there with a look of pleasure on his face. I wanted to throw myself into his diaphanous—yet startlingly strong—arms.

But, I didn't.

Instead, I began to hate myself for these traitorous feelings, the way my heart leaped inside my chest. I reined in and stood strong.

"You're still here," I said and heard wonder in my tone. His presence brought both relief *and* a reminder of the grim gulf between our two worlds. I could no more have stayed in that cemetery every night for a year than I could have flown to the moon. Yet, he'd eschewed the choice of moving on in order to stay here for ... *what?*

He nodded. "Still here."

That voice! So soothing, so familiar. It had once brought such comfort.

"Why? Your business is finished."

"But yours is not."

That quickly, my love for this man leaped into the back seat, and doubt seized the wheel. I hated his attempt to make this situation about me rather than him.

"I'm not your business," I said, my voice even, monotone. "Besides, there's nothing left unfinished. Nothing else to prove or uncover or resolve. Kate died of meningitis. Michael, Seth, and Clay are fine. *Crossings* is empty. Fergus is gone. And, I'm leaving Mason's death alone."

Who was I trying to convince?

Will remained quiet, waiting me out, head tilted, lips drawn in a sad line. His silence made me uncomfortable.

Despite apprehension with who or what he was, my mind betrayed me again as warm memories washed over me. I'd grown to love him as a generous friend and hero from another era, and I wanted to embrace him. However, the warmth warred with the cold notion he may not be as innocent as he seemed.

I flailed my hands through the air in defeat. It was probably stupid to admit to a dead person you suspected he might be tricking you, but I plunged ahead anyway. "I still don't understand if you're a ghost or an angel or a demon or what this is all about."

"That's why I'm still here. To help you understand."

"Understand what?"

"That you need to live your truth whether you can prove it or not."

I glared at him. "What's that supposed to mean? And what makes you think I'm trying to prove anything?"

"Aren't you? You're trying to find proof. Assurances. Verification of what's in your heart, rather than trusting it. You're waiting for certainty, but belief doesn't come with such assurances. It's a choice. Nothing more."

"That's not what I'm doing." Even I didn't believe my curt rebuff as it crossed my lips. "Besides," I added to get the better of him, "what does it matter what's in my heart? Shouldn't we be more concerned with what our minds tell us to do?"

"If you change your heart, you will change your mind. It works in that order. But you … you don't trust. You did once. You learned to trust me. To trust others. To trust faith. Now you're back to trusting only your expectations of the next betrayal."

His words hit me like I'd been shoved. It had been a year since I'd made a move requiring a leap of faith. I'd become suspicious, undecided, and dull. Still, he infuriated me, and I needed to push back. In the calmest voice I could manage, I asked, "Why did you hide from me last year? And why are you so interested in the gold? You chose securing it over helping people."

He frowned. "It only appeared that way. The gold can help a lot of people. I could have gotten it *and* you out of the tunnel and gone back for that Jim hoodlum before the tunnels collapsed. But you insisted I take him as we departed. Taking you both made the exit slower."

It sounded plausible. But then, doesn't evil always sound that way?

I hesitated, organizing my thoughts. "What about Michael? Why didn't you help him when you saw Fergus using him?"

"Things must be handled in a certain way. None of those incidences had to happen. You both could have stopped it."

"By trusting." My tone sounded snarky.

He looked away, one hand rubbing the back of his neck as though trying to draw forth the right words. *So lifelike.* He gazed back, cocking his head in an endearing way. "Yes, by trusting. Besides, Michael wasn't my concern."

"You said I was your concern, and he is *mine*. So he *is* your concern."

"It doesn't work that way."

"Well, how does it work?" I spewed the words, my whole body shaking. "You talk in riddles, Will. Can't you just be normal—"

I broke off with a groan and ran my hand over my head. "Listen to me. I'm standing in a cemetery, talking to a ghost and accusing him of not being normal. I'm losing my mind." Since arriving, I'd stood stiff with mistrust, but now I dropped onto the cold headstone behind me. In the blip of a moment, I remembered where I was and jumped back to my feet. "Ugh. I'm so sorry."

Will smiled. "It's okay. He's not there anyway."

I turned to read the inscription: David Alan Kavanaugh. Born 1817. Died 1882. "Your father!"

Will nodded. "When he and my mother returned from Brazil, they stayed in Alexandria. But they wanted to be laid to rest here. To be near the son they lost."

Moisture filled my eyes. "And your sister …?" I scanned the area around us. "Is she here as well?"

"No, she wanted nothing to do with *Crossings* after I died."

I darted my gaze from headstone to headstone. "These other people, none of them stayed behind?"

"They had no unfinished business. They're all gone."

"Gone …" My strength dissipated again. "… like Kate."

He nodded. "Like Kate."

"Why isn't she here with me, like you?"

"You know the answer to that."

"But she shouldn't have died so young." At my last word, I remembered Will was only two years older than Kate when he died.

"She's content. Happy. She's with her father. She left nothing behind. You're mourning her, but she's moved on. It's time to let her go."

I received his words like a startling blast of air and held them in my mouth before swallowing them with great effort. They contradicted the dream I had the day before. Where had the dream come from, if not my heart? Yet, Will was trying to tell me to trust my heart. Wouldn't doing so merely bring up every pain I harbored?

"Grace, you didn't need to react to any of this." He made an *over there* motion with his head, toward *Crossings*.

I scoffed. "I didn't go looking for it. How could I not react when it landed in my lap?" I pointed my finger at him and jabbed at the air. "You pulled me into it."

"Did I? Or did you pursue it?"

I blinked, and something inside me registered he was trying to deliver a far more poignant message. He continued before I could collect my thoughts.

"Evil will always come," he said. "It seeps through the windows like moisture, grows on the walls like mold, tracks in the door like dirt on your shoes. It will always find you. Test you. Tempt you. Try to pull you over to its side."

I shivered. "You make it sound so sinister."

"It is sinister. And it's well-documented. We've received the warning. Mankind's real struggles are not against flesh and blood, but against the darkness, against the powers of the bleak world and the spiritual presence of evil in the heavenly realms. It surrounds us, and yet it's beyond our grasp. Beyond human understanding. That mystic area most people can't see or touch, but you, Grace, somehow you've been made privy to parts of it."

His words, so ominous and formidable, overwhelmed me. I remembered something he told me after we first met and whispered it now. "A war that's been raging since time began."

He seized on it. "That's right. Every step we take is a decision to fight it … or not. To accept it or not." He jerked his gaze as though startled and looked toward the west. He cocked his head, making me think he heard something or studied a particular spot, rather than the expanse of the horizon. I tracked his gaze but saw nothing disturbing.

In a hushed tone, he continued, "There's more coming … worse than ever. I'm not sure what, but it's coming …" He paused before shrugging himself out of the thought.

"More?" I scoffed. "What more could there be? Haven't I done enough?"

"There will always be more," he said, but his focus returned to something distant, not to me.

I shifted and sighed, attempting to signal that he needed to return to our conversation.

His gaze returned. "Grace, be careful in your decisions, but fight for what's right. Sometimes the trees that endure the worst storms grow to be the strongest and most beautiful."

I shivered at his words and wrapped my arms in an embrace. When I could move again, I paced in a fitful, random manner, trying to clear my thoughts. I was weary of the conversation and the riddles, but I needed to understand one thing: "So what are you saying? What could I have done differently?"

He remained quiet. I'm sure he could see on my face I expected him to repeat the directive to "trust."

Instead, he said, "Like so many others, you don't like anything you can't rationally explain."

I uttered an exasperated sound. "That's called being human, Will. Being normal!" I flailed my arms. "And that's what I need to be. Like other people. Besides, people—all people—only see what they want to see."

"Not you. You see things you *don't* want to see."

I shook my head in disbelief, annoyed at how he'd managed to sum up my situation in so few words and in such a brief and puzzling conversation.

"So what's that make you? Nothing more than a physical manifestation of my ignorance ... or my hope?" I recalled a conversation I had with Seth in which he suggested I may be matrixing what I saw, subconsciously manifesting a familiar image or sound that would otherwise be overwhelming. "Am I imagining you? Trying to make you palatable?" I thought next of Pastor Dale's comments about angels. "Are you a guardian angel?"

He frowned. "I can't answer these questions. It's for you to—"

I turned in disgust and began to storm away. "I'm going now." I couldn't tolerate him telling me again I needed to trust. I needed to be away from him, not to think about his words, but to *not* think about them. I didn't want to brood on what I should have done or should be doing. I'd outgrown that Pollyanna hooey, like an outfit a couple sizes too small. "I can't take you back to the house," I said over my shoulder.

But I want to! I miss you. If I could trust you ...

"I understand."

I stopped, turned. *He understood?* Wasn't he remaining here to help me? So why would he be so calm at the notion I wasn't taking him back to the house? From experience with him, I learned he resided close enough to his location of death to be able to move on should he choose to do so, but not close enough to disturb me at the house.

"Then why don't you move on? Knowing you have to remain here instead of in the house." I made a sweeping motion of the cemetery.

"Time and location are not factors for me. You know that."

"But you have a child waiting for you."

He smiled. "That's the thing about eternity, my child loves me and will be there waiting for me."

"Frankly, I think it's cruel to keep a child separated from his parents for so long."

He pursed his lips then spoke in a gentle, massaging tone. "Are you talking about my situation or yours? Isn't that what this is all about?"

His comment smacked me in that spot again I didn't like, the one where truth reveals itself whether we want it to or not. I'd grown so much since moving here, but I still wouldn't call myself "healed" over the deaths of my family and this permanent separation from them. But then, do we ever heal from such horrible events, or do we learn to live with an altered life?

I looked at this man I loved so much. I wanted to believe everything he told me last year, but I couldn't. "I'm sorry, Will. Not yet. I need to be free of ghosts and odd nighttime behavior."

He frowned. "Julius Caesar said what is out of sight disturbs men's minds more seriously than what they see."

I let his words sink in. He was right. But I'd also learned those who do not remember history are doomed to repeat it. And I was *not* going to let that happen.

Without saying a word, I closed my heart and walked away.

CHAPTER 10

After leaving Will, I returned to the garage apartment and packed my belongings into six boxes I found in the café storage room.

Yes, I did it quickly. Had I thought it through more, I might have lost my mettle.

Afterward, I found Cassie standing with Whit behind the *Time Out* serving counter, laughing. I wondered if her positive demeanor could be attributed to contentment with Whit or if she finally enjoyed her success. Or both? Last year, her son-in-law, Sidney, impressed on me what a crackerjack sense she had for business, but she kept disappearing to exercise, leaving the café to her employees to oversee. Lately, I'd seen her in the café more.

"Sure gonna miss havin' you 'round here," Cassie said as I returned my apartment key. She exchanged it for a house key. "Promise you'll use it a lot."

"You know I will. This is my home away from home."

She winked. "And bring my son."

My face warmed. "I'd like that."

"He's got a big day planned, ya know."

"Is he here?" I looked around at the dozen or so patrons scattered throughout.

"He's still sleepin' like a baby. Jamaar too. They kept me up late last night playin' foosball. Yellin' like two kids. Now they get to sleep in, and I don't."

I laughed, warmed by the notion that Clay wasn't too far away.

Cassie draped an arm over my shoulders, the grasp confirming she was still familiar with weights. "Looks like you'll have good weather. Shame I have to work. I've got cabin fever from all this rain."

"Oh … I'm sure Clay wouldn't mind if—"

She scrunched her face. "Hon, are you kiddin' me? Today is all about you two. Besides, this place is closed Monday, so I'll be outside then, even if the monsoon comes back."

I smiled, having no doubt Cassie would walk, run, or bike in the rain. Except for healing from Mason, she tended to dive into whatever she put in her mind to do.

I nodded toward Whit. "You two looked happy when I got here."

She tracked my gaze and sighed. "Oh, that. He was trying to get my mind off Nidhi."

"Still no news?"

Cassie shook her head. "I'm sure there's a good explanation." But she didn't look convinced.

"She hasn't been gone that long. We're probably over-reacting."

We hugged, and after collecting Tramp and Chubbs, I set out for my new apartment.

Like the day before, I detected nothing untoward in the apartment. Tramp and Chubbs explored their new home, as I wandered through the place, all senses alert, studying the views outside the windows, touching the furniture, opening kitchen cabinets to memorize their contents, and unpacking college textbooks.

My spirits lifted. The changes and fresh, contemporary decor proved rejuvenating, as though I could make a fresh start. Perhaps Michael was right; it was the perfect first step before finally moving into the old house.

I didn't *need* Will to feel comfortable at *Crossings*, and each time thoughts of him crept to mind, I blocked them. Besides, with Sheriff Barnes sniffing around and giving possible credence to otherworldly encounters, it was best I lie low for a while.

Crazy as it sounds, I decided the place smiled at me as if Jack's aura was nodding appreciation for the forward focus created by the revamp. I recalled a time he and I enjoyed a father-daughter outing, and his words came back with such clarity I *felt* as much as remembered them: "Your life can be as joyous or as miserable as you want it to be. It's your choice. There will never be a time when everything is ideal."

His words rang true. Here. *Now*. In short, seize the day, instead of worrying it away or living in the past.

But making the decision to be happy is not as easy as flipping a light switch. Sometimes you must tell yourself you believe it until you do. So I did that, again and again, as I finished unpacking.

Clay called mid-morning to confirm the afternoon, and I opted to take a nap until we met. I could explore the old house tomorrow.

***

By early afternoon, Clay and I secured the safety go-ahead from the Maryland Department of Natural Resources to navigate the churning waters and pulled away from the dock at Williamsport, the boat heading north toward Four Locks. Located on a small peninsula known as Prather's Neck, Four Locks was named for a series of four canal locks—47 through 50—on the C&O Canal, built between 1836 and 1838. During earlier visits to the Canal Visitor's Center in Williamsport, I'd learned these particular locks were built to avoid a four-mile loop in the Potomac River and to handle a 33-foot difference in elevation. A close-knit community supporting the canal once thrived at the site. It was located midway between Cumberland, Maryland, and Washington, D.C., and canal boats frequently stopped at Four Locks for repairs and supplies if the Williamsport docking location was busy.

I glanced sunward and sampled a lungful of the moist air. With blue skies and sunlight buttering the landscape, it was easy to ignore tomorrow's forecast for drenching, relentless rains, as if nature held her breath between sobs.

If we needed a reminder of nature's fury, however, all we had to do was look down into the agitated, racing water, carrying all sorts of debris and branches from upstream. As Clay had said, the boat was sizable and sturdy, but still the water churned with such velocity, I made sure to secure my life vest.

As the fourth largest river along the Atlantic coast of the United States, the Potomac was huge. It narrowed and widened with the terrain, but at all times spread a couple hundred feet wide. Filled with twists and turns through the hills and mountain passes between Maryland and West Virginia, the river often ran southeast in one location before turning sharply and switching to a northwest direction, then back again.

At first, I kept my gaze on the muddy water, watching the swelling, undulating waves and patterns change, and countless ducks waterskiing to a stop to search for food, but the rush of the river proved to unnerve me. I settled on surveying landscape skimming by ... and Clay.

Each time I thought he couldn't look any better, I discovered otherwise. He looked at his finest today. Donned in knee-length cargo shorts, a Polo shirt, and deck shoes without socks, he looked as comfortable and skilled on a boat as anyone I'd ever seen. I loved watching him in action, the rippling of his muscles as he maneuvered the ropes, the spill of dark hair across his forehead as the boat surged faster, the twitch of his lips when he teased me about tying my life vest so tight I might never get it off.

His plan: to sidle Maryland's edge as we headed to Four Locks, then return on the other side, closer to West Virginia. He handed me a pair of binoculars and asked if his agenda sounded good. I agreed, but thought: *Are you kidding me? We could sit at the dock all day as far as I'm concerned. As long as I can look at you and be with you, nothing is going to change the serenity of this outing.*

As it turned out, I was wrong.

In fact, my peacefulness unhinged within a short distance of leaving the dock. As we sped around the first big bend in the river, we spotted the C&O Canal Visitor's Center to our right, then an expansive stone footbridge filled with hikers and other folks gawking at the flooded river, followed by a gathering of people in biking gear standing at a small clearing in the trees jutting over the water. My gaze moved from them to track the slope to the river.

That's when I saw the large and distinctly shaped tree I had crashed into last year while biking with Adriana. I grabbed my binoculars to get a better look. Perhaps it was my heightened awareness of the tree, but whatever it was, as I moved the binoculars to peer closer at the bikers, I spotted a transparent figure and recognized him instantly as Clay's father.

It happened so quickly I had no time to think through my actions, scooting close to Clay and grabbing his arm to yell above the roar of the engine, "Can we move closer? To those people?"

Confusion crossed his face, so I added, "I see someone I might know."

He shrugged and slowed the boat, maneuvering closer to land and dropping back the engine, so it hovered there, but not by much because the strong current kept trying to push us downstream.

All this time, I watched Mason, noting the instant he recognized me. He smiled and raised his hand in a greeting, but it faltered. His smile disappeared. He moved closer to the cliff's edge as if drawn by a magnet, eyes intent and focused on Clay. He tilted his head, confused, wondering. Daring to hope? His gaze darted to me and, thanks to the binoculars, I could see the question on his face.

I nodded, offering him confirmation, but I'm not sure he could see my gesture. My eyes misted, and my breath hitched. I dropped the binoculars to dangle from my neck and covered the lower half of my face with my hands to control the emotions churning inside. Mason looked at his son for the first time in years! He'd been killed when Clay was a mere six or seven years old. Now here he was, a grown man.

"Are you okay?"

I turned to see Clay studying me. He reached out and placed a hand on my shoulder as though he wanted to make right whatever wrong caused me such concern.

"I … I thought I saw someone who reminded me of another time. That's all. I'm fine." I smiled for good measure.

He studied me a moment longer, a dubious look on his face. "Well, if you're done here …?"

I nodded and looked back to Mason. "There's nothing more to do here now."

If he wondered at my odd words, he didn't voice it. Instead, oblivious to Mason, he pointed at a few birds sitting on a small patch of land in the middle of the river. He said the grassy knoll was known as "Duck Island," then he cranked the engine full throttle, and we sped upriver.

I was grateful for the distractions that kept us from having to talk the rest of the way to Four Locks—the rumble of the engine and the roar of the river, as well as the need to be on guard against debris floating into our path. It gave me time to get a grip on the visual of Mason looking at his son.

By the time we reached our destination, I had mostly shaken off the emotions, but the notion lingered that I needed to do the decent thing—visit Mason again and confirm the man he saw in the boat was his son. The problem was, I wasn't sure how I could get away from the meeting without promising to resolve his death. I was weary now of souls I encountered. Will's possible duplicity the year before had left doubt in my mind about the genuineness of *any* soul.

***

Four Locks sported a drive-in campground, picnic area, and boat ramp. We docked, pulled on boots, and toured the immediate area on foot. A park sign announced that a barn, general stores, warehouses, and a dry dock for boat repair once stood along this section of the canal. One lock house still stood from the canal days, but otherwise, the area comprised lush green grass, pristine deciduous trees, picnic tables, and gentle slopes to the river. I'd often heard that following rain, the grass and trees look their greenest. It's true, but it also distinguished the muddy, churning river as looking that much more out of sorts.

Clay had packed a blanket, sandwiches, and iced tea. The saturated ground prevented comfortable seating, so we spread the blanket on a picnic table and climbed on. We talked about memories of childhood and our individual days spent camping and boating. At times, our conversation switched to the odd assortment of items floating by at random—a plastic baseball bat, a chair cushion, a yellow T-shirt—as though the floodwater had reached over the banks upstream to grab a few souvenirs and mark its power as it continued downriver.

Clay set his plate aside and stretched back, leaning on his flattened hands, face raised to the sun.

"You look relaxed," I said. He sported more muscles than last year, and the wind had burned his cheeks during our trip upriver, but under those closed eyelids was the same Caribbean blue shade I remembered.

"I am." He opened one eye against the sun and looked at me before closing it again. "The company is perfect, and the scenery couldn't be better. Don't know why anyone would want to live anywhere else."

I was so wrapped in his comment about me being the perfect company, it took me a heartbeat or two to process the rest of his words. Was he talking about Mason, whom he believed had left his family for somewhere distant? I wasn't about to ruin the mood by asking. Instead, I said, "I agree."

He sat up, scooted his butt back and dropped his elbows to his knees to look at me.

"You *do*, don't you? Michael says you are quite content in this area. That you want to stay here. Permanently, I mean."

I nodded. "This is home now. I was slow to move back to *Crossings*, but that's where I belong."

He rapped his knuckles on the table wood in the space between his legs as he said, "Good deal." Our gazes locked, and judging by the smile on his face, he was pleased. I liked that.

"What are your plans after community college?" he asked as we watched a V of honking Canadian geese cut across the sky.

"Nontraditional, and all the way to Shenandoah University." I laughed, aware that he would grasp my humor. The private liberal arts university was a mere thirty minutes away in Winchester, Virginia, a straight commute down I-81.

"No dorm life? No sororities or Ivy League towers?"

I shook my head. "No interest." I frowned. "I'm lucky, I guess." *Although I've never thought of myself as lucky before.* "There's a good college nearby, and there's no worry about money." *Although I'd rather have my family than insurance money any day.* "So, I can commute, keep my part-time job, and live at home." I pulled my shoulders back. "I'm told all orphans want a home. I guess I'm a statistic."

"Maybe." He nodded. "But I guess when you've been parented by loneliness long enough, you improvise. Lock in security, however you can." He reached over and covered my hand with his. "I get it. And I'm impressed. You've grown a lot this past year."

I looked away, lest I reveal he might be wrong. Hadn't I decided the night before that I'd let a year go by with no growth whatsoever?

He continued. "You mentioned the work you want to do. What's it involve?"

"I'm not sure. Definitely history. Probably business, too. I'm not certain yet how those two can merge together."

"Hmmm." He folded his arms, tilted his head, and spoke in a teasing manner. "Let's see, you progressed from interior design to history to business, and now you're working at Hilson's Antique Emporium. And loving it. Sounds like you've brought all your disciplines together."

To say I was startled would be an understatement. And why did the thought excite me so much?

But the shop belonged to Hilda, not me. And she had two sons with families living in other parts of the country. I brushed away the notion. "I don't know. I wish I were focused, like you and Adriana."

"I think people discover their true callings when they discover their talents. Ade picked up a flute early in life. For me, it took several encounters with injustice, both here at home and in the service, before discovering I had a stomach for studying the labyrinth of the law."

"So what are your plans after law school?"

"Hang a shingle. Here, in Williamsport. Unlike my peers, it's not adventure I crave. I've had that. I want family and stability. I want to pick up clients in the District. Maybe non-profits who need legal help. Then, I'll camp and fish and golf to my heart's content. Raise two perfect kids with my wife—"

"Two?"

"Yeah." He shot a mischievous smile, and I looked away rather than feed his craziness. "Clay Junior and Clayola," he said.

I inched my face back to look at him. "Did you really just say that?"

"I did, and I think it's perfect. Little girls like crayons, so I always thought Clayola the perfect name."

I laughed and threw my empty cup at him. "Why not Claybelle or Claymentine?"

He tilted his head, looked skyward and sang, "Oh my darling, Claymentine ... I like it."

We laughed some more before returning our talk to Ade. Clay confirmed she had a date with Jamaar that night.

"I was hoping ..." I waved the thought away.

"What? You want Michael and Ade to get back together?"

"Well, yeah."

His eyebrows formed an anxious arc. "Grace, stay out of it. Don't play matchmaker."

"Isn't that what you did?"

"No, I asked Ade to show Jamaar around the area so I could spend the day with you. I thought it would take her mind off her job search. He's the one who turned it into a grand evening together."

"She said she might move to Seattle."

"Maybe. Oh, now don't you cry, too." He reached out to hold my hand, and with his other one, tucked a lock of loose hair behind my ears. "You and Mom. She's so upset about Ade leaving, she's calling every school district in Maryland to see if Ade can get a position teaching music."

"Do you suppose she'd take a job like that?" Hope rang in my voice.

"I hope not. She needs to stick with her dream, even if we lose her for a few years."

"A few years is a long time."

"Come on … we made it through one." His tone grew serious. "We could do another if we had to, don't you agree?"

He looked at me with such intense expectation, I felt like our afternoon fun depended on my answer, so I said, "Yes, of course." However, I dreaded the notion.

He smiled, looking content with my answer, and we looked to the river again, both wrapped in our own thoughts, but still holding hands.

After a brief lull, I asked: "When do you start school?" Translated: *So how long do I have with you in Williamsport before you drive three hours away from me?*

He rubbed a line between his eyebrows then looked at the river. "We ought to start heading back. We can talk about school tonight."

"Tonight?"

His lips curled. "I guess I forgot to mention … I made reservations for seven o'clock. At the Airport Inn. If you're interested, that is. They serve incredible prime rib … you're not vegan, are you?"

I smiled. If I were, I might have changed my mind on the spot. "Not even close," I said. "I love red meat."

He pulled his hand away, slapped it onto his heart, and said, "The woman of my dreams."

I laughed and turned away, but he reached out and pulled me around to face him. He looked intent. Was his a look of caring? Hope? "No, I mean it. You *are* that woman. I was afraid you'd wake up this past year. Change your mind about us."

"Me too," I confessed in a whisper. "I mean … that you might change your mind."

"Not a chance." He kissed me, short, sweet, his lips lingering on mine for the briefest moment, but shivers spread down to my toes.

I wished he'd kiss me again. I wanted to elongate the moment, make it last. But we sat in public, too central in the picnic area, for more PDA.

"Come on, let's go," he said and held my hand as I climbed from the table.

You'd think the kiss would linger in my thoughts as we packed and launched again. Instead, I dwelled on why he abruptly changed the subject when I asked about his school.

I also wondered why Seth sometimes popped into my mind when I was with Clay, and vice versa. Did either of them ever hold a true edge with me?

I'd told the truth; I hadn't changed my mind about Clay.

I simply hadn't anticipated Seth crawling into my mind and taking up space, too.

CHAPTER 11

The joy in journeying back on the same path you came: everything looks different, thanks to the new direction. So the return trip proved even more delightful than the outbound trek, particularly since I basked in the thought we still had hours to spend together that evening.

When we neared Duck Island, I glued my gaze to the West Virginia side of the river, determined not to look toward Maryland where I'd seen Mason. Again, I marveled at the steep banks sweeping from the river to the peaks of the land, even higher on this side than on Maryland's edge.

I watched as a rare, bald eagle dove to snag a fish from the muddy water then swept up, up, up, flying beyond the crest of the ridge, at least five stories above the river. Something caught my eye. On a stony clearing at the top of the land and behind several trees appeared an odd symbol etched into the rock. It was circular with swirls in the center. My mind flashed back to the box the bearded man carried into Hilson's Antique Emporium on my first day of work, the one accompanied by an angry-looking ghost. I was sure the symbols were the same. What could it mean?

"Grace?" Clay's voice pulled me back to the present. "You look pale. Is it motion sickness?" He moved closer, no doubt so we could hear each other better. The engine and the roar of the swift river worked as a barrier against easy conversation.

"I'm fine." I pointed. "What's that up there?" The boat had traveled beyond where I'd first seen the symbol, but as we moved, it popped in and out of view two more times while we navigated a bend in the river.

"That drawing? Never noticed it before. I guess the higher water provides a different angle." He shielded the sun's glare from his eyes as he studied the spot. "That ridge beyond is called Chocton Bluff." He gestured to an inlet directly below the rock formation. "Below is Devil's Cove."

Chocton Bluff? That's where Clyde Drury had died on the same night someone murdered Mason. I focused on the other piece of information: "Devil's Cove?"

He nodded. "Never been there. As a boy, I was warned to stay away. Too treacherous." He smiled. "That was in front of Mom. On the side, Dad promised we'd go there one day. Then, when you grow up, the prohibited isn't glamorous anymore, so you don't bother exploring. Maybe I should."

"No," I answered so quickly, his eyebrows rose. I shrugged. "Anything called Devil's Cove doesn't sound good."

"True," he grinned. "Besides, it'd be easier to get to Chocton Bluff by driving south and saddling back on a trail road. People used to do that to go sledding, but I heard the trail's been closed for years. You could also get there across your land. It'd be a treacherous climb, but possible, I guess."

"What!" I ramped my tone down before continuing. "What do you mean, my land?"

"Right there." He pointed toward the West Virginia banks again. "From the ledge, you'd descend a steep trail into a ravine, pass through some thick woods, then cross over a couple rolling hills, to reach the old cemetery on your property. As you know, your house isn't that far from that graveyard. In fact, you'd have to trudge across that tunnel area that burned last year."

There, in his answer, threatened at least three conversations I didn't want to have with him today: (1) the fire in the tunnels and what it meant, (2) my land bordering anything with the devil's designation in it, and (3) the close geography of my property to Chocton Bluff where Clyde died.

As the boat lurched ahead, I moved to its stern to study the bluff and Devil's Cove. I swear I saw a dark shadow move, followed by a swatch of blue, there and gone so fast I couldn't be sure. I could rationalize it away as the shadow of a bird or a ground creature, but the form had been too large. Only a person could cause such a shape.

A whisper of dread unfurled in my stomach. Something about the cliff didn't bode well. Was this what Hilda meant when she said she could "discern" evil?

CHAPTER 12

Clay had tucked dinner clothes in the car, so when we finished boating, we changed at *Crossings* to save time. Like I had done, he wandered every inch of the apartment, focusing mostly on the new windows and voicing more interest in safety than aesthetics. "Impressive," he said. "Looks secure. You still own that rifle, right?"

A flash of memory came: the night we first met when I startled him with a weapon in my hand.

"Yes, it's in the coat closet." I pointed toward the exterior door.

"Good. Keep it handy." Then he threw me a curve ball when he sobered and said, "I'd feel better if you weren't living out here alone since I can't check on you."

"You can on weekends."

Rather than respond, he checked the time on his cell phone and suggested we hurry along. Again, I got the impression he was avoiding a topic, but I decided he must be anticipating a busy school year.

I changed first and walked Tramp as Clay took his turn. I wore a bohemian-looking skirt and blouse. My hair looked tousled and frizzled from the river water and humidity, so I swept it on top my head and let little cascades fall around the sides. He made me *feel* it when he said I looked fabulous. He wore creased navy blue pants and an off-white pull-on short-sleeved shirt, and *he* looked like the fabulous one.

Nick's Airport Inn faced the runways, a few minutes north of Hagerstown and about a twenty-five-minute drive from Williamsport. Clay was right: it served the best prime rib I ever tasted. We sat at a corner table behind white rick-rack room dividers, dining to the strains of classical music, courtesy of a pianist in the next room.

After finishing our meal, we lingered and enjoyed being together. Sometimes Clay leaned back and stretched out, looking like a man at the peak of peace and comfort. Other times, he hunched over the table toward me so far it probably looked like we wanted to get into each other's skin. Before long, the waitress stopped returning to the table, as though she and the rest of the waitstaff abandoned any hope of using our table again that night.

During lulls in the conversation, I marveled silently how wonderful the day had been. I hadn't liked his affirmation we could weather another year or two if necessary, but I admitted to myself it seemed impossible an entire year had already passed since we'd spent time together. Had it truly been a year since we sat on my porch talking? Or traveled to Georgia together? Or danced in the café as music crooned from the rafters?

But thanks to Adriana and Michael and their birthday surprise, I was quite aware a year had gone by. That made me wonder all the more about how drawn to each other Clay and I were. Like we linked in some way. He never once asked about Seth, and I appreciated that. Yet, those same thoughts made me uncomfortable, almost a little guilty, like I was cheating on Seth.

Where did these thoughts come from? Seth was a friend, and that was all. Wasn't he? Each time the thoughts gripped me, Clay smiled or took my hand, again convincing me I was right where I should be.

I found it odd he didn't bring up last year and the tunnels, but maybe, like me, he wanted to look forward, not back.

We talked of our childhoods, swapped stories on travels and middle school antics, and compared impressions of some of the people I'd met in Williamsport. Clay told me more about Jack and some of the wisdom my stepfather shared with him. I loved the fact that this man I loved—so handsome sitting across from me— also had loved the only man I'd ever known as a father.

I said, "I have a couple family albums back at the apartment if you'd like to see more pictures of Jack. Why don't you come over for dinner Friday night? I'll cook. Do you like salmon?"

I hadn't expected my invitation to be a mood changer. He frowned, leaned forward, and laced his fingers with mine on the table. His eyes searched my face as though he looked for words there.

"You know, last year I said I love you," he said, continuing to study me intently. "That hasn't changed. Each time I see you, you take my breath away. My thinking shuts down, and I want to be there for you always. I tried to make today perfect, so we'd have a memory."

I hitched my breath. In his tone and his fumbling words, I detected a "but" coming, and every fiber in me begged, *please don't say it.* I was loathe to hurry the word along, but neither was I any good at waiting for bad news. So I voiced it first: "But?"

He gripped my hand tighter, and his eyes suddenly looked like a stormy sea beneath concerned brows. "But … I'm leaving town."

I waited one heartbeat for him to elaborate, but it didn't come. I finished for him: "Yes, for school."

He blew out his cheeks slowly. "I'm not returning to school this year."

I started to pull my hand back, but he wouldn't let go. I said, "But … you're not coming back here?"

He shook his head.

My insides tightened. "You're quitting school?"

"No. Taking a year off. I hope it's only a year."

"You hope? You don't know? Where are you going?"

A shadow fell across his face. "To search for Dad."

I jerked my hand away, propped my elbows on the table, and dropped my face into both hands.

He reached over, placed a hand under my chin, and eased it up so he could look in my eyes. "Have you seen Mom? Even before this whole Nidhi thing, she's been anxious. Unable to move on.

She finally has a chance at happiness. She loves Whit. The best part is he's crazy about her. He's a good man. An honest man. The problem is Dad. Her memory of him. They had an amazing relationship." He shook his head, let go of me, and sat back, a look of frustration crossing his face. "I remember, as a child, Reaghan and I knew we were loved, but we could tell, even as kids, our parents had something unique without us. None of us understood why he left. It's time. I've got to find him. Find out why. I've got to bring answers back to Mom and set her free."

I didn't say a word. I couldn't. I sat there, staring at the same stained spot on the tablecloth.

He continued. "I owe her that much. She deserves to be happy." He groaned a syllable of frustration, and I looked up to see him run a hand over his head. "Who am I kidding? It's for me, too. Dad's sudden departure from our lives, I can't put it to rest. Not the man I knew. I'm not sure I can be a good husband, a good father until I find out what made him abandon all that. I don't ever want to make the same mistake. I hope you can understand my need to do this."

I understand all too well! I left Boston to come all the way to West Virginia, remember? Not only to leave my aunt but also to find parts of Jack again. I had needed to "feel" him and secure closure. Yes, I understand all too well why you need to do this. But, I don't like it. And Lord help me, I don't know how to tell you that you will never find your answer.

When I didn't respond, Clay continued. "Grace, I won't be gone forever. After I find Dad, I'll be back. But I'm not returning without answers."

"Well then, I guess you're never coming back." I spoke the words in a harsh whisper before I could stop myself.

"That's not true. During my work this summer, our firm worked with a private investigator. I had lunch with him a couple times, and we talked about finding a missing person. That's what put the idea in my head. That it would be possible. The guy said to expect it to take at least six months to a year. Or more, because it's a very old and cold trail."

"Where will you start?"

"Mexico. Rumor says he's there. Makes sense. We vacationed there once. On the Pacific Coast. I recall Dad loved one village in particular. It's logical he would head there. If not, then I'll try Costa Rica. Switzerland. Ireland. All places Dad liked."

No, Clay, he's in none of those places. He's not looking at the sunshine in Mexico or the blue waters in Costa Rica or the mountains in Switzerland. He's down at the Canal, along the muddy river, in a ravine. He was murdered then buried there like a piece of garbage.

"I need to go back to school Monday or Tuesday," he said. "I'll see you before I go. I'll meet with the dean and complete the paperwork for the delay in the degree. Then I'll be back later in the week to say goodbye. On my way to the airport."

That's why you dodged my question about school earlier. And, why you wanted to make sure we could survive another separation. And, why Seth and the tunnels didn't merit conversation today.

"I already talked to Whit and Sidney about going. We are going to tell Mom and Reaghan tomorrow after church. Reaghan will blow a gasket, of course. She'll want me around to play uncle to the kids. But I can be a better uncle if I put closure on their grandfather's abandonment. Mom loves you like a daughter. You might want to stop in and check on her."

I'll try, but I'm going to be awfully busy solving a murder as quickly as possible. "Sure. Of course."

Remember yesterday I said I didn't harbor the energy or gumption to tackle the daunting task of resolving another murder? Clay's announcement changed all that. I had both now in spades.

The problem is, it meant tangling with death again. I'd grown enough to admit I was worming into territory best left to God alone. But I needed Clay to stay and wanted to help Cassie and Whit, so I would take the chance come what may.

I don't remember saying more at the restaurant. I don't recall us paying the bill or driving home or being escorted to my front door. I was so lost in thought and my resolve to solve Mason's murder as soon as possible that when I reached for the latch to my apartment and heaved it open, I startled when Clay reached past me to pull it shut. I could feel his chest behind me, his head to my right. His hands gripped my shoulders, and he turned me toward him.

"I'm not letting the night end like this. Not with this distance between us." He stared at me, then traced my cheek with the back of his hand and said, "Grace" in the same way he might say *enchanting* or *incredible* or *lovely* and truly mean it.

He leaned down and kissed me, gentle at first, then deeper, harder. Our limbs entwined so tightly and so full I wasn't sure where he ended and I began. I couldn't get enough of his warmth, his comfort, his heartbeat, the sounds of his breathing.

After he left, I had a conversation with him in my head as I climbed into bed. However, I wasn't dwelling on what I wished I'd said, or what I'd say next time. Instead, I rehearsed how I would tell him he no longer had to go. Because there was no father to go find.

But no matter what words I came up with, it wasn't enough to soften the blow he would soon be forced to endure.

CHAPTER 13

On Sunday, I rose before dawn and trudged outside with Tramp for a quick walk. The drench and fog had returned overnight, the former intermittent while the latter hovered as though considering permanent residency.

Back in the apartment, I donned rain boots and courage before setting out to see Mason. For good measure, and a little bravado, I pocketed a canister of pepper spray and a flashlight. My mission to solve his murder had begun, and I wouldn't let anything stand in my way.

After parking at the far edge of the Visitor Center lot, I stepped onto the gravel towpath, heading in Mason's direction. Two long miles of shadows and eerie nature sounds, all cloaked in darkness.

A voice floated from the inky blackness: "Your dark-skinned friend?"

I whirled toward it, struggling to remove the pepper spray. Before I could disentangle the small canister, I determined the origin of the voice and froze. In the faint light of a clouded, bloated moon, I recognized the dirty, shabby clothing: a neck bandana, oversized white shirt, tannish-brown pants and wide-brimmed hat—the same type of clothing depicted in the historic pictures in the Visitor's Center of the canal workers from the 1800s. Here sat the same soul I'd noticed in this spot once before, last year when I visited Mason, although I hadn't spoken to him. He had been whittling under this same tree, the first soul other than Mason I ever saw along the Canal.

I abandoned my struggle to retrieve the spray. It wouldn't work with a ghost anyway.

He continued. "The one with the long curly black hair? You rode bicycles with her."

I nodded. "Adriana."

"They's a lotta folks prayin' for her. Tell her to call 'bout the job tomorrow mornin'. 'Tween nine and ten. You got that? 'Tween nine and ten."

My breath hitched. "How did you ... are you an angel?"

He smirked and shook his head in one of those *people-are-so-stupid* kinds of shakes. His bushy beard emphasized the movement. The rest of him remained still, and no wonder. Despite being thin, his arms and shoulders bulged with muscles that must have built up during years of slinging heavy sacks on and off the flatboats traversing the Canal.

I continued. "What then?"

He offered a tentative smile. "A messenger. No more."

I opened my mouth to ask, "For whom?" and "Why?" but changed my mind. It would do no good. I was collecting experience with ghosts. Most of them shared stories of unfinished business before their deaths and of staying here to finish the tasks. Some wanted to save a life (as in the fireman at the collapsed bridge) while others wanted to deliver a message (such as the ghost that saved me from a speeding car in Lexington, Virginia, the year before). I wasn't sure what this ghost's intent was. Could I trust him—or any of them—given how Will acted last year?

"What's your name?" I asked.

"Mule."

"Mule?"

"Yes'm ... Mule Chasen."

I exhaled in frustration. "Is that a joke?"

His shoulders jerked back, indignant. "Ain't no joke."

"So ... what? You chase mules?"

"Nah, folks said I's strong 'n' stubborn as a mule. Me given name's Lemule, but only me ma ever called me Lem." He looked back toward the river.

"Well, Mule, is there anything else I should know?"

He shook his head, without looking at me, so I turned to go.

"Wait, maybe …" he began.

I turned back and waited.

"That ranger friend of yourn?"

Again, my breath caught, wondering what he might announce. "Seth? Sandy hair, about my height and age?"

"Yeah, him … sprung from bad seed, that one … but it ain't my choice, and it ain't his fault. Tell him not to take the money. It's tainted." He turned his head to shoot me an intense stare. "*Real* tainted."

I had no idea what he meant by "bad seed," but I registered the gravity of his message, the warning it implied. I took a deep breath. This soul was sharing poignant information with me about Seth, details making my heart race, my fear escalate. I became afraid for Seth and wanted to talk to him immediately, but I needed to speak with Mason before dawn sapped him of optimum energy. I hated that circumstances, once again, forced me to choose between Seth and Clay.

Either way, time was limited, and I thought it wise to be kind to this soul, to maybe understand him a little better so I could talk to him again later. I followed his gaze as it focused toward the river.

"You must have seen a lot along these banks."

"Worked on the river from 1823 to 1835. That's when the Canal reached us. So I did that 'til 1881."

I longed to drop to my butt on the soggy ground, curl my legs under me, and share a long talk with Mule. His stories, his firsthand experience with history and having lived it as he did, that is what made history come alive for me. But there was no time.

He continued in a slow manner as if he had all the time in the world. "Seen births, deaths, duels, murders, fights, theft, gamblin', weddin's, partyin'. Brung soldiers north, just to have 'em killed by soldiers we brung south. The canal, this river, it was a rough place. Rough people livin' a rough life. Women too."

"Why did you stay? Couldn't you find work elsewhere?" I hoped he wouldn't take offense at the question.

He shrugged. "A travelin' preacher saved me. Made it bearable. And, there was other good folks too, don't get me wrong. But wasn't many of 'em. One I liked was a fur trader, trying to git back to them big lakes up north. Another, a giant of a guy ... he fell clean through the ice over there." He gestured his head toward the darkness, and I assumed he meant the West Virginia side of the river. "We had a devil of a time pullin' him out. River never was a dull place."

His words conjured an image I'd had before. One Will had described, and I envisioned it again. The ice giving way. A man going under, arms and legs flailing to no avail. His scream extinguished as he dropped beneath the cracked surface, disappearing into the demanding, black water. His friends panicking to save him.

I had to know. "Asa. The man who fell in the ice, was his name Asa Garett?"

He shook his head. "No, they called him Bear. I 'member 'cause he was named after an animal, like me."

"That's him! Asa was known as Bear."

"Big guy, but gentle as a lamb. I 'member him. I'd never met someone so kind. Humble, too."

"Do you remember William Kavanaugh, too? The friend with Bear?"

He tilted his head and said "Kavanaugh" as though trying to read a memory in the air. "Yeah, I met that family. Took 'em 'cross the river several times. Good people." He shook his head. "Good people livin' in a bad place."

I had a million questions, but no time to ask. I backed away. "Mr. Chasen ... Mule ... I must go. I need to meet someone ..."

"Mason Baxter?"

Again, I stopped cold. *Did this soul know everything?* "How did you ...?"

"I listen. I see. He was local, too. I seen him down at the river a lot with a boy … back before he became one of us."

His words bored into me the way carpenter bees must destroy wood. I covered my mouth with a hand to hold in the wave of sorrow and agony coursing through me, the picture of Mason and Clay together, sharing father-son rituals as they enjoyed the river together.

Stifled by the images in my mind, I struggled with the need to get away to think, despite the wealth of information this soul had to offer.

"Mule, I'm sorry. I need to go … but I'll come back. May I talk to you again?"

He didn't look as I stumbled backward, away from him, but he offered, "I ain't goin' nowhere. Got me center here." He pointed to the ground, and I saw the tip of a rusty metal cleat sticking out of the ground. I recognized it from one I'd seen in the Visitor's Center. People would tether their boats to cleats to keep them from floating away in the heyday of the Canal.

Satisfied, I turned and started walking again.

His voice cut through the still air. "Be careful over there."

I stopped but didn't turn around.

"There's somethin' brewin'. Somethin' that's gripped this town for centuries. It'll make that fire of yourn look mild."

I whirled around, but he was gone.

CHAPTER 14

With *nine and ten, bad seed, good people in a bad place,* and *somethin' brewin'* diving and swirling in my head, I reached my destination without further thought of what to say to Mason. I had intended to have an apology at the ready, an explanation for my elusiveness, and I expected to take a few minutes locating him.

However, I barely stepped two yards off the towpath before Mason stepped close. His translucence and the first vestiges of dawn rendered the flashlight unnecessary.

"It was him, wasn't it? Clay? My son?" He fired questions with such speed it was as if he hoped the urgency would make it true.

He looked the same as I remembered—polo shirt, jeans, a full head of dark hair and thick beard stubble. The only thing different was the distinct expectation and hope in his demeanor.

"Mr. Baxter, I'm so sorry for not giving you a heads-up. I had no warning it would happen."

Mason shoved his shoulders back and donned one of those *are-you-crazy?* kinds of looks. "You brought me my son. A grown man." He shook his head in wonder. "I saw him once or twice when he was younger. He would have been ten or eleven years of age. On the towpath, with another man. They were biking."

"Jack." It had to be, based on the stories Clay once told me. "He was my stepfather." Mason would understand Jack's connection to his family and the area because I'd already shared much of my story with him.

Mason nodded. "Jack was a good man. I'm not surprised he reared such a lovely young daughter."

A lump lodged in my throat, hard as a stone. Tears moistened my eyes.

"Mr. Baxter, I haven't been back in the past year because—"

"Because you suffered a fire."

I hesitated. "How did you know?"

"I saw it. And I overheard stories from the hikers. Enough to ascertain you were fine, but a young woman died. She was your friend?"

I nodded and looked at the ground. "Kate Fletcher. She died of meningitis. Nothing to do with the fire—" I broke off as another thought sprouted. "Wait a second … you said you witnessed the fire. How?"

He pointed across the river, in the same direction Mule had nodded a few minutes earlier. "I can see across to your estate in winter when the leaves are off the trees. The fire occurred late summer, September, so visibility was limited. But, the flames shot high above the treeline, and the alarms echoed through the valley. Oddly, though, I judged the fire to come from the grounds, not the house."

"That's right. The tunnels underneath. But it destroyed part of the attached apartment, so I lived with Cassie—" Alarmed, I broke off again, throwing my hand over my mouth so hard and fast, it stung.

"Cassie! *My* Cassie? In the garage apartment, right?" He grinned, pulling on a memory. "I built it for her mother, knowing full well it would prove handy as my children grew."

"You were right. Clay lived in it for a while."

"And now he's in law school?"

It was a rhetorical question. I'd already updated him the year before on Clay's plans. "He is, yes, but he's had a change of plans, and that's why I'm here. It's time to … to settle your death."

He blanched, and his shoulders drooped, a beleaguered stance. "Grace, I appreciate that. This life of limbo is hollow. But it's too dangerous. Remember, you may be dealing with a murderer who may still be living in Williamsport."

"I'm aware of that."

"We should let the natural course of things occur. My murderer will pay the ultimate price when it matters. Judgment isn't ours. And I don't believe intervening is a smart—"

"Clay is leaving school and putting his life on hold to find you. He still hurts from losing you. From not understanding why. And Cassie ..." How could I couch my delivery on this next thought? Finding no way to soften the message, I plunged ahead. "Cassie is in love again. Finally. But she's finding it hard to trust. To move on. She carries you like a heavy weight on her shoulder."

He dropped onto a rock behind him.

"I'm sorry." My voice was a whisper of sorrow, but in the shadowed stillness, it reached him.

"My beautiful bride." His voice was hoarse. "My life began the day I met her. And our children ..." he shook his head, "... they made life so complete. I was so blessed. I often thought it wrong one man could experience such happiness. Sometimes I feared waking up to discover it all a dream."

My heart ached. I moved to him, dropped to my knees and placed my hand on his arm. It felt cold but familiar. I'd touched Will several times and was aware that when a soul wanted to, he could manifest his composition as solid as any living person's.

"Please, Mason," I choked out the words, "... please help me to help your family."

His gaze moved from my hand on his arm to my eyes. "My son loves you, doesn't he?"

"He says he does."

"And does he know you love him?"

I smiled. "I hope so. Please tell me your story."

He gestured to another rock situated about a yard to his left. I settled onto it and braced myself for the agony of his tale.

"On the day I died, I participated in a career day at the high school in Hagerstown. The snow began to fall so quickly they canceled school and ended early. The ground wasn't even frozen yet. But the snow accumulated, and we got concerned about getting home. I made it to Williamsport and stopped at the bank to tell everyone to go home. Nidhi ... that's Nidhi Michelson ... my secretary—"

"I've met her. She's the branch manager now." There seemed to be no point in mentioning her missing status at the moment.

He smiled, looking pleased about her promotion. "Nidhi handed me several messages. Two of them suggested urgency. One was from our wealthiest client, old man Mint. The ole codger had as much money in his safety deposit box as in his accounts. He reminded me every chance he got he didn't trust the banks. He wanted $100,000 removed and brought to him that night. He'd signed paperwork once authorizing me to do his bidding for him. Rather than lose his business, I agreed. The other message came from Holland Greer."

My muscles tensed, but I kept my voice calm. "The local historian."

"You know him?"

"I've met him. We've had words. To be honest, I find him kind of slimy."

He nodded. "You have good instincts. He'd been hounding me for months about a loan to build a one-of-a-kind museum and educational center. It would be located on the outskirts of Williamsport."

"What does 'one-of-a-kind' mean?"

"The theme was to be the paranormal. He presents himself as a historian, but that's only one aspect of his work."

My nails bit into my palms, and I swear my nostrils flared. "He's a charlatan. Nothing more than a ghost hunter."

Mason's eyebrows rose at my comment. "He's also very calculating. Give him an inch, and he'll measure it. But worst of all, he's an accomplished thief."

I gasped. "How do you know?"

He raised a delaying hand. "I'll get to that. His message said he demanded to talk again. He was threatening discrimination because I turned him down on the loan. Technically, he had no argument. The bank trusted me to make these decisions and to take only acceptable risks to the board. But the truth is, he was right in that I found his museum repugnant. Against my faith and better judgment. I began to wonder if I judged too quickly. If I'd made the mistake of bringing my personal beliefs into my work. I tried to assess the merits of the loan and the potential it could prove profitable, but I decided I needed to do more sleuthing into this guy. To figure out what he was all about and whether he could be a good investment or not."

"What did you do?"

"I walked into Clyde Drury's office, beside mine. He was an associate … and a good friend. Salt of the earth kind of guy. So much so, in fact, that a day or two before, after I'd seen a program on TV about a family that lost everything when the father died unexpectedly, I told Cassie to go to Clyde if anything ever happened to me. Meanwhile, I had shared with Clyde all the details of my investments and insurance. I figured Cassie would be distraught if anything ever happened, that she'd never remember.

"That night I told Clyde my plans on going to Holland's, and I encouraged him to leave early. He said he would because he wanted to take his daughter sledding. I called Cassie. Said I'd be late then drove to Greer's place. Unannounced. It's in the middle of nowhere, outside town. Surrounded by gravel … everywhere. Quite unimpressive."

I shivered at memories of my encounter with Holland at his house. I didn't share this with Mason. It would serve no purpose. Instead, I said, "So what happened?"

"When I got there, it was already dark. I knocked at his door, but there were no lights and no answer. So, I started back to my car and noticed lights around the back. In a shed. I walked back there, thinking I'd find him doing woodwork or fixing his car."

"But he wasn't?"

"No."

"What was he doing?"

Mason moved his gaze from the ground to rest on me. "Looking through his stolen goods."

"What! How do you know?"

"Because I recognized the items. They were part of a traveling display at Antietam. All sorts of artifacts, worth tens of thousands of dollars, from the Civil War era. Cass, the kids, and I had gone to see the display. From there, they were scheduled to go to Gettysburg for a few weeks, but the paper reported dozens of items stolen."

"Nidhi said the police investigated and decided you never showed up at Mint's or Holland's. She said Mint accused you of never delivering his money."

"She's right. I never did make it to Mint's. So I don't know what happened to his money or my car."

"What did you do after you saw the stolen things?"

"I was so startled, I wasn't sure what to do. I backed away from the window and sneaked back to my car where I had a car phone … back then, we didn't have those little mobile phone gizmos everyone carries around today—"

"Who did you call?"

"Clyde. He was in his car, driving to Chocton Bluff to take his daughter sledding."

"Did you say his name out loud?"

He raised his eyebrows at my unexpected question. "I'm rather certain I did."

I remained quiet about Clyde dying that night. I didn't want to distract him from his memory.

"What happened next?"

"I was struck on the back of my head."

"Holland!"

"It would seem so, but even as I dropped, I remember wondering how he heard me and how he got behind me so quickly. Funny I would focus on that rather than on what he might do next."

"And that's it? You don't remember anything else? I mean, you must not have died there, or your center wouldn't be here."

"I died from the blow, but not right away. The pain was excruciating. Darkness pushed into my skull, and a roaring vibrated through my head. I wavered in and out of consciousness for a while. Enough to remember being placed in a car trunk. At another point, I was dragged through endless trees and weedy terrain."

"Here? The canal?"

"I suppose. It's hard to tell. The pain was unbearable, and I couldn't fight back. I couldn't see. The last thing I remember was a voice … an odd voice, almost high pitched, due to my head wound, I guess. The voice certainly didn't fit the strength dragging me. Whoever spoke accused me of meddling. Said I could rot there and see what all my meddling couldn't stop."

"What did he mean?"

"I don't know. I assumed he meant across the river. To Devil's Cove."

I prodded. "What did he mean you could watch? He had to be aware you were dying, right?"

"True. In fact, within seconds, I did die, and they buried me."

"They?"

"They. He. I'm not sure. At one point, I thought there were two. Perhaps I imagined it. I was disoriented. Dying. The roar in my head muddled everything, especially sound. By the time I rose in this form," he looked down upon himself, "they were gone."

"It had to be Holland. He had the motive and the opportunity." Too agitated to sit still, I climbed to my feet and paced. "He stood the most to lose if you acted on what you saw. And he would have been strong enough to drag your …" I cringed at the insolent tone in my voice and the harshness of my words. "Sorry … your body."

"But to murder? Over *things*?"

I shrugged. "He probably panicked. As for watching across the river, Holland probably meant you could watch him dig up the gold that's buried over there. Maybe it was his way of saying he'd get the money without your help."

Later, as I hurried back to my car, I was convinced Holland murdered Mason. He may not have done it alone, and there certainly was more here than what we knew. But one thing was certain: Holland was shady and ruthless and had "murderer" written all over him. That should be enough to bring the sheriff to Mason's body. Sheriff Barnes could take it from there and piece together the puzzle that remained.

CHAPTER 15

Daylight fought its way into the clouded sky as I hurried from Mason to the parking lot. I hoped to find Mule, but he was nowhere in sight. Probably just as well. Already too many people milled about to hold a conversation with a ghost.

At home, I fed Tramp and Chubbs, showered, and headed to church. The services provided peace and personal reflection, and I loved the joy and the warmth the regulars exchanged. The whole experience reminded me of the comforting warmth of a blanket. However, today my attendance also involved urgency to deliver messages to Adriana and Seth. And, of course, I looked forward to seeing Clay.

Despite my best efforts, I arrived with only minutes to spare before the service started. A cropping of saturated, open umbrellas festooned the vestibule, and people muttering about the rain blocked the entry to congregational seating, so I headed to the balcony.

I stepped onto the platform and proceeded to the front row to get a good view of the others below. Like radar, my eyes honed in on Clay. He held both nephews in his lap. I swear he sensed me staring at him because within seconds he turned from talking to them to look around. We made eye contact. I shot him a small wave and a giant smile. He cocked his eyebrows and smiled back, his grin spanning ear to ear. One of the twins tugged at his shirt, so he turned around to attend to them again. Beside him, a hand moved, and I watched as Whit draped his arm across Cassie's shoulders. She leaned into him, looking every bit like a woman tasting love again. A rise of sadness tightened my throat, thinking about the news Clay planned to divulge that afternoon. She would be hurt, perhaps even angry, about his decision.

"Hold on, Cassie," I whispered under my breath. "I'm doing everything I can to stop him."

Next, I spotted Seth sitting with his mother and two of his four sisters. *No Celeste.* Why was I happy about that? A few rows behind them, Adriana and her family conversed with the people seated behind them.

I sat back, waiting for the service to begin. The rain began to fall stronger and faster, pinging off the roof, about ten feet over my head. I peered left, to watch it cascade down the stained glass windows, and noticed Hilda sitting on the other side. She smiled. I picked up my umbrella and bag and moved quietly to her. A half-dozen other people shared the gallery seats with us.

I hesitated before sitting. Hilda made it clear long ago she considered me as much "kin" as employee, but I wanted to respect her space. "May I sit with you?"

"I'd like that, dear." She moved her cane to her other side. Her tailored dress suggested quality, and her flat shoes, practicality. She sat ramrod straight, pushing her head of coiled braids high.

"This is a surprise," I said, making a mental note to maintain good posture. "I never saw you here before."

"Oh, I've seen you." She patted my leg. "I'm not one of those who feel convicted to come every week. Sometimes my service involves me and God and nature, or a little reflecting time. But it's good to join together from time to time, so when I do, I sit in the balcony."

I wondered if she told her whole story. It would take quite a bit of effort for a woman using a cane to climb those steps. Yet, she chose not to sit downstairs, back row, near the door.

By now, we'd both turned to look forward at the people and activity below. I broke the silence. "It's quite a different perspective from up here, isn't it?"

"That's exactly what I like."

"Do you … ever feel separated from them?" I meant physically, but Hilda's answer revealed another focus.

"At times. But most of these folks are trying to be good. They have talents to serve, to help, to teach. Some of them are great cooks. Others are builders. We all have gifts." She hesitated. "Mine is to discern things. Sense them. Feel them. 'Course, the sensation is strongest when I close my eyes and let my other senses take hold. But some of these folks don't like anything they can't understand or find in the Bible. I think that's sad because the Good Book is filled with miracles and the supernatural."

Why was she saying these things?

She shifted her body to get a broader view of the gathering below. "'Course, there are some real gems down there, too. The Baxters are real good people, but I suspect you know that …?"

I blushed under her stare.

She continued. "And the Barrones. Also the Carters, the Haugetos, the Jaffreys. All beautiful people. The others have a hard time understanding my … gift. And they will yours too, Grace."

I snapped my head back to look at her, and we locked gazes.

"Don't ever apologize for the gifts and the talents you're given. Learn how to use them wisely. Mostly, learn *if* you should use them. And how."

Her words were weighty, and I didn't realize they made me physically shrink into myself until she reached over to pat my leg again and said, "Posture, dear."

I sat back up as music poured from the pipes behind us, and the service began. I absorbed little of it. My conversations with Hilda, Mason, and Mule Chasen kept replaying in my head.

I caught Pastor Dale announcing a prayer for "one of our own citizens here in Williamsport," and I assumed he meant Nidhi.

Then, I thought of Mason again.

Next, Pastor Dale said something about no purgatory. That Jesus taught there are only two roads and two destinies.

My thoughts flitted to Mule and his warnings for Seth and

Adriana.

At some point, Pastor Dale referenced First John, suggesting we not believe every spirit, but rather test the spirits to see whether they are from God.

Again, I wondered how this pastor always managed to reach me personally.

Later, he captured my attention when he said Daniel had supernatural powers. Hilda reached over and squeezed my knee.

Continuing, Pastor Dale said faith itself has no power, but rather it's what you put your faith in.

Next thing I knew, everyone stood for the closing hymn. Hilda whispered a quiet "Goodbye, dear" and left. I found myself alone in the balcony.

When the music ended and the congregation began to disperse, I hurried downstairs and maneuvered through the crowd to reach Adriana. I pulled her from the others.

"Ade, you've got to call the D.C. Orchestra tomorrow between nine and ten o'clock."

She looked at me like I spoke a foreign language. "Why would I do that? They have my resume, my audition tapes, my pictures. If I call them, they'll get annoyed."

Stymied, I hesitated. She was right. The way I presented it, out of the blue, made me sound like a simpleton. If Mule—a ghost, no less—hadn't told me to do this, I never would have made the recommendation.

Then again, it's always incumbent on job seekers to take the initiative, to demonstrate eagerness. Isn't it?

"I can't explain. It's a hunch. No, it's more than a hunch. It's something I ... sense." I lowered my voice. In an urgent whisper, I pleaded, "Please, trust me on this."

She shifted uncomfortably, and I could see on her face she was at war with herself, convinced it would do no good, but hoping against hope. Finally, her internal sparring broke, and she shook her head in a huff. "I fail to see what good it will do."

In the calmest voice I could muster, I countered, "I fail to see what *harm* it will do. Otherwise, we both know they're not going to call."

We took each other's measure for a heartbeat or two. She frowned. "I'll think about it."

I nodded. "Please. Do it for me. I don't want to lose you."

"I said I'd think about it." She sighed. "Honestly, Grace, I can't talk about it any more right now. I need to get home to meet Jamaar. We're going to a movie this afternoon." With that, she turned and left.

I exhaled. Round one complete. I spotted round two across the room, but before I could make it to Seth, someone grabbed my hand. I turned to see Clay.

"Hey, beautiful," he said.

"Hey, yourself." I smiled.

He looked around. "Look, I can't talk now, and I can't invite you over."

"I know. The family pow-wow."

"Yeah." He sobered and rubbed the back of his neck. "I'm not looking forward to it. Mom's going to be all sorts of ballistic. And Reaghan." With his hands, he mimicked a bomb exploding.

I nodded and bit my lip to keep from responding.

He studied me. "Thank you for being so understanding about what I have to do." He reached for my hand and squeezed it. "I confess, I didn't think you'd take my plans this well. It tells me you trust me. That you believe in what I'm doing."

I tensed at his words, but still I plunged forward with, "Of course, I do."

He excused himself with a promise to see me before leaving town. When he moved, I had a direct view of Seth. Our gazes locked.

I walked to him, and he smiled, but it didn't strike me as one of those genuine efforts I'd seen on him before.

"Can we talk?" I looked around. "Maybe outside? The rain

seems to have stopped for a bit."

He nodded but said nothing. To avoid the crowd, we skirted out a side door and walked to the back of the church where the basement emptied onto the lawns. We gravitated to the picnic pavilion.

Seth looked handsome in a tie and sports coat. For the first time, I noticed beard stubble, a leaner face, and the slightest hint of creases at his eyes. His physique, too, had changed in the past year, and I startled at how *aware* of him I was. He smelled of lemony shampoo and cherry Chapstick, the latter evoking a memory of a kiss we shared last year.

"What's up?" His smile was warm but hesitant.

I shook my head to dislodge jumbled thinking. "Thanks for sacrificing our time together yesterday. I want to make it up to you. I—"

He laughed, startling me.

"It's okay," he said. "I took Celeste, and we had a great time. You and I will have other chances, especially since we'll be in college together."

"Oh." *Why did his mention of Celeste bother me?* "Well, good."

"Look, don't worry about it." He touched my arm in a reassuring way. "How about this: after we're done with the attorney on Wednesday, we'll go to ZiManti's for dinner? They serve great pasta."

"That sounds nice. I'd like … no, wait, we can't. Seth, about that college money …"

"What about it?"

"I don't think you should take it."

He looked startled. "Why? It's free and clear. No strings."

"I understand." I nodded, watching as he tensed, his jaw, clenched.

"You don't even know enough about it yet."

I shrugged, afraid to say the wrong thing.

"Why would you encourage me to take the harder route? Do

you not want me to stay in the area?"

"What? Of course, I do."

"Then, you want me to go into debt? Rack up all sorts of bills? Spend ten or twenty years paying them off?"

"Seth, that's not fair. None of that's true."

"Then why do you say not to take it?"

"It's a hunch."

His composure faltered, and he raked both hands over his face as though trying to pull patience from them. "Grace, I'm going to go now. I guess I wasn't as honest as I thought I was. I didn't like you spending the whole day with Clay, and I didn't like you waiting until now to talk to me." His voice remained steady, rational, with a mature annoyance rather than the little boy jealousy he used to display. "And I don't like that you don't trust my judgment on this financial situation. I'm not like you, Grace. I can't count on a trust fund to see me through. It's easy to pass along pearls of wisdom to others when your life is set."

"That's not fair. I had to lose my mother and father to get that trust fund. At least you—" I sucked in my breath to stop myself.

"At least I what, Grace? I have my mother and father? Zing, wrong again. Yes, an awesome adoptive mother and a nasty adoptive father are in my life, but I have no idea who the biological parents are who left me. Now, if you'll excuse me, I need to leave before this gets ugly."

He stood to go, but stopped and turned to look at me. In a gentler tone, he said, "I'll call you next week. We can talk after I've calmed down. And *after* I've seen the attorney." He hesitated, before adding, "Alone."

As I watched him walk away, I wondered if I were happy or sad I wouldn't be going with him on Wednesday.

CHAPTER 16

I hurried home, donned jeans, and printed off a black and white photograph I found after much searching online. Next, I found Sheriff Barnes' business card in the pocket of the sundress I wore Friday night and called him.

He answered on the third ring.

"Barnes here."

"This is Grace MacKenna. We spoke at the *Time Out* Friday night. I wondered if we could talk."

"Go ahead."

"In person."

A blip of silence followed. I imagined curiosity breeding in his mind.

"When?" he asked.

"Now?"

"Must be urgent to call me on a Sunday."

"I'm holding a photograph of the man who saved Jerome Knight ... at the bridge collapse. But I don't want my name associated with this."

Another pause.

"Are you familiar with the Municipal Building?" His voice sounded re-energized. "I'll meet you there in fifteen."

* * *

The inside of the unimpressive Municipal Building smelled of the same musty, stale moistness as the outdoors. Sheriff Barnes' office was institutionally boring: plain metal desk, filing cabinets, and garbage can surrounded by a backdrop of mountains of files. None of the furniture matched, and I suspected even Goodwill would have turned it down. Nothing on the walls or his desk offered insight into the man, except one picture featuring a woman and a boy of about ten.

"Your family?" I asked, nodding toward the photograph as he rounded the desk and dropped into the squeaky chair behind it.

"It was. She wanted me to be an accountant." His jaw twitched. He looked uncomfortable, like someone who'd inadvertently shared a small portion of himself he had heretofore pledged not to reveal. "A cop's life can be hard on family. Especially in N'awlins."

At a loss of how to respond, I kept quiet.

"Before I forget," the sheriff said, "You might want to know that James Bender has been located ..."

My heart raced. Greasy Jim was back?

"... in prison. Wyoming."

"Wyoming? As in the state of Wyoming?"

"That's right. Sentenced for armed robbery and grand theft auto. That'll trump our breaking and entering charge for a good long time. His sometimes sidekick, Henry Nesler, is trying to make a new life for himself in Illinois. Apparently, he studied plumbing somewhere along the way. Now, you said something about a picture?"

I pulled it from my backpack and placed it in front of him.

His smile vanished, and he looked back at me, a tired look in his eyes.

I fidgeted in my seat. "That's the gentleman who saved Jerome Knight."

He pulled open the right top desk drawer and retrieved the sketch. Placing it beside the one I brought, he studied them. His gaze lifted to look at me then returned to the pictures. Something in his expression, like he was returning to a place he didn't want to go, told me to wait until he spoke.

He leaned back in his protesting chair. "This," he pointed at the picture I brought, "says our hero's name is Nate Carter."

The sheriff held my gaze. I shrugged. The name meant nothing.

The next bit he said with pointed emphasis: "And that his obituary appeared in the local paper in 1962."

I swallowed and nodded.

"Now, Ms. MacKenna, I'm no physicist, but I don't believe this man coulda' been on the bridge the other night. Most folks can't do these kinds of things after they're dead. Wouldn't you agree?"

I matched his continued gaze. He wasn't mocking, but rather pushing back against this information I'd laid in his lap, no doubt reminiscent of things he'd experienced on the force in New Orleans, a different reality to which he abhorred giving the slightest credence.

I said the first thing that came to mind, borrowing a line from so many of the souls I'd encountered: "I'm just the messenger."

He nodded slowly. "Well, blast it. What am I supposed to do with this? I mean, you denied knowing him the other night—"

"I wasn't lying. I don't know him."

He tilted his head and shot me a look that declared I was playing with semantics. "I have a pretty dang good built-in BS meter, and it was ringing Friday." His eyes, slit; his lips, flat-lined. "So why bring it now? You don't strike me as the sort who stirs the pot needlessly. Why now?"

I took a deep breath. "Credibility."

"With …?"

"You."

"You're too young—and probably too smart—to want a job here. So why do you want me to find you credible?"

"I need your help. I can … *see* things."

He remained still, offering no reaction. "Go on."

I gestured at the picture. "I saw him in the street last year."

The sheriff's jaw tensed. "And?"

"I can see others, too."

"Others … and that's why you're here." He spoke slowly. "I'm guessing it's one other in particular you want help with."

"Mason Baxter."

His stare intensified as though trying to decide whether to hear me out or lock me away in an asylum. He looked back at the picture, and I waited as he digested the information. Parking his elbows on the desk, he steepled his fingers and brought them to his mouth, never once breaking eye contact. More time passed before he shook his head and thumped his hands down on the desk—a man trying to digest the impossible.

"Well, blast it," he growled.

"Mr. Baxter was—"

He waved it off. "I knew him. Met him in Hagerstown at a career days event. The day before he allegedly departed the area. That afternoon we laughed about the snow like new friends. The next, I had to investigate his disappearance. It was my first month on the force here in Washington County, a few years before becoming sheriff."

He leaned to his right again, pulled open the bottom drawer, fished out a file, and slapped it on the desk in front of me. "That's Baxter's file. It's a cold trail, Ms. MacKenna. I turned over every rock, opened every door, and looked under every obstacle to solve it. Nothing. It was like going up a down escalator. Futile. You wanna know why his file is so front and center here? Because there is a handful of cases that bother me. His is one. I never once believed Baxter skipped town. Now you're telling me you've seen him, and I'm guessing from this effort at establishing credibility …" he said, gesturing toward the picture I brought with me, "… I'm guessing you don't mean you saw Mr. Baxter alive."

"He was murdered," I blurted.

The sheriff dropped his head and massaged his forehead with the tips of his fingers. "Well, blast it all." He looked up and said, "I suppose you know by whom, too."

"Holland Greer." I squared my shoulders and raised my chin. "Well … okay, I don't know that for certain … but it's the only logical conclusion."

More silence.

"So you want me to go arrest Greer?" His voice revealed a chill. "As much as I'd like to, I have nothing to go on. No body, no stolen bank money, no car, no nothing. So let's not get ahead of ourselves. Besides, in my line of work, jumping to conclusions usually doesn't make for comfortable landings."

"I can take you to the body."

Up until now, he'd received and digested my pronouncements like a good poker player, but he broke under this latest tidbit I'd offered. I could see astonishment in his eyes. He rubbed his chin again and spoke in slow delivery. "And you know where the body is, not because you saw it but because ...?"

I squeezed my hands together, but I didn't let my gaze falter. "I've ... communicated with his ghost."

"Uh-huh ... and that's why you brought the picture of Nate Carter. To prove you have this ability, and to convince me to trust you?"

I shifted again, feeling curiously and unfairly exposed. "Well ... I ..."

He smiled. "It's okay. I admire your approach." He tapped the fingers of his right hand swiftly on his desk as he thought about what to do. "Raleigh!" he yelled.

A lanky man of about thirty appeared at the door. "Yeah, boss?"

Sheriff Barnes grabbed a pair of scissors and cut Carter's name off the obituary. He grabbed a business card from the credenza behind him and handed them to Raleigh. "Call this Knight guy. Get his email. Tell him I want to send him a picture. Then scan it and send it."

Raleigh left to do as he'd been told.

"Cup of coffee while we wait?" The sheriff asked as he stood. "Something tells me I'm gonna' need it."

"Umm, is it any good?"

"No, it's lousy, and it's cold, but it's all we have."

"I'll pass, thanks."

"Suit yourself, but it's probably a wise decision on your part."

As he left to get a cup, I found myself liking the sheriff more and more. He was one of those people who dealt in facts, patterns, tangibles, but who had seen enough to know he needed to be open-minded about the shadowy and abstract parts of life too.

Within five minutes, he plodded back into the office yelling, "Transfer it in here."

He picked up the phone and said, "Mr. Knight?" Silence. "Uh-huh. Is that right? That conclusive, eh?" More silence. "No, no, he's not around anymore. Apparently he was only passing through and wanted to remain anonymous." Silence again. "Well, the thing is, the man ... is dead. Yeah, that's right. Yeah, definitely a quick turn of bad luck. Who? ... Oh, just a good Samaritan brought it to my attention." Silence. "Yes, I'm sure it's changed you forever. Sure. Sure. Ah, yeah, God bless you, too. Yeah, I'll do that."

He placed the phone on its cradle and studied me before speaking. "I'll try to keep this on the QT as much as possible, but I need to solicit help, and a couple permits to dig. So, Ms. MacKenna, how positive are you we'll find a body?"

Could Mason have misled me? I thought of Will and his possible deceit, and of Pastor Dale's warning not to trust every spirit we encounter, lest they be cunning demons in disguise. But, I was so driven by wanting the truth to come out, I decided—however illogically—that sometimes a lie was indeed justified to bring about the truth. "A hundred percent," I said and firmed my jaw.

Still, before he agreed to proceed, he peppered me with questions about Mason and the location of the body. I described bits of Mason's trip to Holland's house that night, too. Sheriff Barnes referenced his notes and confirmed that none of what I shared contradicted his notes from all those years ago.

He sat back, beleaguered. "Ms. MacKenna, I'm the elected sheriff for this county, which means I've got a lot of good men and women reporting at my disposal. Typically, I'd turn this over to my chief deputy, or directly to one of my detectives. But I'm not going to because I live in Williamsport, and I don't like when things happen in my sleepy little town that I can't figure out."

I blinked, wondering why he was telling me this. Was he justifying? Venting? Explaining why he planned to push the limits in police procedures? He continued, and I decided it was a little of each.

"Remember that BS meter I mentioned? It never went off when I talked with Baxter. The guy was as genuine and honest as the day is long. He talked about taking his son to a football game in Baltimore the next day. My gut, my training, told me he intended to do that. So why would he suddenly decide to leave the area?"

He paused again, and I could tell he wasn't expecting a response. I served as his sounding board.

"Through the years, I've made it a point to watch out for that family. Cassie … Mrs. Baxter did a good job as a single mom. Reaghan never caused a bit of trouble, and Clay … well, there was only minor stuff in middle school, but once he joined the football team, he grew into responsibility." He raised an eyebrow and scratched his forehead. "But I guess you know all that."

I fidgeted in my seat again, waiting for him to continue. When he didn't, I said, "So what happens now?"

"You and I visit the site. I need to check the area to make sure I secure the right equipment. Good news is, the ground is soaked. Easy digging. I'm guessing you don't have a problem going there in this weather?"

I shook my head. "Then … you dig?"

"Then we dig. The area you described sounds like private property. Any closer to the canal, it would be federal or state land, and I'd have to get the Maryland Criminal Investigation Bureau involved."

He continued describing the jurisdiction. I heard something about the Criminal Investigation Command and allied law forces and a forensic sciences division, but little more. Instead, I wondered how long all this would take. On TV, crime investigations were swift and conclusive. I doubted it was that way in real life.

"So, how long before you dig?"

"It's a little more involved than grabbing a shovel." He looked at his watch. "Five hours until sunset. I'll make some calls and see what we can do by tomorrow morning."

"But that's so long. Why not this afternoon?"

He shook his head. "It's Sunday, and the river is flooded. The Canal towpath is crowded with gawkers who love to watch the Potomac pour over its banks. We don't need the attention. Besides, exhuming the body may take a while. We'd end up in darkness, which would mean also lugging along plenty of expensive lighting. Much as I want to get this moving ... no, first thing in the morning is better." He raised an eyebrow. "You'll be available tomorrow, too? To show us the actual spot without much of a to-do?"

I didn't know what he meant by "a to-do," but I figured he meant I better be exact about where to dig, so they had to do it only once. After nodding, I cringed before asking my next question and tried to block my own vision of what the actual body must look like now. "How long before Mason's body can be identified, since it will be so ... so ..."

He raised a brow. "Official identification? Could take weeks, maybe even a month or two."

I exhaled with a groan and slumped back in the chair.

"Unofficial ID?" the sheriff continued. "I'll know in short order. Baxter had a knee replacement. Each medical gizmo that's placed into a body carries a serial number." He patted the file. "I've already got that number here."

Renewed hope surged through me, and I sat straighter as the sheriff explained the digging process in more detail, interrupting our discussion several times to take calls and barking orders through the doorway to Raleigh. After about fifteen minutes of this, he led me to a crude lounge area where I drank lousy coffee and waited another half-hour under bright institutional fluorescent lighting for him to accompany me to the Canal.

CHAPTER 17

Sheriff Barnes and I reached the Canal parking lot by 2:30. Raleigh must have been busy making calls because the park rangers had a roofed mini truck ready for us to drive to the site.

The sheriff had been correct; gawkers crowded at the river's edge. Despite wearing raincoats and carrying umbrellas, most of them looked soaked.

As I surveyed the mingling crowd, I spotted Mule, nonplussed by the multitude of people and sitting under the same tree as when we talked earlier. Despite his transparency, he appeared enough that I could tell the rain pouring through him was a non-issue. He looked up from his whittling in time to watch us drive off.

It took about ten minutes to reach the site. The towpath was rutted and flooded from five days of rain. Other than lame comments about the weather and the few diehard hikers and bikers passing opposite us on the trail, we rode in silence. I spent most of the time wishing I had given Mason a heads-up about our visit.

When I indicated we'd driven far enough, Sheriff Barnes pulled the vehicle to a stop. From the back, he retrieved the two pairs of oversized rubber boots he'd brought along. We pulled them on, and the sheriff followed me into the ravine.

The saturated ground prevented quick movement, and at times, our floppy boots sank into soggy layers of decaying leaves.

To my dismay, I didn't see Mason, so I turned to the sheriff and said, "Okay, this is going to seem weird to you—"

He raised his palms toward me. "I've seen it all. Just do what you gotta do."

I inhaled a breath to calm my nerves, and yelled, "Mason!"

Bless that sweet soul, he appeared instantly to my right, about three yards away.

"You've decided to proceed," Mason said.

Conscious of Sheriff Barnes beside me, I made some klutzy eye movements, hoping Mason would understand the awkwardness of talking in front of the sheriff.

"Is that Deputy Sheriff Barnes?" Mason asked. "I know him."

"He's the sheriff now." I looked back at Sheriff Barnes and watched as he stiffened and spaced his feet into a gunfighter stance. His gaze searched wildly in the direction I had been talking, but he didn't say a word.

I swallowed again, aware of how odd I must appear to the sheriff. "Mason ... where's your body buried?"

Mason hesitated, and it concerned me. Was he worried about his family? Concerned about my reputation in Williamsport? Discomforted this might all finally be coming to a close?

He beckoned me to follow with a wave of his hand and proceeded farther from the river about twenty yards. We were hindered in our movements because, whereas Mason could pass through anything with ease, we had to step over fallen trees and pull our boots free of briars, vines, and slurping soil.

Mason stopped and pointed to a mound of grass that looked like any other inconsequential spot around it. Nature had reclaimed it through years of erosion and an accumulation of debris—leaves, weeds, acorns. And, as Murphy's Law would dictate, the patch was topped with remnants of a huge oak tree that fell at some point through the years. The trunk looked to be more than two yards in circumference.

I pointed to the spot. "It's there."

Sheriff Barnes raised an eyebrow. "You're sure?"

I looked at Mason. He nodded, and I glanced at the sheriff again. "He's sure."

"How deep?"

Again, I looked to Mason for the answer.

"Then?" He shrugged. "Probably only four feet. Now, under these layers? Perhaps five or six."

"Around five feet," I said.

"Okay …" the sheriff cleared his throat, "… I'm assuming we're not alone here."

I shook my head.

"You understand how … unusual this is?"

"I do."

"So then, you understand how foolish we'll look if this is wrong. So ask the …" He paused, scratched his head, and cleared his throat. "Ask Mr. Baxter what tie I wore the day we met."

I flinched. "That was almost fifteen years ago. You can't—"

"A Jerry Garcia tie," Mason said.

I looked at Mason, startled. He bopped his head toward Barnes, urging me to repeat his words. The sheriff drained of color when I repeated Mason's answer.

Mason continued. "It was bright yellow—"

I echoed, "It was bright yellow."

Mason continued: "… with colored swirls. You said it was the only tie you owned that wasn't institutional black or blue."

Again, I repeated Mason's words, and before I even finished, Sheriff Barnes had covered his mouth with his left hand, rubbing. A man trying to digest the unfathomable. He glanced behind him, eyed a stump, and dropped onto it.

I waited him out, not wanting to say anything that might cause him to disbelieve this moment.

"What …" the sheriff began, but it came out hoarse, so he tried again. "What else can he tell us? Who did it? How many? Why? If we dig, will we find other evidence?"

I already knew the answers, but I looked at Mason. He nudged one of those okay-go-ahead-and-tell-him kinds of motions.

So I did. I recounted everything he had told me earlier: the exchanges at the bank with Clyde and Nidhi, his trip to Holland's house where he identified stolen goods, the call to Clyde from his car, being clubbed over the head and coming out of his fog in the ravine long enough to hear them say he could rot there and watch what his meddling couldn't stop.

"What'd they mean by that?" Sheriff Barnes asked, repeating the question I voiced earlier. I didn't need Mason to supply the answer. The words had reverberated through my core ever since I'd heard them.

"He thinks they meant activity at Devil's Cove. Across the river."

The sheriff rubbed his chin. "Ask him—"

"He can hear you. You can ask him directly."

The sheriff glared, not in an angry manner, but rather in a way that said I was crazy if I thought he might do so.

He continued. "Ask him if he thinks there could be any link between his death and the possible disappearance of Nidhi Michelson. She left an odd message on my voice mail. We tracked her phone to the weeded area behind the bank."

And there it was. Another reason the sheriff had so readily agreed to hear me out. I stiffened but held my gaze, wondering what possible scenarios could be racing through his mind.

He nodded, an urge to proceed.

I turned to see Mason frowning. "Nidhi is missing?" he asked. "I don't have an answer for that. I can't imagine a link after all this time. As far as I know, I was the only casualty from that night."

I swallowed, the weight of all the secrets and confusion wrapping around the three of us. "That's not true. Clyde died, too." I turned to the sheriff and said, "He doesn't know anything about Nidhi."

Mason said, "Clyde Drury? He died the same night as me?"

I frowned. "There never was a good time to tell you."

Now standing, the sheriff scowled and plopped his hands on his waist. "Blast it. This is the oddest questioning I've ever done. Sure can't log it in a report." He exhaled, making a decision. "I need to go. Set some wheels in motion. Typically, it'd take a while to coordinate this, but I'll do what I can to hurry it along. I'll need you to be here since you're the only one who can get answers on the fly." He turned to go but looked back. "Oh, and …" he gestured in Mason's direction.

Mason nodded.

"He'll be here," I told the sheriff.

CHAPTER 18

That evening at *Crossings*, thoughts of Mason and his murder hovered foremost on my mind. Focus on anything else proved futile.

I paced like a caged animal, sitting and standing a half-dozen times in the span of about fifteen minutes, circling the apartment, looking but not seeing. The serious nature of what the morning might bring overshadowed interest in activities. Nothing on television appealed to me, and school hadn't started yet. I had no appetite, so why bother to cook? The time dragged, the minutes stubbornly refusing to move.

Restless, Tramp and I walked through the drizzle to the river. Once home, I took a shower.

I thought of inviting Adriana over but feared she would argue her way out of calling about the interview.

Clay's family needed him.

Seth was annoyed with me.

Michael didn't answer his phone.

By eight o'clock, I dropped in my chair, wishing Will was with me. I missed him. What was it about me that when he wasn't here, I longed for his company, but when he was here, I hated being dependent on him?

And then there was the issue of trust. He'd given me plausible answers to my questions about last year. What's more, I'd learned firsthand from Nate the fireman how helpful and altruistic some souls could be. So why my hesitation?

By nine o'clock, I decided the only thing able to distract my mind might be the piano. I hurried to the connecting door between the apartment and house, pulled it open with a flourish, and waited. For what, I wasn't sure. I didn't expect anything to happen. This was the first time I ever entered the old house without Will's presence; I guess I needed to let the gravity of it wash over me. Michael had said the house now had electricity, so I searched near the door and found a dimmer switch. I clicked it on and cranked down the harshness.

The subdued lighting cast a beautiful illumination. I had labeled the room "the library" but had always considered it an activity room as it sported both a study and music room vibe, with a considerable collection of old books, desk for writing, and huge grand piano.

The year before, Michael had used the room as a bedroom for several months, but his bed and scattered furniture were gone now, and the room was restored to the original 1800s furniture, surrounded by signs of change—saw horses, electrical tape, and switches, dust, and debris from plaster where it had been removed to accommodate pipes for plumbing or wires for electricity.

I wondered if the other rooms revealed such progress, but I wasn't interested enough to explore. Instead, I moved to the piano and removed its dust covering. Eighty-eight black and white keys called for me to bring them to life.

I played from memory, song after song, and lost myself in it. For a while, there were no angry loved ones, no unresolved murders, no demons hiding in the shadows of the room *or* my life. There was only the sound of the notes mixing together, and they reverberated into my core.

When I exhausted the songs I knew by heart, I reached for the pile of books and sheet music sitting on the piano's corner ledge.

The book I'd purchased when I first moved to *Crossings* sat on top, folded open to "Lorena," the song I played when I first met Will. My breath caught. Was it a sign?

I sat back with a sigh and looked up, stretching my neck and shoulders. The house felt empty without Will. My eyes scanned the furniture, the bookshelves, the old Kavanaugh Bible sitting on a corner table, covered in dust. I had never touched it; it seemed too scary, like the shadows of the house. I stood and moved to it, compelled to conquer my fears. The long ribbon attached to its top marked a page toward the back. Curious, I lifted the monstrous pages. It fell open at the ribbon to Hebrews 13. A passage was marked: "Be not forgetful to entertain strangers: for thereby some have entertained angels unawares."

The song "Lorena." The Bible passage. I laughed, and it came out more hysterical than comical.

Perhaps a wise person knows when they've been defeated.

Without another thought—which probably would have afforded wiser decision-making—I returned to the apartment to find my boots and flashlight.

Within ten minutes, I reached the cemetery, found the coin behind the headstone where Will had said it would be, and tucked it in my jeans pocket.

He appeared.

In a gruff tone, I said, "Don't ask."

He didn't. Didn't smile or smirk either, and for that I was grateful. If anything, he looked disappointed and thrilled all in one, like a father who is sad to hear a child admit defeat at a local bully or a math problem, but simultaneously thrilled the child still needs his help to resolve a situation.

In silence, we moved, side by side through the still darkness, back to *Crossings*.

***

With one glance at the contemporary changes in the apartment, Will turned and proceeded into the old house, saying he preferred to stay "in the more familiar." Chubbs had dashed into the bedroom the moment Will entered, but Tramp merely lifted his head before shifting into a more comfortable sleeping position.

Together, Will and I strolled through the house, noting

damage to plastered walls that awaited installation of wiring and plumbing before being repaired. Most of the furniture was pushed into groupings in the middle of the rooms and covered in sheets, allowing access to the walls.

The room least changed, on the opposite side of the house, was where he and I sat up late talking many nights after I moved here. I'd started referring to it as the drawing room after learning the term derived from the antebellum references of a withdrawing room and withdrawing chamber, meaning the space to which one could "withdraw" for more privacy.

Will asked me to leave the old coin, his center, in this room. For safekeeping, I tucked it under a vase perched on the fireplace mantle.

He denied the renovations would bother him, but previous conversations had taught me that each change and new item brought into the space, from repairs to furnishings, would weaken him bit by bit. However, the work wouldn't start again for several months, and he probably would have no reason to stay by then anyway.

Perhaps for old time's sake—or because I shivered against the damp weather permeating through the walls—Will built a fire as I rearranged furniture to make room for two to sit and hold a conversation. As though we shared an unspoken agreement, neither of us mentioned the riddle-ladened conversation we shared at the cemetery.

Once settled, I told him about living in Cassie's garage apartment and how Kate's death affected me. He assured me again she was fine.

"I've also begun working at Hilson's Antique Emporium," I said. "It's on Canal Street in Williamsport. The owner—"

"Hilda Hilson. I've heard of her."

Startled, I hesitated. "But, how could you?"

"Jack. He talked about her occasionally."

I touched my face, surprised, pleased, all in one. "Of course.

She said Jack would stop there from time to time."

"Yes, he was always on the search for anything from the 1700s. That period of time fascinated him. Me too. So I especially enjoyed anything he brought back with him."

"That's funny."

He arched his eyebrows. "Funny? Why?"

"You ... from the 1800s. You *are* history to me. I guess I never thought about you being interested in what came before you."

He nodded. "We're all just here for a blip of time. The country had a long, rich history before I came along. Before the Civil War."

"You're right." I ran a hand over my head. "I always think of the soldiers from the Civil War as having been the first to walk across the grounds at *Crossings*.

"They merely walked where many pioneers and explorers already trekked. And, before them, thousands of years of Native American tribes."

"It's daunting when you think about it," I said, tucking my legs under me. "Everywhere you go, people have been there. They've walked where you walked, lived where you've lived, maybe owned something you buy ..." My mind drifted to the angry soul that would have accompanied the purchase of the box if Hilda had commissioned it.

He nodded. "You never know what you might innocently step into. That's why you need to seek protection and blessings as you go. Ask, and it will be given."

"Did you and your family do that, before you built here?"

His gaze dropped to his lap where he rubbed his hands across his pants leg. "I don't know if Father did or not ... I don't think so. Sometimes we're better at giving than following advice."

I don't know why, but the moment had soured our discourse, so I changed focus and asked him about his son, the child he never knew existed until we confronted his dead and deranged wife Naomi in the boondocks of Georgia. Will said he met with him several times, in the dimension. Will once said that when a person dies, the subtle body still exists and moves into another dimension before it moves on. He'd said, "It is meant for crossing over. Souls go there to welcome someone home. If you have remained behind and become aware someone is dying, you may be able to enter the dimension at the same time they do, but then you must leave immediately thereafter, either by crossing over or returning to earth."

I updated him on Mason, explaining my hope to give Clay's father the opportunity to close out his unfinished business as well.

"I understand," he said, his voice ringing with the gentleness I remembered.

His geniality and tenderness comforted me. I thought about the various souls I had met and couldn't stop from voicing what festered in my heart: "Mason is a good man, but you're the soul with whom I'm most familiar. The one I love. But also, the one I'm most afraid of."

He frowned, leaned forward and clasped my hand. As always with Will, the comfort of solidness and power came through in his touch, but it lacked the warmth of life circulating through his core. Instead, his touch was cold, lifeless, as though the solidness emanated from a thick air mass.

He spoke in a caressing voice. "We can change that. Remember what I told you about Julius Caesar. About that which is out of sight being the most disturbing. Now I am here, in your sight, so we can tackle your concerns."

I wished it were that easy. "Let me remind you of another famous quote from Caesar: 'The die is cast.' You can't change what you are, Will. You're dead. So I have to trust that you were an honorable and forthright man."

"I can't make you trust me. You have to decide that on your own. But consider this. You met Braxton. You must have learned from him that sometimes the love that frowns is the one which proves to be the deepest."

"Perhaps. But you *were* right about him. He was an amazing

man, and I judged him unfairly." I'd often told Will his friend Braxton scared me. He was a brooding sort of soul, and it made me nervous. In the end, I learned Braxton—a surgeon during the Civil War—was one of the kindest, most generous individuals I ever met. The horror of war had robbed him of joy and all the people he loved. I inferred Will's comments now as meaning love, on the surface, isn't always wrapped up in a pretty package and tied with a neat bow. Sometimes it's messy, confusing, hurtful … even forbidden.

"Have you taken steps to clear his name of those false murder charges?"

I cringed. "No, but I will. I promise."

We lapsed into silence, listening to the crackle of the fire and the steady beat of rain against the house.

Will stood. "Before we get tangled up in your plans, will you do me one great honor?"

I met his gaze. "If I can."

He grinned. "Dance with me. The last time I danced with a beautiful woman, it was Naomi. As we know, she married me but dreamed of Fergus. I would like to hold a lovely lady in my arms who wants to be there. Is that possible?"

His words, both painful and beautiful, touched me, and I wiped away a tear. My lips twitched into a little smile. Yes, it was possible. I wanted to be nowhere else at this moment than with this gallant soldier from another century. "I'd be honored."

He extended his hand.

"Wait, we have no music," I said.

"Can you hum?"

I groaned. "Let me get music." I started toward the apartment but hesitated. What kind of music should I get? I couldn't recall the names of any dance songs from the 1800s. "Do you have a preference?"

He tilted his head. "I can pick any song?"

I laughed and nodded. "Yes, technology has come a long, long way."

He thought about it. "There is a song. I heard it on the television once with Jack. It was by a man … his name escapes me … King … no, Nat King Something-or-other."

"Nat King Cole?"

"Yes, that's it. It's called 'Unforgettable.' Do you know it?" He reached for my hand again and pulled me closer. "That's what you are, Grace. Unforgettable. It seems appropriate."

My breath hitched, and I felt warm all over. "I'll go download … err, I'll go get it. Be right back."

I hurried into the apartment, retrieved my cell phone, and downloaded the song. As I turned to go back to the house, I grabbed my mini Bluetooth speaker. Reaching the drawing room required me to cross through the old parlor then the wide foyer. It was in the latter I remembered technology would weaken Will, so I placed the phone and the speaker on the steps of the grand staircase before returning to the drawing room. The words, "Unforgettable, that's what you are …" poured forth.

"That's it. That's the song," Will said. "This modern age is amazing."

I stepped into his open arms. "I put it on repeat, so we can dance at our leisure."

And we did.

Three times.

And on one of those replays, I told him Naomi was a fool. That had I lived and met him then, I never would have left.

"Thank you for that," he said, pulling back a little, but not letting go and not breaking our movements. He lifted a coil of my hair in his hand and ran his fingers down its length. "And I always would have been there for you."

"I know," I said, pulling closer to him and resting my cheek against the expanse of his cold chest.

When the song ended the third time, he pulled back. "Grace, I need to say something. Can you turn the music off?"

I did, and when I returned, he gestured to the seats again.

We sat together on the settee, and he took my hand.

"I need to be fully honest about something. I never lied to you last year. But I wasn't as forthcoming as I should have been."

"You're beginning to scare me, Will. What is it?"

He looked at my hand in his. "Everything I told you about my exchanges with Jack was true, except …"

"Except?"

"On his last visit, he said goodbye. Not goodbye for now, but goodbye forever to our interactions. He said he had a change of heart, and when he returned next, he wouldn't care if I was there, but that he didn't want any more conversation or sleuthing to solve my murder. He said it prevented him from focusing on his life and the future. And, that he felt it was wrong."

I let go of Will's hand and sat back, startled.

"Are you angry with me?" Will asked.

I thought about it. Was I mad? Startled, yes. Perhaps a little disappointed, too.

But mad?

"No. No, I'm not," I answered truthfully. I thought about the secret I'd kept from Clay. How could I fault Will for doing the same?

I reached for his hand again. "You should have told me. But, in all honesty, I don't think I would have done anything differently."

He smiled and squeezed my hand.

"Now come." I pulled him to a standing position again. "I have a ton of good dancing songs on my phone. It's time you learned some modern music."

I started the music again, and we returned to dancing, but only after I tucked Jack's words into my memory.

CHAPTER 19

On Monday morning, the sheriff called early and asked me to meet him at the Canal towpath parking lot at eight.

I attributed this quick turnaround in digging not to any convincing appeals on my part, but rather to the sheriff's own unfinished resolve, made years ago, a desire to stamp "final" on a case that troubled and eluded him. Also, because the sheriff suspected a possible link between Nidhi's work at the bank and Mason's death. When I asked about her, he confirmed her as officially missing and said officers had been pulled from other duties to investigate.

The morning unfolded gray and dismal; the rain continued, intermittent. Fog hovered over the river length like it feared dropping, lest it, too, would be swept away by the racing water.

At 7:55 a.m., I pulled into the parking lot at the C&O Canal and spotted Sheriff Barnes talking to a man in a park uniform. Behind him, five men donned boots and loaded a surprising amount of gear into four Canal mini trucks: tarps, bags, hard-sided cases, shovels, chainsaws, photography and videography equipment.

I cringed at the reality of what this meant. Six men removed themselves from other work to dig up a body they knew about only because of me. I wasn't naïve. Despite the sheriff's assurance of this being on the QT, chances remained that with this many witnesses to the dig—even if they were law enforcement personnel—word would spread. If I were wrong, I would be humiliated. If I was right, I might be discussed in restaurants and coffee shops this week with the same disdain people used when talking about witnesses to alien abductions.

Rather than drive across the lot to park near them, I pulled into the first spot, beside Canal Street. I liked having that separation.

I climbed into one of the vehicles with the sheriff and a deputy. The other men—I missed their names but caught their ranks— climbed into the other vehicles.

I now associated Mule Chasen with the entryway to the canal but didn't expect to see him at this time of day. Still, as we pulled away, I turned to look behind us. He stood by a towpath mile marker, watching us go.

We rode in silence, the awkwardness accumulating with the distance. I spent the time wishing I'd gone to the site in advance to ensure Mason's presence. The sheriff had said he might have more questions. I would be the talk of the town by nightfall if I had to call for Mason in front of these people. "The crazy girl who hollers to ghosts" is what they'd label me. Either that or "the brazen girl" since most people liked to discount or ignore what they didn't understand and couldn't prove. As it was, a few of the men in the group looked at me with curiosity, like they wondered how I could have knowledge of the whereabouts of a body, especially one that disappeared when I was in kindergarten. Still, Sheriff Barnes had assured me my name would be left out, where possible.

Near the spot, we abandoned the vehicles at the towpath to hike into the ravine, the slope of the land and the saturation of the ground preventing us from driving closer. The sheriff mumbled something about it being a good thing our little "dig" wasn't visible from the towpath. "It'll cut down on the gawkers from upriver," he said.

An hour passed before they began clearing the site. It took considerable time to unload and haul the equipment to the location, tape a perimeter to the crime scene, lay tarps, and prep the videography equipment and plastic bags.

The sheriff advised I remain outside the bright yellow tape. It read, "Crime Scene—Do Not Cross," and I intended to obey the directive. I folded onto a hollow tree trunk about eight yards from the taped line, and within minutes, my skin prickled awareness of a new energy nearby. I turned to see Mason, a frown on his face. He nodded, and in it I read acceptance and sadness we had to get to this point.

Another hour of waiting followed as the men chain-sawed through the fallen trees and cleared the site. No one appeared in a hurry to dig. But perhaps that was my imagination or my anxiety. The atmosphere lingered as somber and hushed as a funeral. Mason and I watched in silence.

The sun gained, peaking through scattered, bloated clouds and cresting the treeline to the east, sending stretched shadows toward the west that came and went as sunlight and clouds battled for dominance.

When the digging finally began, the ground offered little resistance, thanks to the saturation. Each shovelful of dirt was inched out, placed onto a tarp, and documented with video equipment. Every thrust made my breath hitch, and I wondered if it would be the one which made contact with a body.

I was so absorbed in the activity at the site that when I heard my name, I expected Sheriff Barnes to be calling. It took a heartbeat to register the sound came from behind me *and* from the last voice I wanted to talk to at that particular moment.

Clay!

I stood and whirled toward his voice. Dread unfurled from my stomach and scorched through me with lightning speed.

He arrived from the direction of the towpath, stepping over the thicket into view, and stopped within two yards of me. His smile confirmed incomprehension as to how the scene behind me involved him.

"Hey, beautiful," he said. "Glad I found you. What's happening?" His gaze darted to the dig and back again.

"What are you doing here?" I asked, catching Mason's astonished look in my peripheral vision.

Clay reacted to the panic in my voice by arching back, surprised. "Told you I'd see you before going back to school. I headed to your place but saw your car by Canal Street. Thought you might be walking Tramp. One of the rangers said you were with the police. I got concerned." He paused to look toward the digging again. "What's happening? What are they looking for?"

"Clay." Sheriff Barnes spoke, a concerned tone in his voice. I turned and watched him duck under the tape to come closer. He raised his eyebrows at me, as though asking, "What is he doing here?" and "Did you tell him to come?"

"I didn't say anything," I blubbered.

Bad choice of words on my part.

Clay stiffened, and his gaze darted between the sheriff and me. "Larry? What's this all about?"

Sheriff Barnes rubbed his head as he muttered, "Blast it." He exhaled as if the effort was necessary for him to change personas, morphing from his man-in-charge-of-a-dig mode to his man-responsible-for-delivering-bad-information mode.

"Son, we're merely acting on a lead here. We've received intel that a body may have been buried here. We believe the victim may have been murdered and—"

"Sheriff!" The voice came from within the taped area, a plea for the person in charge to return immediately.

"Blast it," the sheriff muttered and air-pulsed a palm at Clay. "Wait here."

After the sheriff left, I inhaled a deep, shaky breath, hoping to wait this out, but Clay gently grabbed my elbow and turned me to face him.

His gaze pierced into me. "What is this? Who do they think is buried there? Surely they don't believe Nidhi—"

"Clay, I—"

"Just say it." His voice grew urgent.

Flicking my gaze to Mason and back, I confessed, "Your father."

He stood ramrod still as he reacted to this development, his face draining of color and his gaze intensifying. He said, "Okay," but in a voice that suggested, "something's missing here." Letting go of my elbow, he ran the same hand over his face and mouth as he turned away and processed the extent of the information.

"I'm sorry," I muttered, panic growing.

"It can't be true." He turned back and flailed his hand. "I mean, what happened? Why weren't we told? This makes no sense. Someone made a crank call. That's all. What kind of a sick person …" His voice dropped off as he stepped back, as though he needed space to process this turn of events.

"Tell him it was you while I'm here to help you," Mason urged.

Without thinking it through, and trusting Mason knew best, I followed his directive and plunged ahead. "It wasn't a crank call. It was me."

"You?" He didn't sound angry, but rather, confused. "But why would you do that? I know you don't want me to leave, but Dad left town—"

"No, Clay," I interrupted, hearing the panic growing in my voice. "He never left. He's here." My voice faltered, and I continued in a defeated whisper, emphasizing each word: "He's right *here* with us."

Clay's hands fisted, and his face grew red. I suspected his core battled between denial and anger. He shook his head. His tone grew hard. "Grace, don't do this. It can't be."

"It's true."

"Really? Then why can't I see him? I saw that deranged Naomi ghost … or demon … or whatever it was in Georgia, and—"

"She wanted you to see her."

He looked at me like I'd lost my mind.

"What about Terrance?" I asked. "The guy you said you lost in Afghanistan. You saw him after he died!"

"He had been killed *that* day, Grace. Right in front of me." He turned away, one hand on his head and began an agitated pace.

Mason said, "I won't reveal myself because I don't want him to be left with such a memory."

I repeated Mason's explanation. Clay smirked and rolled his

eyes as though to say "of course," and "how convenient."

Mason continued nonplussed. "Ask him if he still has the red flyer wagon he got when he was five."

I relayed the question. Clay halted and snapped his head to stare at me. Then his gaze searched to my right and left. He squinted in disbelief and shook his head. "That doesn't prove anything. Mom probably mentioned the wagon at some point."

My heart sank. His words were born from shock, but still, I was hurt by his doubt of me. "Why would I lie?"

Clay pulsed his palms at me in defeat. "I don't know … I need to think a moment." He stepped a few yards away, rubbing his forehead.

"Clay—"

Mason touched my arm. "I love you, Scout." He nodded toward Clay.

I echoed, "I love you, Scout."

Clay whipped around, his eyes big as walnuts. "What did you say?"

I started to shake at the intensity of his glare but repeated the words.

Mason continued feeding me lines as Clay walked slowly back, his head cocked as though considering something he'd never fathomed before.

With Mason speaking next to me, I repeated his every word. "Did you ever ask your mother about the time you broke your toe when you were seven?" I took a shaky breath. "We decided your mother shouldn't know. She'd worry too much. There's nothing can be done about a broken toe except let it heal on its own. You were such a big kid about it. So grown up. I told you, you were already an ace Eagle Scout. Always called you that afterward."

Clay returned to within a yard of me, absorbing each word of the explanation as I relayed it. In a hoarse whisper, he said, "I never told anyone about that. Not in football. Not in boot camp. Not even during those long, lonely nights in Afghanistan." He swallowed. "I didn't even tell Sonya, and I almost married her."

He moved a few steps away again, before turning halfway back. I thought he was going to say something, but instead, he dropped to his knees. My breath caught as I watched him scrub his hands over his head, a look of anguish distorting his face. Tears flooded his eyes, and he brought his palms to rest over them.

I stepped forward, determined to go to him, to plop onto the ground and surround him with a hug, but Mason caught my arm and said, "Give him a moment."

Clay looked up, but not at me. Rather, he looked at nothing in particular. His face was distorted by grief; his lips pressed together as though sealing in a sob. His anguish came spilling forth. "I'm sorry … Dad. I loved … love you." He shook his head as though he couldn't believe he was talking this way. When he continued, he spoke to me instead of the man he couldn't even see. "He was the best father anyone could ever have … I should have known he'd never leave us …"

"Tell him I love him. And all is forgiven," Mason prodded. "It's important he understand that. Tell him I love him more than he will ever understand until he has his own children. And we'll all be together one day. To keep his faith strong. Tell him."

I repeated Mason's message. Clay folded farther to the ground as though each word were another grain of pain being added to a sack of sorrow and regret he'd carried on his shoulder for more than fifteen years.

I couldn't stand it any longer, and I hurried to him. This time, Mason didn't stop me. I dropped down behind Clay and wrapped my arms around his shoulders, resting my cheek against the breadth of his back.

I don't know how long we huddled like that, but it was long enough to share grief, to learn this pillar of a man had loved his father immensely. When his hand reached up and covered mine where they clasped around his chest, hope surged through me. Hope that he recognized I was a messenger only in this matter.

Unfortunately, the hope was short-lived.

"Son," the sheriff said. I hadn't even heard him return from the crime scene. We looked up to see a Ziplock baggie in his hand. "You'll want to see this."

We stood, but Clay rubbed his face in a swift motion before looking at the sheriff. Without saying a word, he received the baggie and studied it. I looked closer too, to see a gold wedding band within the bag.

Clay held the bag toward the sky. In a hoarse voice, he read: "JMB and CES forever." He let those words sink in before adding, "Dad's wedding ring."

"Most likely." The sheriff frowned. For the first time, I noticed how pale the man looked, a reminder that a fifteen-year-old corpse would not be visually appealing. "'Course, it proves nothing because it's not a permanent part of a ..." Sheriff Barnes cleared his throat, "... a cadaver. What's more convincing is what we found on the remains."

Clay's gaze snapped from the ground to study the sheriff, his eyebrows scrunched in curiosity.

"Son, we found a metal plate ..."

"On his left knee." As Clay spoke the words, he closed his eyes, letting their meaning sink in. "Dad had knee replacement surgery when I was five."

The sheriff nodded. "It would seem so."

"How long before official ID?" Clay asked.

"Weeks to do an autopsy, confirm the plate, get dental records. All procedure."

Clay exhaled a defeated sigh. "But we already know what it's going to say, don't we?"

"If I were a betting man, yes," the sheriff confirmed.

"Are you done with me?" Clay asked. "I need to tell Mom and Reaghan."

"Son, I can't let you do that." An unmistakable tone of caution sounded in the sheriff's voice. "I need to be there. To witness her reaction. So … no phone calls either. Part of police procedure."

Clay's head jerked back in surprise. "What? Larry, you know Mom had nothing to do with this."

"Just doing my job. This means a new investigation. All this," he gestured behind him, "suggests your father was murdered, and I intend to find out who did it. I'll call your sister to meet us at your mom's in about an hour."

Clay hesitated then spoke to the sheriff. "I'll wait for you at the *Time Out*. It's closed for Labor Day. Mom won't be there." He gave a long, tired sigh, looked at me and shook his head, then left, stomping toward the towpath.

CHAPTER 20

"Clay, wait, please!"

He continued moving, ignoring my plea. My heart sank, wishing he had asked me to accompany him, but I suspected his pain and struggle for understanding drove him.

"Sheriff?" I shot him a pleading look.

He waved me on. "Go. I have your number. Be available." He headed back to the taped area.

I turned to Mason, but he spoke first. "Give my son time. He's reeling from shock; that's all."

I bit my lip to keep from crying.

Mason shifted. "I'll have to leave now." As he spoke, he turned his gaze to the activity within the taped area, and it struck me: the police were removing his body, his center. He had no choice but to go with it, or move on.

"No! You can't go yet. Please … wait!" I pulled Cassie's house key off my key ring. "Here, use this."

He looked at it. "What—"

"It's from your house. Cassie said she never changed the locks, so it's got to be from before you … you know."

He hesitated.

"Please," I urged. "You must trust me. I will protect it. But don't come out. No matter what you hear."

He tilted his head as though not understanding.

"It gets confusing, trying to talk to people and souls at the same time." I jerked the key toward him again. "Please."

He nodded and stepped into my hand. A burst of energy vibrated over me as he settled into the key. Tucking it in my jeans pocket, I scrambled toward the towpath.

Clay appeared ahead about thirty yards, moving at a slow pace, as though dazed.

I called his name, but he didn't respond.

When I reached within a couple feet of him, I said, "Clay, let me go with you."

Still no answer.

I fell in step behind him, and for a few yards we walked in barbed silence.

Then he turned, his movement so abrupt it startled me, and I bumped into him.

"How long, Grace?"

"What?"

"How long have you known?"

I tensed, frightened by his determination. "Please ..."

"We spent the day together Saturday. What could have happened yesterday ..." He broke off, shaking his head. "I'm trying to figure out ... how long have you known Dad was dead?"

My mind raced, but there was nothing I could offer him but the cold, hard truth. It felt frightening, this harrowing moment of long-awaited revelation. "A year."

"A year? A year, and you didn't think I'd like to know about this?" His voice grew louder and angrier as he continued. "We talked on Saturday about there always being honesty between us. Was that merely a lark—"

"What did you want me to do?" I countered, my voice quivery. "Walk up to you and say, 'Hey, by the way, your dad's dead body is down by the river?' How would that have made you feel?"

"Not much different than now," he growled. He looked away, shaking his head. When he looked back, it was clear he was trying to restore his composure. "So ... what's different? Why now?"

When I remained silent, he continued.

"Have you learned something new? Do you know who did it? What, Grace? What's different about now?" His questions came so rapid fire, I shrank back.

"I couldn't before now. There was always something else happening. I wanted to wait until I could figure out how it happened. Who did it ..."

"But yet you didn't," he said in an eerily calm voice. "You still don't know who killed my father, do you? Yet you decided to go to the police. Why now?"

In an anguished whisper, I said, "You were leaving. I don't want you to go."

He took a deep breath and pulled his shoulders back. "So you bring it up now when it helps *you*. It's not about me and my family and what this might mean. It's all about you, is that it?"

I winced, his words hitting too close to home. "It's not like it sounds. I've agonized over what to do. I didn't want you to be hurt … there was no good way … it's not about me—"

"But it is. Don't you see you're playing with fire?"

"What's that supposed to mean?"

"Grace, do you hear yourself? You know about my father's death because my dead father told you? In anyone's book, that's lunacy. And let's not even get into how you're stepping into weirdness … into things best left to God."

"If I hadn't acted on what I know, you might never have found out!"

He scoffed incredulously and shook his head as though he couldn't believe I said what I did. "Maybe I wasn't supposed to find out! Did you ever think of that?"

"But then you would have left and lost months … maybe years searching for a man you would never find. It would have been such a waste of time."

"A waste of time? I would have traveled, seen the world, found my own peace, come to my own conclusions. Maybe that was part of my path. I'd have been growing and learning and discovering during that time. That's not a waste."

"But wouldn't it have been cruel of me to know, and to still let you go?"

"Grace," he ran a hand over his head. "You shouldn't know. You shouldn't be talking with the dead."

I took a deep breath, an attempt to calm my voice. "What was I supposed to do? Turn and walk away from these … these souls who come into my path?"

"Yes!" He delivered that one word with all the crash and finality of a judge's gavel smacking down on the court bench.

A heartbeat or two passed as I panicked. Tiny ticks of painful time. I spoke and heard desperation in my voice: "Don't you think maybe this is God-given, this subtle vision I have? A gift, this ability to communicate with ghosts? It's not like I went to the store and bought it."

"We've all found ourselves in situations that look like opportunities, but they are traps in disguise. You've heard the pastor. You shouldn't converse with witches and fortune-tellers, and certainly not the dead. It can rule your life, take you away from living in the moment."

"But people talk to fortune-tellers all the time. Call psychic hotlines. Some have incredible stories of how accurate those spiritualists are. You're telling me those abilities aren't God-given? Then what are they?"

"I don't know. I do know there's a lot out there that looks appealing, that holds great promise. But we shouldn't look there for answers."

Anger overcame me. "I have been trying to help you. But you're so ungrateful." I stomped my foot and crossed my arms. "It wouldn't have been loving of me to turn my back on what I know. Why can't you see that?"

For a harrowing moment, he remained quiet.

"Clay?" I prompted, despising the tremor in my voice.

He shifted, rubbed his neck. "I need to be with my family."

"I'll go with you."

He grabbed hold of my folded arms, and shook gently, his face awash in confusion. Pain. And, worst of all, defeat. "Grace, I'm sorry. I don't want you to have any expectations … between us, I mean."

My breath hitched. "What are you saying?"

"We have a fundamental difference in beliefs here. I've loved you for a long time now. But there always seems to be this push-pull between us. Maybe we assumed too much."

"Clay—"

"And when will it end? I thought it was over last year, with Will. But there will always be another and another."

"But that's my problem, not yours!"

"It *is* my problem if I love you. But I can't protect you if I can't see what you're fighting."

"I can protect me!"

"Grace, couples who love each other are supposed to help one another fight their battles. That's what they do. But I'll always be locked out of this!"

A tense pause fell as if one of us ought to say more, and it felt significant, this moment of finality. But I couldn't argue. He was right. My supposed ability was mine alone.

He broke his hold and leaned back. "You seem to choose death over life, Grace. That's not a future I want." He ended with a note of sorrow in his voice, turned, and left.

His words prompted a pain so harsh it rendered me incapable of thought. I stood there, stunned. Words wouldn't come. And what could I say anyway? He was distraught, addled by shock, so allowances had to be made, right? He was floundering from grief and anger, but he'd be back.

Wouldn't he?

I watched him walk away as the drizzle began again, the perfect weather to mirror the gloom in my heart.

CHAPTER 21

B y the time I stumbled back to the parking lot, I felt broken, hopeless. I didn't even look around for Clay. I was certain he had left by now, so I headed to my car, determined to go home, shower, and report to work. Hilda wasn't expecting me. The shop was closed for Labor Day. However, I hoped she'd be inside stocking shelves or crunching numbers on her calculator. I could help her, and I needed the distraction. Mom once said that when you need help the most, help someone else, and in doing so, you'll get it. I hoped she was right.

I almost made it to my car when a voice called my name.

"Grace!"

I turned to see Cassie and Whit approaching from the opposite direction.

Of all people!

"Hi, hon," she said in that Southern accent of hers. "We didn't see you on the towpath. You callin' it quits because of the rain, too?"

"The rain?"

She laughed, lifting a lock of my hair. Moisture beaded on it. "Yes, silly, you look like a drowned rat."

For the first time, I noticed she and Whit wore rain gear and hoods. They always had the right gear for any occasion, avid athletes and outdoor people that they were. They both looked ten years younger than I suspected they were.

"Oh ... it caught me off-guard." I gestured north. "I was up the trail when it started."

Cassie's eyebrows pulled together. "You hiked north? But that direction is closed off." She pointed behind me.

I tracked her gaze to see a police barrier blocking the path. Beside it, a sign read "Do Not Enter." I'd been so lost in thought when I came back, I stepped around it, unawares. That's why the sheriff's concern was limited to people seeing us from upriver; he'd closed the path to hikers from downriver, from Williamsport.

I stammered, "Oh … well …"

"The rangers said the police were investigating a crime scene," Whit said.

Cassie shivered. "Someone on the trail said they found a body buried up there. Can you imagine?"

I looked down and remained quiet.

"You know something, don't you?" She tilted her head and studied me in one of those ways people do when they're trying to figure out what's wrong with you. She gasped. "Oh, my word! This has something to do with Nidhi, doesn't it?"

Whit frowned. "Cas, darlin', how did you jump to that conclusion?"

She flailed her hands. "She's missing—"

Whit shook his head. "Don't go there. We could guess all day and still be wrong."

I touched her arm. "I don't know anything about Nidhi's whereabouts."

"But—" Cassie began.

Whit cast her a quelling glance. "Cas, not everything that happens around here involves us or our friends."

You're so wrong, Whit. This definitely involves Cassie. Unfortunately, I wasn't at liberty to say so, nor could I figure out how to change the topic, so I looked at the ground again. The next voice was Cassie's.

"Then why are you looking so glum, Grace, and acting so …" Her tone changed. "Oh, I know."

I jerked my head up to see her park her hands on her hips and frown.

"Clay found you, didn't he? You were with him."

"I … yes, he was here."

"And he said goodbye, didn't he? I knew it. He told us his plans yesterday. Mexico! There's no stopping him when he gets an idea in his head." She blew a resigned breath. "He's determined to find his father."

Whit grumbled. "Makes no sense to me, a man leaving his family. I'd never turn my back on Francesca." She was his daughter and lived in Rome near her mother, Whit's ex.

Cassie touched his arm and nodded sadly like she agreed with him. Turning back, she said, "Hon, I'm sure you're disappointed. I am too. But he'll be back. Eventually. Come to the house tonight, and we'll have our own little pity party. I'd invite you now," she looked at Whit, "but we're drivin' to Hagerstown to—"

"Cassie," I said, "you need to go home. Now." I turned and began fumbling with the key fob to my car door, but my hands shook so badly it required several efforts. "Clay will be there."

"Clay … at home? Why? Grace—" she began, stepping closer and trying to make eye contact with me.

Tears surfaced. I refused to talk or look at her.

She touched my shoulder. "Oh, hon." Her voice revealed fear, regret.

I pulled away and yanked my car door open. "Trust me. Go home."

Her cell phone rang. "No, Grace, wait …" she read her phone and looked at Whit. "It's Larry Barnes. The sheriff."

I panicked. "Gotta go."

"No, let me take the call first!" She punched the button on her phone like she was mad at it.

"I can't. We'll talk later." I shut my door, started the engine, and backed out as she answered the phone.

"Mason," I said out loud, "I'm sorry you had to experience that. They don't know the truth."

The key vibrated in my pocket. I imagined it as his way of

saying he understood.

I heaved a sigh as I pulled onto Canal Street, as though I had held my breath for the last several minutes. I pictured myself throwing a massive rock in the proverbial pond before callously running away, leaving the ripples for everyone in the water to ride out.

***

At home, I left Will alone because his presence was weakened by daylight. Instead, I showered and walked Tramp before driving back to Williamsport.

As I passed Cassie's house, I imagined the scene unfolding within. The family gathering, pulling close, sharing shock and sorrow. I hated how the tide had turned against me. I should have been with Clay through this, not excluded for being the messenger.

A few blocks farther, I arrived at the Antique Emporium and entered through the back door.

"In the showroom, dear," Hilda called.

I smiled to myself; the woman must have seen me driving by. *There was little she missed.*

I found her standing by the front windows, hands on her cane, studying the First Potomac Bank and Trust across the street.

"What's up?" I asked, crossing the expanse of the showroom and moving to her side. I saw nothing questionable through the window that would cause her to look so pensive.

"Nidhi Michelson. I'm worried about her."

I wasn't aware Hilda knew Nidhi, but then again, why wouldn't she? It was a small town, and Hilda knew a lot about it. During previous conversations, she'd kept her tidbits about local residents to a social level, never revealing anything seedy or passing along assessments that shed people in a bad light, although I suspected she had keen opinions about them. Instead, she'd make a *pshh* sound and wave a dismissive hand when a customer tried to rope her into gossip. The one exception had been Holland Greer, of course. She'd made it clear she didn't like the man.

Sometimes I wondered if Hilda kept alert to the activities outside her door because she imagined herself as the town's memory keeper. She once told me she gets "a little too excited about solving problems ... and heartaches." I could use her wisdom on both counts right now.

I turned to study her more intensely, hoping to gauge her mood and level of concern. She looked downright stressed: eyes troubled, brows scrunched together, and skin pinched at the throat. What's more, I noticed her right hand rubbing over her left in pointless movements as they rested atop her cane. I'd never seen her look so plagued with disturbing thoughts.

"You know her well?" My energy seeped away. Hilda's comments about Nidhi heightened my concern. But there was more. I ached at the stress I read in Hilda's eyes. This woman had grown quite special to me.

Hilda shrugged. "As well as the next person in town." She met my gaze and opened her mouth to say more. Instead, she halted and tilted her head as though assessing me. Her body posture tensed.

When I opened my mouth to ask about it, she shook her head in two fast beats, as though dislodging her thoughts. She backed up a couple steps and folded onto a stool by the window, her face paler than when I arrived. She gestured to another stool, and I pulled it close. I sat with my face toward the window, too. I was still a little discomforted by Hilda's reaction to me, and I didn't want to provide her with easy eye contact.

"Nidhi only works there," Hilda said gesturing toward the bank, "but that makes her my neighbor. She's a good person and I—"

She broke off, and I stole my gaze from the street back to her face. She was staring at me again, her eyebrows furrowed, as though trying to figure out what was different as if I'd changed my hair color or sprouted a wart on my nose.

I swallowed. "Is something wrong?"

She leaned back, tilted her head again. "What makes you ask that?"

"The way you keep looking at me."

She shifted on the stool as if embarrassed. "Forgive me, Grace." She looked indecisive but continued, "There's something different about you. Something … came through the door with you. I can't pinpoint it because I can't see anymore."

She couldn't see anymore? What did she mean? The woman had keen eyesight for an octogenarian, so I ruled out poor vision. She'd alluded to an ability to discern or sense things before. Was that what she meant?

She prodded. "It's true, isn't it?"

"I … don't know what you mean."

"Do you remember last year when you first visited the shop?" She gestured to the entryway. "I sensed something then, too." She leaned in and studied my face as though trying to memorize it. "Like you didn't come alone. But when you came to inquire about the job, I sensed you were alone and have been each time since. Until now."

Her words, her gaze, together intimidated me. I lifted a negligent shoulder. "I don't understand. You know I was alone. I walked by, and when I saw the mirror you displayed in the window, I got this notion to …"

My body jerked back, and my gaze turned to the window as it hit me. *She was right!* The notion had been born from Will! I'd gone into the shop at what I believed to be his urging. His center had been in the gold coin I wore around my neck. At every visit afterward, I hadn't worn the coin because it was at the cemetery near *Crossings*.

She tapped her cane, up and down twice. I looked back. As always, she wasn't being rude with the effort. Rather, she sat quietly poking at the floor and waiting for me to process my thoughts.

"You're remembering something," she said.

"I …" I shook my head, trying to make sense of it.

Instead of waiting for me, she plunged ahead. "It's alright, dear. I'm not angry. Quite the opposite, because both times it has felt *safe*." She said the last word like she'd thought about it for hours and had come to that calculated conclusion.

Safe? With a ghost around my neck? Only she would say such a thing. Perhaps her ability to sense was quite remarkable. Or, completely out of whack, because in this instance she was wrong. I was here alone solely because I was worried about Clay and Cassie learning about—

"Mason!" It came out of my mouth before I could stop. His center resided in the key I'd reattached to my key ring, now in my backpack, sitting on the floor beside me. I looked at Hilda. "How did you know?"

"I thought so, dear." She stood. "Let's move upstairs where we will be more comfortable and people won't look in at us. We are closed, after all." She didn't wait for a response.

I followed on wobbly legs.

She continued talking as she moved along, the cane thumping at every other step. "Rather than us beating around the bush and you keeping things to yourself, I want to tell you a story. It's time. And, you are the person who should hear it."

"A story?"

"About the town and when its atmosphere began to change. You could say a chill set in and never left." She talked over her shoulder as she regally thumped along.

Dread flooded over me, but I decided I had reached a point of no return when she added, "And you can bring your friend with you, too."

I followed her to the back of the building, past the lengthy storage room—more like a warehouse—the packing/shipping area, and loading dock, to reach the small elevator that carried us up a flight.

***

The building housing Hilson's Antique Emporium looked bland and boring from the outside, a two-story structure of red brick, built fifty-plus years ago. The first floor carried indoors the same insipid look of the exterior, with its aged floors, walls, doors and shelving, the oldness contributing to the atmosphere of the antique business and the treasures showcased within.

I expected Hilda's personal space on the second floor to be likewise dull and dated. When the elevator came to rest, and the doors opened directly into the living area, my jaw dropped. The apartment—and I use the term loosely because it looked more like a posh penthouse in New York's Upper East Side—featured vaulted ceilings and an open concept with a wide expanse providing views of a spacious living room, formal dining area capable of seating twelve, and a modern chef-style kitchen. Rather than floor-to-ceiling walls, spaces were defined by decorative beams, shelving units, and glass partitions. I noted the latest in subway tiles in the kitchen, massive artwork around the dining table, and Oriental rugs atop polished hardwood floors. The décor was eclectic and upscale, and clearly no expense was spared.

Most startling was the sweeping staircase. It led to a loft practically floating above the dining area, as though supported by hidden beams. Rows of books lined the exterior walls of the loft. A door led to what I assumed must be a rooftop patio.

"Hilda, this is amazing," I gushed, with genuine admiration. "I had no idea this was up here."

"What did you expect, dear? The place to look old, like me?" She chuckled. "Shag carpet, perhaps?"

I blushed, deserving the wisecrack.

"Most people are surprised when they see my flat. I like to redo it every seven or eight years."

I followed her into the kitchen. As I admired the brick arch above the range and the hanging copper cooking utensils, she filled a teakettle and removed two cups from the custom-designed white cupboards. While the water heated, she gave me a tour. We walked through a home office, theater room, and three master suites each with its own bathroom, walk-in closet, large-screen TV, and computer workstation. "I like my boys and their families to be comfortable when they visit," she said.

I couldn't help but admire the video game collection on the living room floor, placed strategically in front of the large-screen TV. Controllers for the Octagon 720 sat scattered about.

"My favorite is Skyraiders Revenge 2. I'm already at level ninety-three on expert." She shot me a prideful smile. "'Course, it's a complete waste of time, but I love to relax here at the end of the day, put my jeans on and get lost in the kite savages and the drone destroyers."

"You wear jeans?" I threw my hand over my mouth. *Talk about harboring a stereotype.* "I mean, you never cease to surprise me."

"Hmpf. I plan to give Grandma Moses a run for her money. She didn't start painting seriously until she was seventy-eight. Died at 101."

As we returned to the kitchen, I told her about the changes Michael made in my apartment.

"It sounds lovely," she said and poured steaming water into our cups. "Personally, the contemporary look is too minimalist for me." She looked around at the busyness of her home. "But I plan to remodel the showroom in a contemporary style."

Surprised, I asked, "But shouldn't the backdrop for antiques look old, too?"

"Balderdash." She pointed to the dining area. "Look at how those modern paintings and pillars make the antique hutch stand out. Such good contrast."

She was right.

"Besides," she continued, "I want people to develop a comfort with antiques. They're works of art. Even though they're old, it doesn't mean they have to harbor secrets or haunt our lives.

Wouldn't you agree?" She tilted her head in a knowing manner.

This sounded like a segue into her reason for bringing me upstairs. I nodded and followed her into the living room with my tea to listen to her story.

CHAPTER 22

Hilda's Story, as told by Hilda

I was a little girl in the 1930s, the time of the Great Depression. Like so many people, my family was quite poor; my mother, father and sister, Lavidia. Our house was nothing more than a crumbled shack up the road from here. It's long gone now, but like this shop, it had a window facing this same street, too.

I loved to watch the people go by. What a sight, too! For such a little town, there was always something going on. Horse-drawn carriages. Bums hiking through, all their possessions in a sack on their shoulders. Barefoot children playing in the street. Occasionally, a motor car or truck would rumble by, but that was rare. Those mostly belonged to rich folks passing through the area.

I longed to be outside playing, but as I said, we were poor, and it demanded we all do what we could to survive. My daddy worked at the brickworks outside town, but it wasn't steady work because few were building during the Depression. So he was laid off a lot. As a result, we had little money, and none to spend on pleasure.

My greatest joy came every winter when Mama and Daddy would take us sledding across the river at Chocton Bluff. The place was hard to reach and had a reputation for being mysterious, but no one gave it much credence and paid little attention to it. From time to time, someone would repeat the legend about gold being hidden in the area during the Civil War, but there were few veterans from that war still around by then, so no one ever proved or disproved the story. But the challenging times kept the story alive.

Daddy would borrow a sleigh, and the four of us would pile

on with blankets and lanterns and extra clothing, our sleds stacked in the back.

When I was six ... Lavidia would have been only three ... we went to the bluff one Saturday night. It was so cold we had the hill to ourselves. We'd been there for at least an hour, going up and down the slope. Only the moon and a few lanterns to light our path.

We heard a noise, beyond the ridge, in the direction of the nearby *Crossings* estate. Your home, dear. It sounded like a long, drawn-out moan.

At first, we thought someone was hurt. Well, you can imagine it concerned my parents. Daddy told us to stay put while he investigated. We had no reason to suspect danger or anything untoward. Perhaps we were naïve, because people around here were desperate for money, for food, like everywhere else in the country. Many of them would have sold their souls for a better life or to keep their families from starving. It wasn't until years later I understood how such desperation and lack of faith in a better future could render the door open for evil to come in.

Ten minutes passed, and Daddy was still gone. Then fifteen. Finally, after about twenty minutes, Mama couldn't stand it any longer, and she asked me to climb up the bluff to find Daddy. She told me not to go beyond the reach of the lantern light.

I climbed and climbed and kept calling his name. There was no answer. I got scared. I was ready to run back to Mama when I heard a noise a bit ahead, in the darkness. I thought it was Daddy, so I defied my mother's warning to stay in the light.

I inched around a huge rock. The top of the bluff was filled with crevices and entrances to little caves. In the dim light of the moon, I saw my father standing at the edge of the cliff. In front of him stood a ... creature. I don't know how else to describe him, but he appeared to be covered in fur. His body was sleek and thin, like a cross between a man and wolf. Maybe that's what made me think it was a "him" covered in fur. I was so stunned, not much more registered with me except his large fangs and long, thin fingers with talon-like fingernails. Oh, and a smell of decay hung in the air. I was so scared; I didn't even notice the odor until I sucked in my breath as the creature pushed my daddy over the ledge. With the smuggest, nastiest smile I'd ever seen, the creature turned and looked at me.

Well, I screamed and raced as fast as I could, slipping in the snow and tumbling as much as running down the slope toward Mama.

Daddy disappeared that night. Forever. I tried to explain to Mama and to the police what I saw, but everyone decided I was in shock. They found his body two days later on the rocks, at the edge of the frozen river. Daddy's death was ruled an accident.

That quickly, my father was gone, and I became the second grownup in the house. I tended to my sister while Mama got various jobs cleaning houses and taking in laundry for money.

Not long after Daddy died, I discovered I could see ghosts, apparitions of dead people. Before long, I could hear them talk as well. By then, I'd already been designated as delusional, not clear in the head, because of what I described from Chocton Bluff.

I became the most aloof child in the town. Afraid of everyone and everything. I was scared to go anywhere for fear one of those ghosts would walk right up and talk to me, or worse, snatch and kill me. At the time, I didn't get close enough to see that many of them were actually gentle, kind. That didn't occur to me until much later.

So from age six to about thirteen, seven years, I watched the town like a hawk from our front window. As I said earlier, the tone of the town changed. One day things were calm, and the next, fear hovered everywhere. I suspect most folks attributed it to the damage the Depression caused. But people locked their doors and stayed home more at night.

That seventh year after the accident, we experienced a warm winter, but terrible flooding. It rained day after day for almost a week. Fog was a constant. Day and night. The weather this past week has been an eerie reminder of that time so long ago.

I would stay awake into the late hours while Mama and Lavidia slept. I sat there staring out the window. For what, I don't know ... all I ever saw was rain falling, fog swirling, night passing.

Then one night, I spotted something. Actually, it was the seventh anniversary of my father's death, near eleven o'clock, about the same time he fell off the cliff. The creature stepped out of the foggy shadows and into the light of the street lamps. Oh, he looked different, certainly. Presentable, for the street. He was dressed like a dandy with a perfectly tailored red suit. Red! He had shiny shoes and carried a long umbrella. Despite the rain, he wasn't using it, and he wasn't even getting wet. It was closed, and he twirled it in his hand as he sauntered. That's what it was, sauntering. Down the street. Like he owned the place. It was the wolf from the cliff. I was certain.

No, I couldn't see any fur. In fact, his face looked presentable, more human-like than what I'd seen on the cliff, but I knew it was he. Knew it from the fangs and the claw-like fingernails.

I froze in my seat. I'm sure I didn't make a sound. Didn't move. I considered myself safe, sitting as I was in the shadow by the window. But he strolled right up to our window and tapped twice with his umbrella.

"Good evening, Hilda," he said, and looked directly at me.

I was so startled, I think my blood stopped flowing. His stare pinned me to my seat, even though I still didn't believe he could see me.

Then, he spoke again. "I like your pink ribbon. Let me in, and I can give you many more. Any color you wish."

Yes, I was wearing a pink ribbon in my hair. When I didn't respond, he laughed and shook his head. He lifted his hand, or his claw, whatever it was, and scratched several swirls on our window. With his hand! Then, he etched a circle around it. He did it slowly. Grinning at me all the while. The sound it made was so horrific.

"Go away," I screamed.

He chuckled. Stepped back from the glass. Said he'd see me again soon. Then, he disappeared.

I don't understand why my scream didn't wake up Mama and Lavidia. I would have thought the neighbors could hear it. But no one rushed into the front room to check on me. Exhausted, I fell to the floor, and I must have passed out. The next thing I knew, I heard Mama stirring in her bedroom, and the sun was shooting its morning rays into the corners of the room.

I climbed off the floor, disoriented, wondering why I would have dreamed such a silly dream. Then my gaze fell on the window. The circle was gone, but the swirls remained. It was like he left enough of a warning sign that I could not forget him, but not enough to alert others. For years, Mama wondered what kind of stone had smacked against the window to create such a design. Meanwhile, I wondered if I had dreamt it all.

But at that moment, it was so real. I raced into my room and changed for church. Needless to say, I dropped to my knees at the service that morning. And from then on, the creature never returned, and I never saw any ghosts again. Ever.

My prayers were answered. What had plagued me for so long was gone. I couldn't see death anymore, but I was left with the ability to discern between right and wrong, good and evil. I still have the ability to sense things, which is much more palatable than seeing them. And it's still that way. I am not deaf, and I only need glasses to read. I have my own teeth and must follow a special diet these days. But my ability to discern is as sharp now as it was then.

CHAPTER 23

As Hilda told her tale in steady-stream delivery, we'd settled in the living room, her on a leather wingback chair, me on the squashy cushions of a plush couch amidst plants and artwork.

When she finished, her lips and cheeks were drained of color, and her white hands were knotted in her lap.

I regarded her in wonderment. "That's incredible. You must have been scared."

"When that gentleman,"—she voiced the title in a way that suggested she thought it undeserved—"brought his wooden box through the door on your first day of work, I recognized the etching. The same as the one drawn by the creature ... man ... whatever it was. But you recognized something else, didn't you? You said you could *see* the evil. You saw a spirit with the box, didn't you?"

"I did. He looked angry. Menacing." No point in denying what Hilda already knew. Not only had she shared a horrific experience from her childhood, but she had also described to a T the one person I heretofore had not recognized in my dream, on my birthday—the wolf-like man.

"And you see others?"

I nodded.

"You've brought one with you now, haven't you?"

I closed my eyes and slumped into the couch. If I couldn't trust this sweet, dear lady, this relative, who had shared an eerie and somewhat similar tale, who could I trust?

I reached into my pocket, pulled out the key, and placed it on the table. "He's placed his energy, his center, in the key."

She didn't look surprised. Didn't even blink. "Who has?"

"You'll hear the news soon, so I may as well tell you. As we sit here, Sheriff Barnes is telling Cassie Baxter they've found her husband, Mason. His body, I mean."

"Oh, my. That poor woman."

"He was murdered. Buried along the canal. I'm aware of this because I …" I took a deep breath. "… I *met* him … his soul … during one of my bike rides. After the police dug up his body this morning, I asked him to place his center in this key. This way he can stay here until his murder is resolved. Or at least long enough to answer questions."

Hilda remained quiet, staring at the key.

I rubbed a hand over my forehead. "I asked him not to come out."

"Goodness. Oh, my. It's okay, dear. I knew Mason. He was a fine man. I always thought his disappearance might have something to do with foul play. It's good that you're helping him."

"I've helped others, too." I briefly explained how I first met Will and Braxton and resolved their deaths, but I left out the details, unsure of her interest. I waited, certain she'd want to utter denials about it happening and warn that I dabbled with something I shouldn't.

Instead, she said, "Those might be isolated incidences, but I doubt it. We need to consider that they might be related. Particularly since your home is so close to Chocton Bluff."

"But Mason's death has nothing to do with *Crossings* or the bluff."

"Don't be so sure." She pursed her lips. "You know, this will continue until they get what they want, or until we get it first and use it against them. It's time we put our heads together." She smiled and stood. "Let's order pizza and compare what we know while we eat."

I wasn't sure who "they" were, or what "they" wanted, or how she even knew about "them," but as she dialed for pizza, I realized

I loved this woman more than ever.

***

We finished our pizza long before our discussion. I described my life since leaving Boston and added the details: Will saving me from Henry and Greasy Jim, both trips to Georgia, the headless Naomi and the brooding Braxton, the explosion that destroyed the tunnels, other souls I met along the way, Michael's possession, Fergus being devoured by demon-like creatures, my suspicions about Holland.

I finalized my story by expressing relief at being able to talk to someone who didn't believe I was batty. "Clay has tried to be understanding about everything, and so has Seth. But they're both angry with me right now. And then there's Adriana. You should have seen her when I told her to call about the audition today. She thought I was butting my nose in where it doesn't belong. She doesn't know—"

My cell phone sounded, and I read the ID. Surprised, I mumbled, "It can't be ..."

Hilda cocked one eyebrow. "Adriana?"

I nodded as a flush of adrenaline tingled through me in a discomforting way.

"Take the call, dear," Hilda said, climbing off her chair. "I'll clean this mess."

When I clicked on, Adriana squealed.

"Grace, I got an audition! I can't believe it! The conductor, Mr. Gamberaldi, said he came in today only because he left papers in his office he wanted at home. He found a note from the concertmaster saying one of the flutists tendered her resignation. He knew he'd need to find a replacement, pronto. I wouldn't be the principal flutist, and there's no guarantee, but I audition on Thursday!"

I was glad she told me over the phone because she probably would have been disappointed by the look on my face. I was happy for her, and thrilled not to lose her, but I was overwhelmed Mule's advice had been sound. How did he know?

"Grace? How?"

Her voice brought me back to her call. "Um, how what?"

"I said, how did you know?"

"Umm … a hunch. It makes sense." And it struck that it did make sense. *Sometimes instinct helps us make good decisions.* Or, was I deluding myself? "Ade, I'm so happy for you."

"Thanks. Dad says practice makes perfect, so I'm not leaving the house until Thursday. I'm going to get that position!"

I clicked off as Hilda returned and settled again into her chair.

She said, "That was a rather fortuitous call, wasn't it?"

"If you mean odd, random, too weird to be believed, then yes, it was fortuitous. Things happen like that a lot."

"What things?" she asked, sounding as excited as a detective discovering a clue in a crime he's been investigating for months.

"The phone call from Ade when I was talking about her. Seeing Kate's face in the mirror last year right before she called. Some helpful soul being at the right place at the right time. Like the musician at the library or young Andrew at the medical museum or Malcolm Prestwood, the research physician in Savannah, or the cop in the pawn shop."

She smiled. "Welcome to my life. What you described is typical for me."

"But I need it to make sense."

She thought about that. "I doubt it ever will, dear. But, let's see … I can't explain the souls. I do believe angels help us in all sorts of ways. As for Adriana and Kate, are the coincidences so unusual? Of course, Adriana would call if she got good news. If we sat here long enough, one of your friends was bound to call, wouldn't you agree?"

"I guess." I stood and began pacing. "What about why I walked into the Emporium in the first place last year?"

"You said Will prompted you to do so. From the coin you

wore."

"But was it truly that, or would I have come in anyway? On a hunch? Were you and I placed together because of Will, or were we drawn together because of a shared history? Or a similarity of which we weren't even aware?" I flung my hands in frustration. "Were we like magnets bound to eventually come together?"

"Perhaps." Hilda nodded. "I told you before; I believe things happen for a reason. We would have met without Will's assistance. Did he help? Maybe. Maybe not. Does it matter?"

"And why did I have those visions when I talked with Mason at the canal last year? I saw Cassie say things before she even said them."

"Some form of reverse déjà vu?" Hilda reasoned. "Again, does it matter?"

I stopped and raked a hand over my head. "I don't know why, but it matters to me. I want to understand it."

"But you probably never will. Maybe that's the point. You're trying to apply logic when sometimes you have to move on in good faith. We're surrounded by a supernatural world. Things are going to seem odd at times."

"I guess."

"Haven't you ever hummed a song, then turned on the radio to discover it playing? Or found a missing object in a place you knew for certain you already checked three times?"

I raised my shoulder in an "I suppose" gesture.

"See? You shrugged off the notion of these coincidences. Why can't you shrug off others?"

"But how?"

"Focus on your bravery. I'm proud of you, dear. You witnessed Braxton's murder. Approached souls on the battlefield near a full moon. Watched a headless Naomi—was that her name?—commit suicide. You saw Clay hurt, Michael possessed, Seth attacked—"

I groaned and dropped back onto the couch. Hearing her list didn't make me sound courageous at all. Instead, it reminded me all those people had suffered because of me. "None of that sounds brave. It sounds foolish, like it never should have happened."

"Yes, well," she said, waving a dismissive hand, "that's true. Perhaps those *are* bad examples, but the point is you were brave when you needed to be."

A silence fell as we sat there lost in our thoughts.

I broke the silence. "I am envious. You grew your faith, and the ghosts disappeared. Mine are still here. I've talked with Pastor Dale. Prayed for guidance. Read scripture. But for me, death won't go away. And please don't tell me it's a matter of faith and choices. Pastor Dale and others have said the same, but it's not true."

She frowned. "No one can do our internal work for us. Focus on the good. You gave Adriana excellent advice. Employers want people who take the initiative. You also advised Seth wisely. Don't overlook that."

"How do you know my advice to Seth is sound? He hasn't even learned the details yet."

"Oh, but I do know." She leaned forward, pulled a red throw from a side basket, and pulled it over her feet. For the first time, I noticed a series of varicose veins road-mapping her legs and understood the need for the walking cane. "Most folks suffer amnesia in small towns. They act like it's kind and beneficial and important to forget. But I believe it's more important to remember."

"I don't understand."

"Seth. He's a Crinshaw."

"Oh … yeah, I know. In fact, it was Nidhi who told me. Last year. She wasn't very impressed with the Crinshaws. Whoever they are."

Hilda's gaze intensified. "Grace, one day last year I was looking out my window, and I saw you walking down the sidewalk. You stopped suddenly. Do you remember? You jumped behind a tree as though hiding from someone."

I wasn't sure why the change in topic or where she was going with this, but I remembered the day quite well. I nodded. "I saw a ghost. In fact, it was the young fireman, Nate Carter. The one who saved the Clarksburg man at the bridge the other day."

"Do you remember anything odd about that moment?"

I chuckled, a sound more of dismay than mirth. "Well, I should respond that seeing a ghost is odd enough but, yeah, it was strange. He jumped back like he wanted to avoid someone. In fact, he looked quite alarmed."

"So that explains it."

"Explains what?"

"I thought *you* were hiding from her, but it was actually the ghost, the soul, cringing away from her."

"Her? Her whom?"

Hilda sat up taller. Her lips pulled together with a suggestion of distaste or disgust. "Gwendolyn Bealle. At the library."

"I don't understand."

"Mrs. Bealle is—"

I lifted my index finger. "That's *Ms.* Bealle, as she informed me." I rolled my eyes.

"That's because she doesn't want people to remember."

"Remember what?"

"She was married for a time. Bealle isn't her birth name."

"But why would it matter? Is her birth name that bad?"

Hilda nodded. "It's Crinshaw. They have a long, sordid history with this town. Benny Crinshaw is her brother. And, Seth's birth father."

CHAPTER 24

Had a steamroller crunched over me?

Seth was Benny Crinshaw's son! *The* Benny Crinshaw? Brother to Gwendolyn Bealle?

"But Benny—"

"Wasn't always like he is."

True. Seth once described Benny as an upcoming young entrepreneur about eighteen, nineteen years ago.

Right around the time of Seth's birth!

Benny had started a chain of bistro-style restaurants and looked to expand into California, where he was involved in a horrible accident. He was left with the mental maturity of a small child. The mother must have gotten pregnant before—

I jerked forward. "The mother! Seth's mother, who is she?"

"Rachel Shepherd. Sister to his adoptive mother, Jacquelyn Shepherd Rendale. Rachel and Benny were engaged to be married at the time of the accident. It happened two weeks before the wedding, and, some said, right after she learned she was pregnant. The wedding was postponed indefinitely. At least, until Benny improved. When it became clear the fiancé Rachel knew was gone forever, she left the area."

I squeezed my eyes shut and gripped the arms of the chair as Hilda's words roiled over me.

She continued. "One year later, the Rendales adopted a baby boy. Everyone believed it to be a logical step for them to take after four daughters. But there was always speculation. In time, Rachel came back. Visited now and then, but eventually, she stopped coming."

"How do you know all this? I mean, if you are aware of the details, then surely most of the town is too. You'd think Seth would have learned long before this."

"Not necessarily. It was quite hush-hush. As I said, some suspected. But no one knew for sure. Except my Arthur. He was on the board of the Mental Health Association until he died. He believed Gwendolyn Bealle maneuvered to keep Seth here. Benny's accident resulted in a tidy insurance payment to the Crinshaws, in other words, Gwendolyn. Arthur suspected she helped with Seth's finances, which is what persuaded Seth's father to go along with it."

"That's incredible. No wonder Ms. Bealle pays such rapt attention to Seth. Do you suppose she's the one who's funding his college?" I stood and moved aimlessly as I talked. "But, it makes no sense then for Seth's dad to be angry about it. Shouldn't he be pleased Ms. Bealle is willing to pay the tuition?"

She chuckled and shifted, the leather reacting with squishy sounds. "I imagine they're caught in a tug of war right now. You said Seth and his dad fought over his intended course of study. My guess is Seth's father was happy with the financial arrangement until Seth declared his major. When Dirk Rendale refused to go along with his son's plan, he threatened to withhold support. Gwendolyn must have stepped in and made other arrangements, merely to ensure Seth didn't move away."

I rubbed my forehead. "All this time, I've disliked her. She always struck me as a snooty busybody. Turns out, she's trying to keep her family together. She provided Seth with an opportunity he never would have otherwise."

"Well, I don't know about that, dear. She also lied and manipulated to do it."

My nerves tensed at Hilda's remark. I stopped moving and turned to look at her. "I'm no one to fault lying. I told some lies when I first got to the area, too. I called them white lies and convinced myself no one would be harmed by them. But they were still lies. My point is, her goal sounds altruistic. For Seth, I mean. And then there's Benny. She took care of him all these years."

Hilda looked skeptical and shook her head. "I don't know. There's something about that woman. When I see her come, I want to hide too, like the soul of that young fireman. Why, the afternoon of your birthday, I saw her. At the bank. You'd already left here. She climbed from her car at the same time Nidhi walked out the side door to her car. Nidhi was wearing that pretty peacock-blue dress of hers. The vintage one? I remember it because she bought it here. She once told me it is Sheriff Barnes' favorite. They were seeing one another, you know. Anyway, I remember wondering if they had a date that night." Hilda frowned. "I was so happy for her until I saw Ms. Bealle call her over. They talked and moved together around the back of the building, out of my view. I thought to myself, 'Look out, Nidhi. You're in for an earful with that one.' It was the last I saw her."

"Did you tell the sheriff?"

"I saw the police searching in the lot behind the bank the other day, so I walked over. They found her cell phone while I was there. I told Sheriff Barnes what I had seen."

"I wonder if Holland Greer has something to do with this?" A new energy coursed through me, and I started pacing again. "Are all these loose ends tied together somehow? I saw Ms. Bealle and Greer arguing in the library last year. Before that, they always looked like they were colluding on something."

Again, Hilda frowned and repeated, "I don't know, dear."

"I always got the impression she was enamored with him. Like she'd do anything to please him. He probably learned her story and blackmailed her to keep quiet. And, in fact, it was a Crinshaw, presumably Ms. Bealle's ancestor, who murdered Fergus Lowe and Thaddeus Fleming Calhoun in the tunnels under my house. Maybe Holland believed Ms. Bealle had some insider knowledge."

"Knowledge about what? And what does that have to do with Nidhi?"

"I'm not sure. It's just that … well, Holland is overly curious about *Crossings* and the gold. He shows up at the oddest times."

She pulled her shoulders back and pursed her lips in a manner of disgust. "I told you; he's a rubbernecker."

"He was there when the tunnels exploded last year. And Mason was at Holland's house the night he was killed. After seeing Holland with stolen Civil War relics, he—Mason—was struck from behind. He came to half-dead, along the canal. Then he died and was tossed into a crude grave."

"How ghastly." She looked thoughtful. "But, dear, things aren't always as they seem."

I looked at her, surprised. "Hilda, on my first day of work you expressed a distaste for the man."

"But not because he's sinister."

"Then what?"

"His intelligence. His acuteness." She shrugged. "Well, his lack thereof. He seems to enter unfamiliar territory if he gets lost in his own thoughts."

I gasped. "Maybe it's all an act."

Hilda looked skeptical. "Maybe … but I don't think so. It's dangerous to jump to conclusions."

On the latter she was right. It's not only dangerous, it's also foolish. But sometimes, when time and answers are in short supply, you've gotta make do with what you know.

CHAPTER 25

I left Hilda's place mid-afternoon. Instead of rain, a muggy mist had settled on the town, although the former appeared to be a mere cloudburst away.

My mind kept replaying the past few days, like a video set to repeat, each viewing producing the same effect—anger toward me.

Clay, because I'd withheld information from him.

Seth, because I'd cast a shadow on his future plans.

What if I thwarted any more hurt or anger by acting on both lessons, in a reverse kind of way?

No more withholding information from Seth, as I had Clay. I would tell him about his parentage.

No more casting shadows on Clay's future, as I had Seth's. I would resolve Mason's murder so Clay could heal and move on, with or without me.

As for Seth, I needed to prepare my thoughts. I owed him an apology and a good explanation. But I could think about that later.

First, thanks to lessons I learned from the intervention my friends conducted months ago, I intended to hold my own encounter with the oddest—and most select—assortment of characters that ever graced a room. If nothing else, from the intervention I'd learned truths cannot be refused, denied, or altered when all key parties are in the same room to dispute or confirm them.

I inched past Cassie's house and the *Time Out*, driving as slow as the cars behind would tolerate. The blinds remained closed. Despite the reason the family pulled together, I wished I could be with them. But, no one inside would want to talk to me right now.

Except Sidney!

I pulled over and called his cell phone. He was Clay's brother-in-law and the career counselor at the community college where I planned to study for a couple years.

When he answered, I said, "This is Grace," although he probably read my name on caller ID. We were in each other's phone address books, having exchanged numbers last year when we discussed online homeschool lessons for my senior year in high school.

"How're you doing?" His tone was genial but hushed.

"I'm … I don't know. Is anyone there still talking to me?"

He chuckled. "I am. Hold on a sec. Let me go into another room."

A brief pause followed.

When he returned, his voice wasn't much louder. "You've helped bring a close to a missing link that's plagued this family for years. I'm grateful for that."

"I don't suppose the others feel that way?"

"They will. Give them time."

"Clay told you I was the messenger?"

"It came up, yes."

I blew out my breath. "Sidney, could we talk sometime?"

"How about now? I'm supposed to meet my mom at the park in about twenty minutes to collect my kids. That is if the rain holds off. We could talk while I wait."

"I'll be there."

"At the swings. The bandstand, if it's raining."

It was. Raining, that is. In fact, it began to pour as I climbed from my car. I thought about leaving Mason's key on the console but decided he might enjoy hearing Sidney talk. After all, he never got to meet the man his daughter married. However, I reminded him, "Do not come out."

A few minutes later, Sidney drove down the entry lane, parked, and dashed the hundred or so feet across the lawn to the bandstand.

Again, he struck me as a man of contrasts. His six-five frame, broad shoulders, and premature baldness—which made him look older than his roughly thirty-some years of age—suggested a man equally imposing on the inside, but such was not the case. Sidney oozed pure gentleness and served as the calm to his wife Reaghan's storm.

"Thanks for meeting me," I said as he hurried up the four steps onto the stand. "I'm sorry to pull you away."

He pulled his drenched rain poncho off and shook it over the railing. "It's probably best they have time to talk without me around anyway. They're going through a lot of mixed emotions. Shock. Survivor's guilt. Regret that they ever doubted him."

"But you're family," I lamented. "Maybe you should be there."

Sidney gestured at a bench, and we sat. "I'm an in-law, but still an outsider in this respect. I never got to meet Mason."

He may describe himself as an outsider, but he was certainly more of an insider than I was. Seeing no point in beating around the bush, I asked, "How did Clay explain me finding Mason?"

"He sorta skimmed over that. But he did say enough to give me the impression you possess some rather unique abilities."

I blew air out through gritted teeth and nodded, resigned. "Do you think I'm odd?" *What an unfair question to ask him.* I backtracked before he had to answer. "I mean, sometimes I think I'll be shunned if people hear I can …" *How much dare I reveal?* "… intuit certain things." *Ugh, vague, but it would have to do.*

He frowned. "I won't shun you. I don't think anyone back at the house will either … in time." He hesitated before continuing. "I'll be honest. I don't agree with this … ability. I believe it's best left alone. But people lie and cheat and steal and bear false witness every day. Yet they're functioning, and they're forgiven if they truly want to be. You can't worry about other people judging you."

"You don't think the others will hate me? Not even Reaghan?"

"Grace, first off, you don't have to worry about her. She will love whomever Clay ends up with if that's your concern. She's like that." He sat forward, parked his elbows on his knees, and joined his hands in a lose clasp. His mouth curled. "She has a wolf-pack mentality. If you're one of the pack, then you're in, and you're permanent, no matter what you do. She'll protect the pack."

"You said 'first off.' Is there a second?"

"Second, you might be happy to hear Reaghan defended you back there." He nodded in the direction of the house.

"Defended me?"

His mouth curled, and it looked thoughtful, born of love. "She's always been tough. Feisty. Self-protective. I often wondered if it grew from being abandoned by her dad. Now she knows she wasn't. I watched her cry today. It was soft, and it was brief, but it was there. I don't recall ever seeing her cry. Not even when the kids were born."

He waited for that to sink in before continuing. "You changed a lot of the reason for her protective wall. The reason she keeps people out. It rattled her, and she's still sorting through it. But when Clay voiced ..." he hesitated, as though choosing his words carefully, "... dismay that you set all this in motion, she pointed out how lucky they were to finally know the truth. She said if it weren't for you, they still would not know."

I slouched back on the bench, letting his words sink in.

"I'll forever be grateful for how you helped the family. I love Reaghan. The kids. They're my life and mean everything to me. Yes, murder is much more tragic than abandonment, but they'll mourn now, and in time, every story about Mason will be good again, whereas in the past ten years it's all been negative. You gave us a different story to tell our children about their grandfather. So shun you? Never."

I wiped a tear from my eye.

The sound of children's laughter cut through the roar of the rain.

"Here they come." Sidney smiled and stood.

I looked up to see Ethan and Elias running and giggling toward us through the rain. They wore yellow rain slickers, but both boys had removed their hoods, and dashed from puddle to puddle as though seeing who could make the biggest splash. Behind them, a woman carried a little girl in each arm. She rolled her eyes and yelled to Sidney, "We didn't think these plans through very well, did we?"

I grabbed his arm to get his attention and said a quick, "Sidney, thank you."

He squeezed my hand, and in it I felt the firmness of his words. "Give it time."

Within seconds, the bandstand was crowded. During introductions Mason appeared, standing off to the side and clearly delighting in the group. I hid my smile.

Sidney's mother insisted they get back to the house to dry off the children, but Sidney countered that the air was warm and the rain no colder than bath water. However, he acquiesced and gathered the girls in his arms. The group headed to his vehicle.

Securing four children into car seats took a few minutes, but they were out of earshot, so I turned to Mason and teased, "I thought we had an agreement."

Without taking his gaze off his family, he shrugged, and it ended in a grin. "Couldn't resist seeing my grandchildren. Thank you for that."

I moved closer to him. I wanted to say something about Sidney's comments regarding Reaghan. To assure him she was fine now. But as we watched them drive away, I remained quiet. Witnessing her family probably offered him more assurance than any words I could offer. He could see firsthand how full her life was now.

"Come on," I said, touching his arm. "I have one stop to make; then we'll go home."

***

As I pulled out of the park, Seth called, catching me by surprise. "Wanted to say I'm sorry about yesterday."

Relief washed over me. "Me too. I didn't mean to hurt you. I don't ever want you to be hurt, Seth."

With a jolt, I acknowledged to myself I meant what I said. Not only as a friend but deep down in my core. My feelings for him were confusing, but through it all, I loved him. It was the nature of the love that remained unclear.

"We both agree I should go alone to see the attorney, right? But I'd like to brainstorm with you, if you're willing, that is, to figure out what information I need before accepting or rejecting the offer."

I liked that he asked for my help. Me, and no one else. He wanted my opinion. But first, I needed to tell him about his birth family. I didn't want him to accuse me of withholding information, as Clay had. If, after hearing about his lineage, he still wanted to move forward, then I could suggest questions he should ask.

"When?"

He hesitated. "How about tonight? I could stop by around ten o'clock after I'm done at work."

"The hospital?"

"No. Canal work. We're doing inventory at the gift shop. I got paid a little extra to help out."

I cringed. He worked so hard to save money for college. He sure could use that money, but still …

"So," he asked, "that work for you?"

"Perfect." Ten o'clock would give me time to set the wheels in motion with my "guests." I would need a breather by then anyway. I could break and meet with Seth then get back to what I hoped to accomplish for Mason.

The distance between the Williamsport Park and the Canal was short, so by the time I clicked off the call, I pulled into the parking lot.

When I first met Mule, he said he could see a lot going on from there. That had stuck in my mind.

I headed toward the river. Very few people were out. Mule sat under the same tree as the other times I saw him. It was daylight, so his energy would be in a weakened state, but I had simple questions, so I forged ahead. I didn't even care if eavesdroppers thought I was talking to myself.

"I spoke with my friends. Thank you. Adriana has an audition Thursday." I hesitated, hoping my first question wouldn't sound too nosey. I wasn't used to ghosts having oracle or clairvoyant abilities. In fact, the notion unnerved me a little. "How did you know about the audition?"

"No voodoo if that's what you mean." He gestured toward the canal. "Folks come from miles away for leisure by this river. The only thing I have to do around here is sit and listen. Been doin' it for more than a hundred and fifty years. I know a lot about plans made and plans broken. That flutist that quit? She runs here every Saturday morning. I heard her tell a companion when she was going to hand in her resignation."

"That's amazing." I wasn't sure if I was more amazed by his recall, the coincidence, or what I realized for the first time must have been an incredibly lonely and solitary life, sitting by the river day after day after day. The depth of the feeling behind why he remained here and his unfinished business seared into me.

He nodded at my comment but remained quiet and kept his gaze toward the river, beyond which sat my property.

I followed his gaze. "So you hear a lot. But have you ever seen questionable activity over there?"

If my abruptness surprised him, he didn't show it. "Yeah," he said and met my gaze before again looking away. "Seen a lot."

I startled at the disgust in his voice and hugged myself to suppress a shiver.

He continued. "Seen even more after I died."

"I don't understand."

"There's the world you can see, and then there's the one that's more real."

I pressed my lips together, holding in a barrage of questions. I wanted to drop to my knees and ask him for every detail about this other world until he ran out of answers. But, I needed to stay on course, and that demanded different questions. "Do you know a man by the name of Enoch Crinshaw?"

Again, he showed no surprise at the question. "Like the back of me hand," he said with a tone of finality.

"There's another man, too. He would have been before your time, but any chance you know about a guy named Josiah Sawyer?"

He chuckled. "Yeah, iffin ya knew Crinshaw, ya knew Sawyer. They's the reason I'm still here."

My mouth fell open. "What do you mean?"

"I can't move on until someone knows their stories." He looked at me again. "Their real stories. After folks know, and Crinshaw and Sawyer are gone, then I'll be able to move on too. But I ain't leavin' before that."

"Mule, today's your lucky day." I reached down beside him and yanked the cleat out of the ground. "Come on, I'm going to help you resolve this."

CHAPTER 26

That night, I took a deep breath of fortitude and opened the connecting door between the apartment and house. Chubbs leaped off the couch and dashed into the bedroom.

Passing through the library and the wide foyer, I reached the drawing room on the opposite side of the house. Will stood by a window, looking at the rain. I was pleased to see he had built a fire. The dreary weather outdoors ushered a chill into the room, and it would only get colder as the souls joined me because the warm blood of life did not course through their veins.

I set Cassie's house key and the cleat on the low table centered by the various chairs. I returned to the apartment, collected my hot cup of tea, and returned to the drawing room.

Will turned as I entered. "Looks dreary out there. Wind is getting stronger. Reminds me of summer storms in 1859."

I bobbed my head but looked around, distracted. With three souls in one room, would "dreary" soon describe the indoors as well? Was I about to penetrate a Disney movie or a nightmare?

The settee and chair where Will and I sat the night before remained near the fireplace. I pulled another tufted chair closer and stood back to assess as if I pondered seating arrangements for a dinner party. The absurdity of it hit me.

A party? They're ghosts. I didn't even know if they would want to sit. They might float on the ceiling for all I knew.

I looked at Will. "Are you ready?"

He nodded and offered a gesture that said, "Proceed."

Stepping back, I took a deep breath, exhaled and said, "Mason … Mule, will you please join us?"

Faster than a blink, the two souls materialized. As human beings do who haven't met before, these souls inched apart, taking measure of one another, the room, and Will. I waited, soaking in the oddness of the situation and the souls gathered, each a pale carbon copy of what once had been a handsome, vital man.

Proper introductions required one to speak to the person you wish to honor first, so I said, "Mason Baxter, I'd like you to meet William Kavanaugh." I gestured toward Will. "He died here, in this house, in 1863. And this," I said, turning to Mule, "is Lemule Chasen. He died in …?"

"1881," Mule said.

"At the canal?" I asked.

Mule shrugged. "Close enough."

I continued. "And, gentlemen, this is Mason Baxter. He died about fifteen years ago."

They exchanged stiff nods and verbalized socially appropriate acknowledgments.

I shook my head. "This is something you don't hear every day … the year of death of the people you're introducing."

None of the souls responded so I added, "I mean, people usually share titles and work positions, you know? Yes, well, never mind. Shall we sit?"

Mason had already wandered to the fireplace and perched one elbow on the mantle. He raised a hand toward me as though to say "I'm fine."

Will sat in the same wingback chair he used the night before, settling his left ankle atop his opposite knee.

Mule's gaze darted around the room before he folded onto the settee. "I ain't ne'er seen a place this fancy before."

Surprised, I figured that was as good a place to start as any. Complete candor was the only workable course now. I studied him. His canal clothes seemed so rough compared to the other two, and for the first time, I noticed that a scar bisected his pale cheek. "You lived by the canal your whole life but never entered this house?" I dropped into a chair that offered a view of everyone and access to my tea.

"My kind didn't socialize"—he said the word like it was foreign to him and, therefore, hard to pronounce— "with this kind. We mostly stuck to the river."

Will's gaze intensified on Mule. "I know you. You're the man who worked on the Chamberlain flatboat before the War."

"That's right," Mule nodded, studying Will. He pointed an index finger like he, too, had a revelation. "Kavanaugh ... your pa's David Kavanaugh?"

"That's correct," Will said.

"Good folks," Mule offered with such certainty that any possible argument to the contrary would have been wiped away right there. "Yer ma and pa was kind to me sister. Let 'er work here a few summers. Long afore the War."

"I remember," Will said. "Her name was ... Daisy?"

"That's it." Mule smiled and sat a little taller.

Well, this is going well.

"You helped pull my best friend from the frozen river," Will said. "Asa Garett. Without your help, he would have died."

Mule shrugged away the kindness, looking amused. "Pshhh, was nothin'. Been worse scrapes on that river."

Will's eyebrows rose in response to Mule's impertinence. I looked at my lap as my lips twitched into a private smile. Even death didn't change deep-seated testosterone challenges and conditioning.

I plunged on. "Will, you were killed by Fergus, for greed and gold. He is gone now, yet a question remains. You said Fergus was rejected by Josiah Sawyer. Can you explain?"

Will shook his head. "I don't have an answer. Fergus said it when he was ill at the prison on Johnson's Island. I assumed Sawyer to be a powerful man, whoever he was. At the prison, Fergus had a terrible fever. He talked nonsense. Mumbled something about having done everything to win Sawyer's favor, and that it had to be different after he got back. When you and I encountered Fergus in the tunnels, I knew it would be a sore spot with him, so I said it."

My energy drained, and I sat back in the chair. Will's answer wasn't the one I wanted. I turned my gaze toward the fireplace. "Mason, you're here because I'm trying to resolve your murder. It strikes me as odd that Holland Greer—the local historian," I said for the benefit of Will and Mule, "is very close to Gwendolyn Bealle and that she is a Crinshaw. The same Crinshaw lineage that murdered Thaddeus Calhoun here, at *Crossings*. I had hoped to start way back in time, to hear about Sawyer and his connection to Enoch Crinshaw—"

Mule smirked. "I kin help ya with that. Everyone in my day knew Sawyer or heard o' him."

Hope surged anew, and I sat straighter again. "Was he born in Williamsport?"

"New York. In the 1750s. His pa died of cholera, so his ma worked in a tavern. When he was still a squirt, maybe five, six, his ma fell in with the wrong man. Tate, I think his name was. She got in the family way, but he refused to marry her. Story goes there was a scuttle. Sawyer watched his ma kill Tate in self-defense. But Tate was wealthy, so they hanged her."

"Such injustice," Will scoffed.

"Sawyer ended up with a family that abused him. Told him he was nothin'. That he had the Devil in him. So he ran away. Musta been 'round ten or eleven by then. There was talk of gainin' independence from England, so he kept heading west.

"This whole big country, yet he came here." I frowned.

"Not surprising," said Mason. I turned to watch him shrug. "I'm a history buff of sorts."

I smiled. Having a similar interest with Mason made me feel good.

He continued. "Williamsport lies on the Great Wagon Road. One of the early Native American trails between New York and the Carolinas. Thousands of European settlers and pioneers followed the route. From the north to Virginia and points south and west."

Mule nodded. "Mostly west, in my day."

Mason said, "Between the time of the French and Indian War and the Revolutionary War, the Great Wagon Road was the most heavily-traveled road in America."

I marveled at his knowledge, and I could tell from the way the other two studied him, they were impressed, too. It flicked through my mind they should have known these tidbits better than Mason, but they were busy being *involved* in that same history at the time.

Mason added, "The first ferry was established in the 1740s to carry settlers across the Potomac River. For years, they came up against strong Native American resistance."

Mason paused, and Mule added to the story. "I heard tale it was wild and rough on that side o' the river in them days." He nodded toward Williamsport. "Sawyer liked that. Learned to steal and gamble for food. Clothes. Even a horse. Wasn't much that was good about him."

I rubbed my forehead. "He started so young."

"Anywhere he went he caused trouble," Mule continued. "Folks claimed he said ... 'course he was an old man when I met him, so who knows if it was true ... but he said he got here in 1772 at age twenty and in three years won a boat in a card game. He started haulin' people and cargo 'cross the river. Made good money. Before long he staked a claim on this side. Right here."

Will frowned. "Young people grew up quickly in those days."

"I think," Mason began, and I looked up to see his gaze on me, "some young people show great maturity long before they should have to."

"Indeed they do," Will said. I caught him focused on me as well.

My face heated at their perusal.

Mule continued, oblivious to our unspoken exchanges. "Sawyer dug tunnels cause o' them Indians. When he had more money, he built a tavern and an inn. Called it *Crossings*. Built a couple sheds, too. And a barn down by the river. Folks could stable horses and store their wagons after crossin' the river. It all connected through the tunnels."

I sat back, startled. The tunnels led to the river? A map I'd secured from Holland Greer the year before depicted a lone channel running that direction. But that would mean the tunnel ran into Devil's Cove!

"Grace, are you alright?" Will asked.

"I … yeah … I'm remembering some things. Don't mind me. Mule, please continue."

"Sawyer had three wives," Mule said, leaning back and draping an arm across the back of the settee, looking like a man who either felt more comfortable or liked the attention. Perhaps both. "One disappeared. Another died givin' birth. Most o' them kids died o' one disease or another. When Sawyer was 'round sixty, he married a gal a quarter his age. She birthed a boy the next year. His only survivin' son. That woulda been 1814. I know 'cause that's when I was born, too."

"Dead wives. Dead children," Mason said, shaking his head. "Amazing the adversity people lived with back then."

Mule shrugged. "I don't know nothin' bout that. I can tell ya Sawyer was angry and hateful wherever he went. Watchin' his mama hang when she was innocent, them crooked laws in New York, the nasty family that reared him. Who could be normal after that?"

"No one," we all chorused back.

Impatience crept over me. "So what's the connection between Sawyer and Crinshaw?"

"I'm gittin' to that." Mule's tone grew hard, serious. He leaned forward to park his elbows on his knees and clasped his hands. "There was still Indian raids 'round here at the time. Folks could git killed by Indians. Or disappear. When settlers moved west, most of 'em said goodbye to families for good. No one ever came lookin' for 'em. Sawyer picked up on this right quick … that people could disappear, and no one would question it."

"Incredible," Mason said, and the loathing in his tone echoed what raced through my mind.

"In 1820," Mule continued, "Josiah was out huntin', and an Indian shot him. In the leg. Gangrene set in. He got drunk and paid a crusty riverboat ruffian to saw it off. Rigged up a stump and hobbled 'round on it the rest o' his life. 'Course, for about a year he kept gettin' phantom pain. So he made his son dig up that leg. It'd been rottin' in the ground all that time. Imagine the smell. Didn't do nothing with it, mind you. Just had it dug up. But the pain stopped. That's when Sawyer began to believe in the supernatural."

"That's coincidence. Nothing more," I said.

Mason asked, "That's what finally labeled him as a crazy man?"

"Nah, it's more what came after," Mule said. "When his son was eight ... Sawyer woulda been in his seventies ... a group of folks from New York was movin' west. They crossed the river and stayed here before pushin' into the Valley. Turns out they'd left up north to get away from a yellow fever epidemic. Sawyer got convinced one of them was descended from Tate, the man who killed his ma. He demanded they pay more than what he'd quoted. They refused. Sawyer got mad and killed 'em. All of 'em. Down at the barn. Made his son bury 'em."

"That's horrible!" I said as Mason huffed a short syllable of disgust, and Will dropped his gaze to his lap, shaking his head.

Mule tilted his head as though looking at a distant memory. "Sawyer knew he got away with evil. Even got rich from it, 'cause they left their belongings and money here. He began devisin' his own worship of evil down at the barn. And let me tell you, they wasn't the last folks who disappeared at Sawyer's hands."

Will slapped a hand on the arm of the chair, rose, and began to pace. "I had no idea any of this occurred here."

Nonplussed, Mule continued. "When his son was fourteen, Sawyer killed the boy's mother in a fit o' rage. Sawyer and the boy fought. The boy grabbed a rifle and shot him. Then he burned down the barn with Sawyer still in it, too wounded to get out. The old man burned alive. After that, the boy went crazy burnin' everything. The tavern. Inn. Sheds. Burned it all. Then, he ran."

"What year was that?" Will asked.

"Ohhh." Mule looked toward the ceiling. "Woulda been 1828 'cause I was fourteen at the time. It was all the scuttlebutt 'cross the river where I lived."

"Sawyer's son, you mean?" Mason asked.

Mule shook his head. "Not the son, the fire. It wasn't until many years later folks learned the boy even existed, that he was Sawyer's son. By then, he was all grown up."

"What happened to him?" I asked.

"He knew no one would know him across the river 'cause Sawyer never allowed him to leave the place. So he headed across the river to Williamsport. Told the town folk he was part of them New York settlers Sawyer killed. Said Sawyer kidnapped him." Mule turned his gaze to me. "The boy changed his name from Sawyer to Crinshaw 'cause one of the folks from New York had been named that."

"Crinshaw? Enoch Crinshaw?" I unfolded my legs and jerked forward in my chair. "The boy's name was Enoch?"

Mule smiled as though he had enjoyed dragging out his story. "That's right. He knew he didn't dare be tied to Sawyer in any way, so he kept quiet about his property, *Crossings*. Iffin he'd tried to claim it, his story woulda been suspicious. In time, he made a livin' as a lockkeeper. This property lay abandoned for over twenty-five years. No one wanted to go near it anyway. Finally, an outsider came along and bought it."

"My father," Will said, rubbing a line between his eyebrows as he paced. "He had no knowledge of its history."

"He couldn't have known," Mason offered.

Will dropped into his seat again, looking beleaguered. "But Fergus must have known ... or figured it out after becoming my friend and visiting here. Crinshaw must have confided in him. Perhaps they even colluded on how to get it back."

Mule nodded. "Truth always seems to come out, in time."

Outside, the wind groaned louder. The sound of agitated chimes clanged and echoed from the apartment porch, on the opposite end of the house.

I stood and began pacing. "We don't know that for sure. So what *do* we know?" I taxed my memory for what I'd learned last year. "Crinshaw grew up and married a woman by the name of Clara Calhoun, sister to Thaddeus Fleming Calhoun." I turned to Will. "After killing you, Fergus left and brought Calhoun and Crinshaw back to the tunnels. Eva ... a soul I met in the tunnels," I clarified for Mason and Mule, "Eva said Crinshaw killed Fergus first, then Calhoun. Crinshaw searched like a wild man for the gold, but he, too, left without it. Although he didn't leave alone. Instead, he took Calhoun's dying body. Probably so he could present it to Clara and point the finger at Fergus."

"Could be," Mule said, "Fergus learned the truth about Crinshaw. Enoch started blabbin' about it in later life. Even bragged about it. Knew no one would do nothing about it, what with the War buildin'."

"Incredible," Mason said, shaking his head. "Will, you died in what year? 1863? That means Crinshaw would have been forty-nine or fifty by then. He must have been filled with intense rage after so many years ... and because someone else was living on what he believed to be his property."

Mule agreed. "Yeah, makin' a livin' on the river was hard. They was always fights with lockkeepers over rules, and tolls, and passage fees. And during the War, the northerners seized a hundred and sixty canal boats in 1862, then the southerners burned about eighty canal boats, in 1864. All this made it hard to make a profit on the river. So after Crinshaw learned about the gold, he got real greedy. He was angry all this money was on what shoulda been his property. He decided it had to be his. He vowed to return for it, but he never could get near it. I heard him talking in the pubs in Williamsport, many a time. He believed it was his pa, old man Sawyer, keepin' him out."

"Part of the barrier was me, I confess," Will chimed in. "I was dwelling here and didn't want the property to be disturbed until my death was resolved. In the tunnels, as I've since learned, it would have been Fergus."

Mason moved closer and folded into a chair as he said, "Crinshaw killed Fergus. So even though Crinshaw's descendants continued to seek the gold for nefarious purposes, Fergus wouldn't let them near. I guess there's no honor among evil." He hesitated, before adding, "What about at the dock? Through the years, there's been a mystery around that, too."

Will said, "I never knew about that. Those buildings were long gone when I lived here. I guess it could have been Sawyer."

"Could have been?" I asked as the hair on my back stood on end. "Or still is? Are you so sure Sawyer is gone? I mean, Fergus knew about him. Crinshaw must have convinced Fergus that Sawyer had powers. Supernatural powers. He told Will that Sawyer rejected him. He must have meant Sawyer kept him from the gold as well. And the area by the river is known as Devil's Cove. Straight up a huge cliff from there is Chocton Bluff. People have died there." I thought of Mason's co-worker, Clyde, and Hilda's father who was killed for no other reason than it had been the wrong place at the wrong time.

Mason nodded.

Mule shook a thoughtful finger at me. "Exactly. And don't forget, Crinshaw hated his pa, so he ramped up the evil. Wanted to prove he was better than his old man. Wanted to overcome what he thought was his pa's lingering power.

Mason leaned forward. "Are you saying he practiced Devil worship?"

Mule laughed. "Nah, Sawyer and Crinshaw both woulda never asked the Devil for help 'cause it would be admittin' the Devil was more powerful than they was."

The rest of us exchanged quick, sobering glances.

Mule continued. "He was sure he could build evil strong enough to overcome whatever it was protected the house and kept it safe. It caught the attention of Satanists through the years too … tried to meet for their rituals. Rumor was they tried to open a doorway to hell. Where they met is what's called Devil's Cove."

"So Sawyer taught evil to his son." Mason rubbed his lower chin, looking like a man who couldn't fathom such depravity.

Mule nodded. "And Crinshaw continued the same, teachin' evil to his son, and on and on down through the generations. Each convinced the story 'bout a big treasure in gold was true …" Mule paused. "Until this latest one. From what I hear down at the canal—you can learn a lot by listenin'—he turned away from the evil. Wanted nothin' to do with it. Started his own business. Done real good. So much so he was goin' to move his work to California. Start a new life. But he got in a bad accident. Next thing you know, his sister moved him back here, and now she takes care o' him."

I swallowed hard. "Gwendolyn Crinshaw Bealle. Descendant of Josiah Sawyer and Enoch Crinshaw. Local librarian. Overseer of a tapestry map she keeps in the library basement that depicts the location of the gold in the tunnels before the fire destroyed them last year." My gaze cut to Mule, before resting on Mason. "She's close to Holland Greer. I'm convinced he used her history against her. To gain insight about *Crossings*."

Mason looked dubious, but then he gestured as though to say he had no better explanation to offer.

"You know her?" Mule asked.

I nodded.

"Then you can understand why I said that friend of yours shouldn't take the money she offered."

I studied Mule. "Understand it, yes. But I don't know how you even knew about it."

He smiled. "The canal is my home, remember? He—your

friend—works there. Heard him talk about it. To a co-worker. Wondering what he ought to do. It was easy to figure out that any hush-hush kind o' help like that would come from her for her own advantage. I don't think he knows he's related to Bealle and Crinshaw."

"He doesn't," I agreed.

A pause fell as we digested the story we'd collectively pieced together. Within seconds, however, a thunderclap rocked the old house, and the wind pelted rain against the structure from all directions, sending it rushing and swooshing through the new gutters. Mule stood and moved to a window, opened a drape, and struck a stance that suggested he intended to watch the elements for a while. "Ain't seen a storm like this since back in the '30s."

I exchanged a glance with Mason. He arched an eyebrow and lifted a shoulder in a gesture that suggested, "Maybe." I took it to mean: *maybe* Mule referred to the same storm that Hilda spoke of in the '30s, *maybe* it was associated with the wolf-like man, and *maybe* at its center was Josiah Sawyer.

Despite the noise of the storm, I heard my cell phone ring in the apartment, so I hurried to answer.

CHAPTER 27

The call came from Seth. He was running late but still planned to stop. I clicked off and walked to the northwest corner of the apartment. I flipped off the light switch, opened the blinds, and looked out the massive new windows as lightning knifed the sky, illuminating the horizon with an eerie glow.

As I watched the storm play havoc with the landscape, I thought about what I learned in the drawing room. Where should I investigate from here? What was I missing?

I still didn't understand what link—if any—there was between *Crossings,* Josiah Sawyer, Holland's search for gold, and Mason's murder. Was it possible Holland callously killed Mason to hide his theft of the Civil War artifacts? But then, why kill Clyde? And what about Nidhi? All this time, I'd been worried about Mason, Clay, and Cassie, yet Nidhi was the one who needed help the most. Were any of these incidents tied together?

I felt, rather than heard, Will walk up behind me. His presence brought a cold waft, and I hugged myself against it.

He said, "I told the others we'd be back in a moment."

I smiled. "I thought you couldn't come into the apartment."

"I can't stay long. But you're here, so I had to come."

I returned my gaze to nature's display outdoors. "How can anything be so beautiful and frightening at the same time?"

"I remember that feeling, static that makes your skin crawl and shivers that chase down your spine. It's energizing. Makes you aware of the life coursing through you."

His response sounded so earthy, so reflective. We turned to look at one another.

"It's something I can no longer feel." He touched my face, his gaze penetrating into mine. "I wish I could experience it with you."

My heart swelled with love for this man. Had it been only two days ago that I had doubted him? I swallowed and whispered. "I wish you could, too."

Thunder sounded again, like cannon fire. He dropped his hand, and our gazes turned in unison to stare out the window. We stood in the darkness listening, watching. Lightning flashes lit the sky in random, staccato blips, like freeze-action strobes, none lasting long enough to enable us to hone in on what we saw. On one burst to my left, I thought I saw a tree being split in two. At a flare to the right, I saw a foggy mist like a lid on the entire valley. The next flash revealed a cruel and merciless wind whipping the trees.

"Did you see that?" Will asked.

The tone of his voice suggested he saw more than vegetation suffering against the wind. I followed his finger to the west. "A strange sort of light."

We watched and waited.

I was anticipating another lightning flash to reveal what he meant. Instead, when it came, the light itself was the anomaly, generated at ground level.

"Is it a lantern?" Will asked.

"The beam is too concentrated. It has to be a flashlight. But who would be out in this kind of weather?"

"Especially there," Will said.

I jerked to look at him and arched my eyebrows, prodding him to explain.

"That's Chocton Bluff, and below is Devil's Cove," he said. We exchanged a look that suggested we both recalled the conversation we had with Mule in the past hour.

My arms goose-fleshed, and I whirled back to the window. I took a deep breath to swallow the silent scream climbing in my throat. "That's the direction that caught your attention when we stood in the cemetery, isn't it? Something there disturbed you then, too."

"I wonder ..."

When Will didn't finish his thoughts, I prodded. "What?"

"It's probably nothing," he said, shaking his head.

"Tell me!"

"Earlier today, while you were gone, I walked through the house again. The second floor looks over the roof of the apartment. I'm able to look west."

"At Chocton Bluff."

"I thought I saw something unusual then, too."

"Like what?"

"At first, it was two shapes moving ... maybe struggling. I'm not sure. So I kept watching, but all I saw was a flash of blue. The color stood out against all the green and brown. It was probably a bird."

I remembered seeing a smattering of blue during the boat ride with Clay. "Blue? But what could be—"

"Grace? Are you alright?"

"Nidhi was wearing a blue dress when she disappeared! Hilda told me. She remembered it because Nidhi bought it in her shop."

"But it makes no sense for—"

"What part of any of this ..." I flung my hands in the air in a wide gesture that included the house, the apartment, him, "... makes sense?" I moved to the kitchen counter and picked up my cell phone.

Will followed. "What are you doing?"

"Calling for help."

Sheriff Barnes answered on the first ring.

"It's Grace MacKenna. Sheriff, I—"

"Ms. MacKenna, I'll have to call you back. I'm sitting here now with—"

"No, wait! You have to come now. It's Nidhi ... well, I think it's Nidhi ... I mean what else could it be? You have to—"

"Whoa, slow down. Take a deep breath." His tone revealed I

caught his attention. "What's this about Nidhi?"

"I think she's at Chocton Bluff. I can't explain now, but that place is evil, and Holland Greer might be involved. He's taken her there—"

The sheriff sighed, long and deep. "That would be impossible."

Frustration filled me. "No disrespect, Sheriff, but why do you refuse to believe Holland capable of—"

"Because I locked him in a cell about two hours ago."

"What?"

"That's right. He's in a cell in this building as we speak."

I dropped onto a counter stool as my energy drained away. "So he confessed? He admitted to killing Mason?"

The sheriff hesitated. When he spoke again, his tone was hushed. "I'm sitting here with the Baxters right now."

"Oh, my gosh; he did confess! So it's over …"

"What? No … blast it … I can't discuss details with you, but his incarceration at this time has nothing to do with Mr. Baxter."

"Then what?"

Another hesitation. I visualized him silently debating what he could tell me with what he'd like to tell me, especially in front of the Baxters. Or, perhaps he was trying to figure out how to get me off the phone.

"As I told the Baxters …" The way he spoke made me think he was trying to talk to all of us at once. "… I went to his place this evening to question him. He tried to distract me with some nonsense about you having stolen a map from him?"

I swallowed as the sheriff waited. Rather than answer, I said, "Go on."

"Is it true?"

I scraped a hand through my hair. "I'm not denying it."

"Uh-huh, well, when I asked him to explain how that could be possible, he was dumb enough to lead me to a room in the back. It was filled with Civil War memorabilia. You know the room?"

"I … yes, that's where he kept the map."

"Uh-huh. Wasn't real smart of you to go into his house alone, was it? Anyway, some of the stuff still had tags attached. Those tags designated them as part of the collection that was stolen from the traveling Civil War display years ago. It didn't take much detective work on my part to put two and two together."

My heart pounded. Mason's death was still unresolved. But what, then, was happening at Chocton Bluff?

"Grace!"

I looked up at Will's voice. He was standing at the window again, waving his hand in a come-quickly motion.

I stepped to his side. Chocton Bluff was aglow with a light that bounced, wavered, and irradiated the sky.

"It's on fire!" In one heartbeat I looked at Will, then my phone, and clicked off the call.

Will studied me. "Why did you do that?"

I jerked a shoulder, agitated. "So the sheriff would take me seriously. To get him here sooner."

"How can you be so sure he'll come?"

I wasn't sure, but I felt it was a good gamble. I figured I had played the best card I had: Nidhi. "Doesn't matter. *Something's* happening at Chocton Bluff that shouldn't be. Looks like a fire, but how could it burn in this pouring rain?"

"There's only one way."

We turned to look at one another. His intensity alarmed me.

"I'm going out there." I tucked my phone into my pocket and began scurrying to collect my raincoat, flashlight, anything I thought I might need.

"I'm going with you."

I stopped and looked at him. "You're not going to try to stop me?

"Would it do any good?"

I shook my head. "I have to go."

Will nodded. "After what I heard in there," he nodded toward the house, "it's time to end this. All of this. Before there are more deaths."

"Thank you." I paused long enough to touch his arm. "I need to get a few things first. Your center, Grandma Sadie's cross—"

"I'll tell the others." He turned toward the house.

"No! They're coming too. They're part of this, and they might be able to help. As you said, it's time to end *all* this."

After collecting what I thought I might need and cinching a fanny pack to my waist, I hurried with Will through the house to the drawing room.

Mason and Mule stood together, assessing a painting hanging above a sideboard.

"I need your help," I said in swift delivery. "Chocton Bluff is burning. Will and I think something sinister may be happening." I retrieved the coin from under the vase and picked up Mason's key and Mule's cleat. "I'll explain as we head there. Mule, this is too heavy for me to lug that far." I looked around for something to replace the cleat and spotted a small silver bowl on the table below the painting. It held several objects. I grabbed a ruby-encrusted cuff link. "Will this work?"

Mule smiled. "Awful fancy for me, but yeah, that'll do."

I put the three objects in my fanny pack. "I promise to be careful with your centers. We can make a plan as we go. Ready?"

Three heads nodded agreement.

It wouldn't be until much later I remembered Seth was on his way to *Crossings*, too.

CHAPTER 28

Within seconds of stepping onto the lawn, a thunderclap pealed, and the sky pelted thicker, swifter sheets of rain. I tossed my umbrella and a few steps later wrenched off my worthless rain jacket and threw it aside. There seemed no sense in bringing them since the sideways-blowing rain had drenched me already. Besides, the thought struck that if the sheriff did show up, he'd have the beginnings of a trail to follow.

Lightning sheared the sky as we hustled across the grounds, over the rolling hills, past the cemetery, and into the scattering of woods near the river, at the base of Chocton Bluff. The distressed trees signaled their objection to being rooted as they flinched from the stabbing light and swayed against the unremitting fury of the wind. Twigs and debris blew into my face as I stumbled along. Twice Will, and once Mason, had to keep me from stumbling over fallen branches or slipping in gullies full from rainwater.

We didn't speak as we hurried along. Besides the gales of noisy wind limiting our communication, I suspected we each focused our gazes and thoughts on Chocton Bluff and the eerie arch of red, orange, yellow, green, blue, indigo, and violet snapping and cascading at its crest.

As we stepped out of the woods into the clearing at the base of the bluff, the redolent smell of river mixed with the earthy, dampened soil changed, replaced by an odor of decay. The flickering, unruly blaze disappeared, too. In its place, a steady light hovered at the bluff's top. Even the sound of the thunder changed, from booming and cracking to more of a rumbling mutter, as though complaining about our approach.

My skin crawled from a static I couldn't explain. The four of us eyed one another in the pouring rain, but no one spoke.

I spotted a smooth, straight approach to the bluff. No doubt it had been the one used by sledders such as Clyde and Hilda, but it looked too slippery from the rain roiling down to be of much good. Instead, I opted for a path off to the left, toward the river. The rain continued to pelt as we moved, and the thunder reverberated down to the ground, through the trees and up into the distant mountains.

The steep, demanding ascent to the bluff followed a cattle path that wound back and forth through thick underbrush. I had enough experience with ghosts to know I was the sole concern among us. They couldn't falter, stumble, or get hurt. But I could, and I noticed they flanked me protectively as we ascended.

After ten minutes or so of this dark, grueling climb, we stepped onto a slope. The sound of the roaring river, so close, suggested the ledge fell abruptly to the water below. Another lightning flash revealed we were only three-quarters of the way to the actual bluff.

I turned to the others wishing I could talk, and a bizarre quiet descended as though nature read my mind. The wind still blew, the trees swayed, the lightning sparked. I could see and feel the elements, but there was no sound, like someone hit the mute button while watching television. The night creatures were quiet as well. The silence engulfed us, heavy, oppressive as if nature expected something to happen and knew it wouldn't be good.

"He's playing with us," Mule declared, an unmistakable hint of warning in his voice like he already knew what lay in wait. I watched his body swell and darken as though an angry tide coursed through him in preparation to fight. I had seen the same thing happen to Will last year when he fought with Naomi and Fergus.

I followed Mule's lead of speaking. There seemed no point in remaining quiet because the muted elements signaled our presence was known. What's more, my skin prickled as though we were being watched, anyway.

I sucked in a deep breath and yelled, "Nidhi! Are you here?"

An elongated, muffled sound came from my right. I darted the flashlight that direction, but stopped when into the light appeared the symbol Clay and I spotted from the boat. At least eight feet tall and wide, the circle and three hook-like swirls looked like an old and permanent etching in the side of the monstrous rock.

"That's Sawyer's doin' alright," Mule said. "I seen it carved on his saddlebag once. His brand, his symbol of evil."

Another moan broke the silence. I turned the flashlight to the sound, but all I saw were more rocks and trees.

"It came from behind that rock," Will said.

"Or in it," Mason suggested.

At my questioning look, he explained, "I heard Hilda tell you there were caves up here."

I gripped the light tighter, and we moved toward the rock. The souls moved easily, but for me the progress proved challenging. For such a rocky terrain, there were a surprising amount of vines, brambles, nettles, and fallen logs. I tripped over something and went sprawling to my hands and knees. Pain surged in my left ankle, and I muttered an inane sound. Will helped me up, but when I stepped, the pain returned.

Will complained about it being too dark for me to see well, and Mason added, "That full moon does us no good."

As though we mirrored one another, Will and I snapped our gazes to Mason. "What did you say?" I asked.

"Full moon. Tonight."

I looked at Will. He once explained that a full moon provides optimum energy for souls. It's the night when the divide between life and death is thinnest. Souls are more likely to walk the earth and act out their torment. A full moon is more dangerous, he had said, because souls' energies are heightened in whatever state of mind they held upon their deaths. If they were evil, it could be dangerous because they might attempt to finish whatever foul thing they planned at the time of their death.

The concern on Will's face equaled mine. On one hand, he, Mule, and Mason would have optimum energy, but on the other, so would any other soul we encountered on this ridge.

Will frowned. "I hadn't realized."

I shook it off. "It doesn't matter. We'd have come anyway. Let's go." I picked up the flashlight and limped with Will's assistance toward the origin of the muted noise.

We wound our way past two rock formations, both with indentations that led to false caves.

I called Nidhi's name again. The muted groaning sound answered back, and we followed it into the mouth of a large cavity.

Mason moved ahead of us, deeper into the darkness. "She's here!"

I shined the flashlight to the back and saw her, bound, gagged, and curled in a fetal position. "Nidhi!" Despite the pain in my ankle, I limped hurriedly to her. Her eyes blinked open, but they reflected a hopelessness and fear that made my stomach knot.

Mule returned to the entrance. "I'll stand guard."

"Here's a lantern and matches!" Will called from the darkness. Within seconds, light filled the grotto, enough to reveal that the immediate area was otherwise empty, except for a metal jug of what looked like water and a couple Styrofoam food containers.

I pulled the bandana from Nidhi's mouth and began working at the ropes tethering her. My stomach lurched when I saw blood on the bindings and on her dark skin. I studied her closer as I worked at the ropes. Her hair was covered with brambles and dirt, and her arms and legs covered with scratches, cuts, and black and blue marks. Her peacock blue dress was torn and rumpled like an old rag.

"You're okay now, Nidhi. We're here." I repeated this again and again as I worked, hoping to calm her, reassure her. After I finished untying her hands, she slumped, making no effort to help me with her legs. I worried that she was too far gone, either physically or emotionally, to help.

She started to cry, and I began choking, overcome by her pain and what she must have experienced. The fear, the hopelessness, the horror of wondering if anyone would ever come.

Hearing her rasping, I began to wonder why she was still breathing. This could have killed her, sucked the life right out of her.

Remember I said earlier that silence fell as though someone hit the mute button on a TV show? Well, whoever or whatever was back, cranking the knob to full volume. The wind roared with a verbosity I'd never heard before, like some presage of doom.

Mule ducked his head in and yelled, "Somethin's happenin'. I'm goin' up there."

"No, we need to stick together!" I glanced at Mason, but he studied Nidhi with such an odd expression, I decided it would be better if he stayed here. "Will, stop Mule, please!"

Will hurried after Mule.

I looked at Mason. "She'll be okay."

He nodded, his face awash with incredulity. But he said nothing. For the first time, I wondered if a ghost could be shocked or filled with new horror. In my experience, they only reacted based on conditioning or to what they experienced while alive. Then again, he had known Nidhi, cared about her deeply as a friend.

Will returned. "I can't reason with him. He's hell-bent on finding the center of this tumult."

Despite the fury kicking up outside, I felt Nidhi move, heard her opening and closing her mouth like she was plagued with dehydration in addition to her other pains.

"Nidhi, it's okay. We'll get help here soon." I pulled out my cell phone. I shouldn't have been surprised to click on and find no service, but I was. I jammed it back in my pocket. Nidhi shifted again, so I helped her sit up.

"Who ..." She stopped and licked her dry lips, before trying again. "Who are you talking to?"

I cringed. She didn't need more confusion. "You, I'm talking to you."

"No ..." She tried to sit taller but slumped again. Mason moved to her side and, without a word, he grabbed her left arm and shoulder, and I held the right. We eased her to lean against the wall.

She looked at her arm where Mason touched her. Her eyebrows pulled together, confused. "You were talking to someone else."

I eyed the other two before moving to her front, to make better eye contact. "I'll explain later. Can you talk? Can you tell us ... me who did this to you?" She seemed to be drawing on a hidden reserve of energy, so I thought it safe to encourage her to continue.

She told her story, slow and steady, between bouts of gasping for a deep breath or licking her parched lips, despite refusing to drink any more water from the jug. "We held a garden club meeting Friday morning, at the library. In the basement. I was the last to leave. When I walked by one of the conference rooms, I heard a noise. Like a groan or a sob. I thought someone was hurt, so I went in. Benny was on the floor."

"Benny Crinshaw?"

"He was curled in a ball, rocking back and forth, staring at the tapestry on the wall. Well, I knew Benny, so I wasn't afraid. I sat with him. Put my arm around him. He kept mumbling, so I asked him what was wrong. He acted like I wasn't even there. Just shook his head and rocked. He kept repeating, "Mason, Clyde.""

My gaze jerked to Mason. He ran a hand over his head.

Oblivious to my exchange with Mason, Nidhi continued in raspy breaths, "It scared me. After a few minutes, Gwendolyn Bealle came into the room. She wasn't happy with what she saw. I asked her what he was talking about. She got mad and said it was nonsense. I didn't believe her. Clearly he was distraught. So I pushed for an answer. She got mad and told me to mind my own business. I left. Went back to work. But the more I thought about it, the more I grew concerned. I decided to call Larry and tell him about it. I was in the midst of calling him as I headed to my car.

That's when she—"

"Gwendolyn, you mean?"

"Yes, she popped out of nowhere. I clicked off in a hurry because I didn't want her to hear what I was about to say. She said Benny felt bad and wanted to talk to me. That he was in the car, in the back of the bank. I followed her. She asked me to climb in the car and talk to him. I refused but turned to talk to him from where I stood. Then something hit me from behind. I came to in this cave. They must have stuffed me in the trunk of her car and drove here by the old trail road."

Mason's body swelled with rage like Mule's had done earlier. "That worthless, wretched—"

His words were drowned out by a clap of thunder that shook the ground so ferociously, I reached out for support. Nidhi winced and cried, "That didn't even sound natural."

She was right. The wind sounded like a freight train, and the rumbling of the thunder more like cannons booming. I shifted, accidentally rubbing my arm against Nidhi. A spark burst between us as if an angry electrical leviathan had seized the escarpment on which these rocks and caves sat.

I looked at Will and Mason. "I know you want to stay with us, but I think you need to go fight whatever is out there."

They looked at each other then back at me. I sensed they were about to argue, so I continued. "I can't fight what's up there, and I don't think Nidhi and I will get out alive until we do."

Still, they hesitated. They both looked like they agreed with me, even had one foot ready to bolt and go fight, but their concern remained with us.

"Mule needs you," I said as convincingly as possible. "He's strong, determined, but whatever is up there is stronger."

"Stay put," Will ordered. He turned to Mason and nodded. Together, they disappeared into the darkness.

I turned back to Nidhi. She studied me with a horrified look.

"Look, I'll explain later." I needed to keep her focused. "What about Holland Greer? Where was he in all this?"

It took her a moment to collect her thoughts, to shake off the conversation I'd had with two people that weren't even there. "Holland? I don't know. He's not involved in this as far as I know."

"But that's impossible. Gwendolyn Bealle and Benny never could have done all this on their own."

"You don't think so?" The voice came from the entrance.

I looked up to see Ms. Bealle holding a revolver, and it was pointed at me.

CHAPTER 29

Gwendolyn Bealle was a mere wisp of a woman, short, frail, late '60s, and blonde hair courtesy of a bottle, but the gun in her hand gave her an advantage that her sneer suggested she enjoyed. "So, you don't think me capable, Ms. MacKenna?" She let out a dismissive snort. "You may be surprised at what I can do."

"You won't get away with this," I said in as brave a voice as I could muster. "The sheriff is on his way."

She laughed. "Well, then I better hurry. It's quite fortuitous that you showed up tonight. Makes my plans easier. Once you're gone, I can finally claim what is rightfully mine."

"*Crossings*? Or is it the gold you're after?"

"All of it. It belongs to the Crinshaws."

"You mean the Sawyers, don't you?" Why I would egg on a woman holding a gun pointed at my heart I didn't know, but it seemed like the only way to draw out the time.

As though she read my mind, she rolled her eyes. "Ahhh, yes, this is where you ask a bunch of inane questions hoping to buy time so that you can figure out how to get this gun out of my hand. But look around, dear. We're in a cave. We're in the eye of a storm. There's no help coming, little girl, because no one knows we're here. I saw you arrive alone. Besides," she said as she flicked her gaze around wildly, "he will protect me and let me in, finally ... once I've gotten rid of you."

I assumed she was speaking of Josiah Sawyer and his supposed black magic or supernatural power, but I wasn't about to ask for clarification.

She sniffed in disdain. "I will oblige your questions. Then you can think about it as you die."

Nidhi gasped. I slid my hand on top of hers.

Ms. Bealle continued. "When that idiot Holland Greer moved to Williamsport, it seemed like an answer to my problem because he was a ghost hunter, a phenomenological researcher. Nobody before that had been able to get close to *Crossings*." Disgust oozed in her voice. "My father used to tell Benny and me it would take somebody the spirits would trust, so I thought sure Greer would be that person. It would merely take a while. A little courting along. But the waiting turned into years, and then you moved right in without a problem. That's when I finally accepted Greer was worthless. He couldn't find his way out of a paper bag. But I could tell you distrusted him, so I let it alone. I figured if you were distracted by him, you wouldn't notice what I did." She scoffed. "Turns out, I was right."

Anger boiled in me. "And yet here I sit, so you must not have been too right."

"You're nothing but another obstacle to deal with."

"Like Mason? And Clyde? You killed them, didn't you?"

She laughed, looking so pleased with herself I had my answer. But she must have had help by someone strong enough to move him, to drag Nidhi …

The truth hit me like the sting of a slap to the cheek. "You made Benny help you, didn't you?"

Her smile dropped to a scowl. "I did all this for him, and for his son. The gold, the estate, it belongs to us, not you. Once you're gone, we will be restored as rightful owners. So yes, Benny was there. It's only fair he take part in it."

"How could you! He's big and vulnerable from his challenges, but he is a gentle giant. He wouldn't hurt anyone on his own."

"He would if he believed it was the only way to protect me."

And there it was. She had tricked her brother into helping her cover the murders. She manipulated his immature and innocent understanding of right and wrong.

She continued, and the joy she experienced at sharing her murderous deeds reflected on her face, the curled lips, the glitter in her eyes, the eagerness in her voice. "On the night Baxter went to Holland's house, Benny and I arrived to see Baxter peer through the shed window. All those years ago, I knew what Greer kept hidden in there. The worthless items the idiot had stolen. I knew if Baxter reported him, Greer wouldn't be available to help us gain access into *Crossings*. So, I had to stop Baxter. It only took one blow. I made Benny wait in the car while I drove Mason's vehicle down the road and hid it in a thicket of woods for a couple days. Then I jogged back to my car, and we drove to the canal. The snow was falling in buckets, so our tracks were covered everywhere we went."

As Ms. Bealle told her story, I watched Mason's soul arrive at the entrance behind her. He put a finger over his mouth and stepped to stand beside her. I had no doubt he would move when the time arrived. Would he manifest himself? Will had once told me ghosts could do that if they wished. They could use all their energy to materialize to someone who didn't have subtle vision.

Hope blossomed, and I struggled to hide it. "But Holland must have heard the cars outside his shed. He had to be an accessory to all this."

"He knew nothing! The door to his shed was closed to keep the warmth from the space heater in. He had a radio on. It was so simple. A few nights later, I drove Mason's car to the airport. Left it there. Took a taxi home. As I hoped, people assumed he skipped town."

"How did you get Benny to cooperate?"

She uttered a whimpering sound. "Benny struggles with reality. He gets upset at times, and it all comes back to him."

Nidhi mumbled in an astonished whisper. "Like the morning I found him."

"That was quite inconvenient." Ms. Bealle's shoulders drooped. "Benny has lapsed a few times through the years. You happened to catch him at one of those rare times."

"What about Clyde?" I asked. "Why did he have to die?"

She shrugged. "That may have been a misunderstanding. Right before Baxter died, he came to, enough to mumble for Clyde's help. I was able to determine from his babbling that Clyde knew where Baxter had gone that evening and that Clyde was sledding that night, here, on Chocton Bluff. That infuriated me. Not only was Clyde another loose end, but he was sledding on my property. So, he had to go, too."

"And, as Mason died, you told him he could rot there in that grave and watch what his meddling couldn't stop."

She looked startled, and her hand faltered, but she caught herself. "How do you know that?"

"Because I told her," Mason said and stepped into her sight, manifesting himself in full.

I heard the air rush out of Nidhi like she'd been punched as Ms. Bealle screamed an unintelligible sound and stepped back. "You're dead! I know you are." She wrapped her arms around herself protectively, which meant the gun now pointed at the cave wall beside her.

"Grace! Where are you?" Clay's panicked voice reached us through the storm.

"In here!" I yelled.

Mason disappeared from view before Clay entered. He took one look at Nidhi and me cornered on the floor before his gaze jerked to see Ms. Bealle with a gun in her hand. In a flash, he jumped at her, pulling the gun away and knocking her to the ground. She acted dazed, moaning and curling into a fetal position.

He scrambled to us. "Are you alright?"

His question was barely audible above the ruckus of the storm, so I cranked up the volume to respond.

"Yes, but Nidhi needs help. You have to get Sheriff Barnes because—"

"He's outside," Clay yelled. "Mom and Whit, too. We were

with him when you called." In a booming voice, Clay bellowed, "Larry! In here. Quick!"

In seconds, Sheriff Barnes entered the cavity. His gaze assessed Gwendolyn Bealle before darting to Nidhi.

"Larry!" Nidhi called, and he rushed to her.

Their reunion distracted me and, too late, I looked up to see Ms. Bealle stumble out the opening. "She's getting away!"

"She won't get far," the sheriff declared. "Storm will stop her. Worse than anything I ever saw in N'awlins."

The ground beneath us rumbled, and Clay yelled, "Come on, we've got to get out of here!"

Once outside, the full force of the elements hit us. It was a storm of such exaggerated proportions, I thought I was stuck in a cheap movie set. The rain fell in heavy, stinging sheets, and the knives of wind cut at our skin, thwarting our progress. Then too, Nidhi could barely walk. The four of us—Clay, Nidhi, Sheriff Barnes, and I—tried to hold onto one another as we battered forward against the beastly weather.

Clay pointed to higher ground. Although he stood at my side and gripped my arm, I strained to hear him when he yelled, "That path is washed out! We'll have to go higher, then down a crude trail on the other side. I hope that's what Mom and Whit did."

The wind and rain continued to fight us each step. Every few seconds, the ground shook with violent tremors, sending us jerking to the side and falling in a unit as we attempted to move together.

What kind of storm was this? I had never heard of a tornado hitting this area, but the roar of the wind sounded like a train barreling down, the same noise of destruction a twister makes, I'd been taught. Was it a tornado? An earthquake? Flooding rain? Was this a horrible storm or something much more diabolical?

"Let's go! Hurry!" Clay urged.

"Stick together!" Sheriff Barnes bellowed.

We came to a rubble outwash of a chasm in a wall of rock where the rainwater roared with such intensity down the steep and narrow ravine that ascent by foot became almost impossible. Instead, we had to crawl to climb and pull ourselves and one another over the jagged rocks as dirt, stones, and other debris crashed into us from all directions.

Clay ascended first, throwing up a leg and hauling the rest of himself after. He lay on his stomach, his upper chest reaching over the edge, and waved for me to follow. It was hard to see even at that close distance. Airborne particles smacked into my face, and our soaked hands made locking grips almost impossible. Ruing my mediocre upper body strength, I grabbed whatever support I could find among the outcrop of rocks and roots, and stretched to grab his hand. He pulled me up. Together we attempted the same for Nidhi with Sheriff Barnes assisting from below, but a sizzle of lightning lit the sky, and the sudden blaze startled her, causing her to lose her grip. Between that, and the weight and awkwardness of her rain-soaked dress, she fell back.

On the second try, we moved with greater speed and strength, as though panic fueled us with a new energy. Finally, we hoisted her onto the ledge. Once the sheriff scaled the rim, we turned and raced around the cropping of trees to step onto the wide expanse of a rampart that served as the top of the monstrous bluff.

The hair on my arms rose when I took in the scene in front of me. In the center of a massive inferno appeared a figure so grotesque, it took a moment for me to realize it was the wolf-like creature from my dream, his fangs and claws now exaggerated in size. Here hovered the being Hilda had described. The one that had originated the odd, demonic symbol. The one I somehow intuited was Josiah Sawyer. I say he *appeared* because I couldn't tell if he was standing in the fire or drifting over it.

Surrounding him on three sides, and oscillating as though to confuse or disorient him, were Mule, Mason, and Will. Their feet remained rooted to the area outside the fire, but their upper bodies enlarged and wavered freely, ever-moving and changing, dodging right, left, then swelling high into the sky before swooping low to cut under the wolf creature. Each time they surged in and clashed with him, the ground shook, and the sound boomed like thunder.

Off to the right stood Whit, Cassie, and Seth like frozen statues, watching the fire as if mesmerized and oblivious to the souls clashing in and around it. The rain pouring down on their faces and funneling across their foreheads and cheeks must have served as a startling testament that this fire was beyond ordinary. My friends couldn't see the souls or witness the strength or vehemence of these supernatural movements, but I wondered if they could feel the electricity in the air or sense the loathing between the clashing forces.

"Mom!" Clay bellowed, but she didn't respond. He called twice more before Seth looked over and touched Cassie's arm to get her attention. The three stumbled toward us.

"Come on," Clay shrieked. "We're not safe on this bluff!"

Cassie and Whit reached us, but Seth stopped midway and stared at something in or beyond the fire, I couldn't tell which.

Clay shouted again for him to hurry. Seth screamed something about Ms. Bealle and Benny needing help. He turned away from us as though he was going to run to them.

In the opposite direction!

Panic prickled my body. In the distant recesses of my mind, my brain screamed for clear thinking. For action.

Please, Seth, don't do it!

But, I couldn't move or speak. I had been so bold and brave when I faced Naomi in Georgia and Fergus in the tunnels. Yet here I crouched, frozen, watching the conflict unroll in slow motion before my horrified eyes.

What's more, the odor in the air reeked of burning carcass, such that I struggled to breathe, but the others didn't seem to notice! I was reminded again they were witnessing only a fraction of what I was, and it struck me that this was how demonic forces worked. Always there, behind the scenes, generally invisible to the human eye, but always ready to pounce and devour at any detection of weakness or lack of faith and conviction. We can't *see* their moves and their plotting, but their spiritual battles continue.

The others in the group yelled for Seth to stop, but at the same moment, the souls clashed again, this time in a collision that sent a mammoth oak tree crashing down on the bluff, missing the fire and Seth by inches. Ms. Bealle emerged from the side of the blaze, stumbling to Seth and calling his name for help. Her voice squawked and shrieked as though she were panicked, desperate. Benny ran behind her, a confused and frantic look on his face.

As the souls continued their scrimmage, I looked up to see the wolf creature's eyes flicker with a diabolical sparkle right before he extended a talon-like claw and swiped at Mule, sending Mule's upper body roiling out in a wide arch that must have stretched a couple hundred yards into the glowing sky. I knew the others in our group couldn't see this. The most they could comprehend was that some elemental force beyond human understanding was at work.

In as fast as a blink, other shapes appeared and surrounded the fire. Dozens of them. Their bodies swelled as they moved in. I don't know who or what they were, but my mind resonated they were the souls of the people Sawyer killed, back finally to exact revenge and eradicate the evil. In that second, I wondered about Enoch Crinshaw, but I knew he had died elsewhere and, therefore, at best he could only present his soul here as a residual that would mean with weakened and incomplete strength. But if he participated, would he have fought for or against his abusive father?

I would never know because the new figures battled Sawyer with such coordination and intensity, I sensed his demise was imminent. Mule, Mason, and Will dropped back, drifting into the backdrop and hovering to watch the unfolding scene also. It was as if they knew the new souls were working in a planned attack, perhaps one born from years of waiting for this moment to complete their unfinished business against the evil that had ended their lives. As two souls swooped low to strike at Sawyer, three dove from above to pummel blows to his bent shape. He'd no sooner jerk back in reaction when two more would hammer him from behind.

As though he knew he was defeated, Sawyer let out a strangled cry toward the sky, a screeching wail of fury and frustration. He folded and faltered as though weakened and defeated.

The ground rocked with his fury, flinging several of us to our hands and knees. I looked around and saw that we were all still together, before jerking my gaze to Seth, Benny, and Ms. Bealle. The ground had moved them, and in that split second, my breath caught as I realized Ms. Bealle and Seth were teetering on the edge of the cliff, struggling with their balance and precarious grips. Another tree had fallen in their direction, but its girth was too large to offer a secure grasp.

In that horrible second as time morphed between rapid speed and slow motion, I witnessed Benny's fear, saw it register on his face, the hideous moment he realized he had *one* chance to save *one* life.

He screamed, "No!" and reached out and grabbed Seth's hand as Ms. Bealle plunged over the cliff and down the sheer walls of rock into the depths of the deep river valley below.

Benny pushed Seth full force to safety, turned, yelled, "Gwennie!" and jumped after her.

It happened so quickly, all our group could do was gasp and scream.

The sheriff yelled for Seth to move away from the cliff. Seth scrambled backward on his butt several yards before struggling to his feet, all the while keeping his stare locked on the abyss of darkness where Ms. Bealle and Benny disappeared. The firelight washed over the dazed, incredulous horror on his face.

The sheriff's voice cut through his stupor on the second call. He turned and hastened to us, stumbling repeatedly on fallen branches and rocks. Of our group, Whit crouched the closest to Seth, so he crawled to help, pushing him toward the rest of us. He reached us, but Whit's foot got caught in the base of an uprooted tree. Before any of us could react to help him, lightning struck another tree. It exploded into a second blaze of fire, and flames began to shower on Whit.

Mason moved with such speed that no one in the group had a chance to scream or move to help. Mason swooped in and dragged Whit to safety, depositing him near Cassie. Later, I would think back on that moment and realize that, to the others, it must have looked as though Whit was simply moved by a blast of wind.

Cassie screamed Whit's name and crawled to his side. She pulled him into her arms, stroked the wet hair from his face, and cradled him in a tight embrace. Despite the chaos around us, I saw the edges of Mason's lips lift, and I sensed a melancholy closure and a comfort emanating from him at what he observed.

I looked back at the fire. Sawyer's soul was now clumped at its base, like an abandoned ragdoll. The figures that had come to assist Mule, Mason, and Will floated higher and higher until they were out of sight.

As had happened with Fergus last year during his defeat in the tunnels, Sawyer's body changed and shriveled, spotting over before turning sickly yellow, then skeletal. His frame deteriorated, his face melted, and his eyes emptied to mere sockets.

Dark cloaked figures with hollowed faces and no eyes moved in to claim and devour him, screaming and squawking piercing sounds that seemed to come from the depths of hell itself.

The wind ceased. The rain stopped. The fire died.

Then, the rock formation crumbled beneath us. I had one fraction of a second to see Will's face and hear Seth's cry before I hurtled over the edge behind us.

CHAPTER 30

At first, I saw light. A soothing, radiant light, captivating me and beckoning me to choose.

Choose what?

Confused, I waited, and the light faded to dark.

Still, I waited.

A sharp sound intruded at the edges of my mind. I sat up and looked around, but didn't see anything. Nothing but darkness. I couldn't hear anything either, except a rumble in my ears.

I did not know where I was or remember how I got there.

And why was I alone?

I stood. The movement proved effortless.

What was I supposed to do now?

I continued to wait. Seconds. Hours? I wasn't anxious. Somehow, the emptiness felt soothing, free of troubles, and the dark, rather than intimidating, full of potential.

A noise sounded from my left. I turned toward it.

"Will!" I relaxed. I would be okay. I trusted him. I loved him. He was kind and handsome and good to me. I knew he loved me, too.

He took my hand. Kissed it. Looked into my eyes.

"You have to make a choice," he said. His voice was softer than I ever heard before. From him or anyone.

"A choice?"

"To live or die."

"Then right now …?"

"You're in between. Alive, but quite weak."

I thought about that.

He must have read my confusion because he continued. "Your loved ones aren't sure what's happening. And the medical team? Limited understanding of *all* the healing powers available. Of a person's will to live. So, your decision will not come as a surprise."

"But isn't that like choosing suicide? Giving up all hope?"

He smiled. "Not this time. You've been hurt. You could get up and return to your life and be better than ever. Or, you might be in dire pain, perhaps living on the edge of death."

"But it's my choice?"

"In this instance, yes. We are given free will. At this unusual juncture, you have that choice."

"If I die, you will be with me?"

His gaze bored into me, and he gripped my hand tighter. "Come with me now, and we will be together forever."

I grinned. I could go with Will and be eternally happy. I could touch God. Actually reach out and touch His indescribable, glorious, exalted face. I could see Mom, Jack, Julie, Grandma Sadie. The thought overwhelmed me.

"What about the others? Mason and Mule and—"

"We are here." It was Mason's voice. I turned to see him and Mule standing where Will had entered.

I touched my chest. So happy! "Will you be there as well?"

"I hope," Mule said. He reached out, took my hand from Will, and kissed it. "I've been waitin' longer than this scoundrel," he said, nodding at Mason. He sobered and added, "Sawyer's evil was no match for the collective power of those agitated souls 'round that fire. Now that he and his evil are destroyed, and the others moved on, I must make an accounting of my own. So I'll be moving on as well. Thank you for what you did."

I remembered the phrase other souls had said during their departures, and I repeated it now: "Godspeed, Lemule Chasen."

He nodded and disappeared from view.

I closed my eyes to relish the moment. When I opened them, Mason stood before me. I was surprised to see my hand already in his.

"I echo Mule's gratitude," Mason said. "By setting me free, you set my family free to move on. To heal, to love again."

"You saved Whit."

He chuckled. "Yes, I saved Whit. Imagine that. It's the least I could do for my beautiful Cassie. She deserves the best."

I nodded. "She does." I glanced at Will and back at Mason. "What do you think I should do?"

Mason pulled his shoulders back. "I can't answer that." His gaze, too, flicked to Will before returning to me. "I know my son loves you. I could see it on his face. On the boat. At the Canal. The bluff." He paused, pondering. "Think about what young Andrew Crowell told you. At the medical museum. Do you remember telling me about that?"

I did. Andrew Crowell was a soul I met at the Civil War Medical Museum in Frederick, Maryland. He had no left arm and no hand on his right arm. He told me that he never should have destroyed himself by leaping off the cliffs at Great Falls because he still had feet to carry messages, eyes to see his family, and a mouth to teach and offer hope. So, with that reminder, was Mason suggesting I return to life? Or, was he saying to think about Andrew's limitations?

Could ghosts hint?

Mason, too, kissed my hand. "Goodbye, Grace. It has been an honor meeting you."

"Likewise," I choked. I had grown to love this soul. "I am so glad I got to meet you."

With that, he too disappeared.

I covered my face with my hands. Sometimes, that was the only way to *feel* the joy gurgling inside. Mason was satisfied, his business complete, and finally moving on.

I was left standing face to face with Will, my friend, my soldier, my confidante. The man who, given another time, another place, another century, I would have married in a heartbeat.

"Gwendolyn Bealle and Benny. Are they …?"

He nodded. "Dead. Gone."

I frowned. So tragic. "The others okay?"

He understood. I didn't need to explain who the "others" were. He nodded. "The sheriff broke his arm when the precipice crumbled, but he and Nidhi can heal together."

I nodded as he continued. "Whit is sporting back pain because Cassie fell on him. I doubt she'll give him much pity, however, because she suffered a few bruises too. As luck would have it, Clay fell on the leg that was damaged in Afghanistan, so he'll be nursing it for a while. Seth has cuts and scrapes but is fine. However, emotionally he went through the most tonight, so he'll need time to heal."

I sighed. "So I'm the only one they're concerned about now."

"At least you didn't plunge off the same cliff as Benny and his sister. Instead, you were tossed over the same rampart you and the others climbed to reach the top. But it was still a good eight feet to your fall."

I thought about it but couldn't remember the fall.

"Grace, it's time to make a decision. Try not to find your answers in this fog, in this mystic haze of unknowing. Step out of it, choose your answers, and find your path."

He offered good counsel. Step from the murk and the mystic and find your answers there. Yet, I could sense him urging me to go with him now.

It was enticing, this notion that submerged beyond the surface of the visible world were mysteries too amazing to comprehend, and that I could witness them. *Now*.

But, somehow, I understood: God was right there, on the other side of that veil separating one world from the other. He always was and always will be.

I reached for Will's hand and pulled it to my heart.

"I love you so much," I said, feeling the warmth and the truth of my words bubbling inside.

He frowned, but not in a sad way. Instead, it looked wistful.

"Will, I choose to live. No matter what life brings, no matter what hardships, I know that what you describe will be waiting there for me. That it has been from the beginning. It will get me through anything. And, even if I feel pain … even if I have a long road back … I will still have a mouth to talk and teach and help others."

As I said it, I knew it was true. I wanted to continue to live to be the person I was created to be.

Will frowned and kissed my hand again. "Then I guess we will part. First, I will help you return to the others."

"What should I do?"

"Simply wake up. We'll be at *Crossings*. The others carried you from the rubble back to the house. A long trek, filled with confusion and crying. Storm damage has delayed the ambulance, but EMTs hiked in to help. They had to order two very anxious and demanding young men to keep out of your apartment. The sheriff is making sure they do. Remember, I said they're not sure what your status is. All this," he gestured around the darkness, "has taken but a second of their time. You'll find Seth on the porch to the apartment, and Clay in the old house."

Seth on the porch. Clay in the house. I memorized it. "May we go now?"

He nodded, and his eyes sparkled. "Yes. Just lie down and close your eyes."

I dropped to the ground, closed my eyes, and opened them again to see the ceiling of my refurbished apartment. Tilting my head slightly right, I saw Cassie on the couch cradling Whit. A twig protruded from her hair, and a wound darkened her cheek. Nidhi sat near her, hugging her knees and staring blankly into space. Beside her, the sheriff yelled into his cell phone for someone to "Hurry up, blast it!" His other arm was in a sling.

The moment of truth had come. I focused on my right hand, and it rose into the air.

Someone gasped.

I attempted more. I sat up.

Some pain, but bearable. Will stood by my side.

From my left, Cassie choked. "Whit!"

Whit jerked his gaze to me, startled, and winced as though the movement brought pain.

Everyone around me sprang to life. EMTs leaned back in shock as Cassie and Whit struggled to their feet. The sheriff clicked off the phone and wiped a shaky hand across his mouth as he stared at me.

"Grace!" Cassie's voice trembled.

I smiled at her as I resisted the pain to inch to my feet. The EMTs barked warnings and demands that I be still, but I ignored them. They couldn't see Will helping me from the side. "It's okay. I'm fine."

They looked at me awestruck as I limped past.

I didn't stop. Didn't hesitate. The man I loved was waiting for me. My friends would understand my priority.

Seth on the porch. Clay in the old house.

I proceeded to the front door and stepped onto the porch.

CHAPTER 31

Seth scrambled to his feet and watched me approach. He covered the lower half of his face as though shocked, or doubting what he saw. Scratches and dried blood covered his arms, and a rakish lock of sandy-colored hair tumbled over his forehead. When he dropped his hands, I saw again that beautiful smile and high cheekbones that I'd grown to adore.

He shook his head when I reached his side. "I thought you were—"

"I know …" I touched his face. "… but I'm not. I'm here."

He smiled before embracing me. The hug was gentle and frantic, all in one.

Pushing back to arm's length, he studied me. "I can't believe this."

"Believe it." I smiled, but it dropped to a straight line as I thought about my next words. "Seth, I—"

"No." He sighed, shook his head, and spoke in slow, thoughtful delivery. "No, don't say it. Let me speak first, please. Let me save my pride." He swallowed. "I love you, Grace. But I see now that I can't be there for you. Not for a long time. Nidhi told me everything that happened on the bluff tonight. Benny was my father, and I never knew it! He saved my life, Grace. My father saved my life. Yet, he lost his. This is going to take a lot of years and head work to get over."

He paused, and I saw moisture in his eyes. I reached for him, but he shook his head. I could not imagine how he felt, learning the truth of his ancestry. His birth family had been composed of liars, frauds, murderers, and masters of evil, with the exception of his father, Benny. Worse than all this, Benny was now dead, and Seth had been cheated out of a chance to acknowledge him.

Lights flashed us, and we turned to see an ambulance and police cars pulling into the lane.

Seth's gaze darted to the house then back to the emergency vehicles. "They'll give me a ride home. I'm going to go now. I hope you understand. It's only goodbye for now."

"I do. Thank you, Seth. I love you, and I hope you remain a part of my life forever."

He nodded, looked toward the house once more, and frowned. "I will," he said, as though he determined to make it true.

"And Seth? If you get the chance again, take the money. Benny would want you to, now that it's no longer tainted." I smiled. "Your *birth father* would want you to use it for school."

With a nod and a smile, he kissed me on the cheek and walked away.

"Bravo," Will said from my side. "He needed to hear that."

I watched Seth a few seconds before turning to look at the house.

What would I find inside? Would Clay embrace me or push me away?

I took a deep breath and, with Will's help, hurried—as much as my injured body would allow—across the apartment porch to where it connected with the house's porch and entered *Crossings*.

Clay sat on the grand staircase, his clothes torn and stained with mud. He'd dropped his head to between his knees, his arms crisscrossed over him like a lid trying to hold the anguish in. I didn't know if he was praying or crying.

I decided it didn't matter. "Clay."

Startled, he dropped his arms and looked up. Scratches grazed both his right cheek and upper lip. His face paled as he climbed to his feet, favoring his injured leg. He tilted his head, studying me. I could see shock, wonder, a dare to believe, all of it written on his face.

"Grace …?" His voice was hoarse. He firmed that rugged square jaw of his as though afraid to believe and preparing himself for the worst.

I chuckled through tears and nodded. "It's really me. I'm not a ghost."

He took one step down to the floor, but still hesitated, dubious. He ran a shaking hand through his dark hair, and it flopped back into place. Had I ever seen him unsure before?

My, "I'm sorry," collided with his, "Can you forgive me?"

And the next thing I knew, I was in his arms. No more words were necessary.

From behind me, I heard the clearing of a throat. I pulled from Clay to look back at Will.

If a ghost could blush, he was doing it, and I laughed.

"Lucky man," Will murmured.

Clay said, "Is that Will?"

I turned back to him. "Yes, he helped me get here. Now, where were we?"

He straightened, but before reaching for me, he said, "Um, Will?" and flicked a go-away gesture with his hands.

"Ah, yes," Will mumbled. "I'll just be outside. I won't leave until later."

When he was gone, I moved into Clay's arms and knew I would only be away from that spot for short spurts for the rest of my life.

CHAPTER 32

One year later

"**R**eady? Here she comes!" Reaghan's voice sounded from the hallway, and I turned from the hors d'oeuvre platter to watch Cassie step into my kitchen. With a smirk, she struck a coquettish pose that proved more comical than runway suave. Her ivory, tea-length wedding dress, three-inch heels, and festoon of tiny pink roses softened the gym rat that I knew lived beneath the lavish wrapping. A tiny silk pillbox hat, perched stylishly off-center, sported a small veil that reached across her forehead. Reaghan followed her into the room, clapped a couple times, and said, "Whoo-hoo, work it, Mother!"

I laughed but offered an honest assessment. "You look beautiful!"

Cassie rolled her eyes and resumed her normal stance. "I look ridiculous." She tugged at the lacy bodice of her dress as though it irritated her skin. "I never should have let y'all talk me into this shindig. City Hall woulda been just fine with me."

Clay entered the kitchen from a different entrance, fidgeting with his cummerbund. He jerked to a stop when he saw his mother. "Whoa!" With a scrutinizing look, he said, "What did you do with my mother?"

She smacked him with the bouquet, causing Reaghan to gasp as one flower broke off and fell to the floor. Clay laughed and pulled her into a hug. "You look great, Mom. Whit's a lucky man."

"Yeah, he's lucky I agreed to this hoopla," Cassie muttered.

Clay snatched a crab-stuffed pinwheel and popped it in his mouth before I could stop him. I grabbed a dishtowel and swatted him. "My turn," I added.

"Okay, ladies, no more hitting the best man," he scolded, straightening his bowtie. "I need to be in top form to carry out my duties."

I chuckled as he leaned down to kiss me, cupping my chin in his hands. I drank in the familiar smell of him, his presence and affection, delighting in the way he loved me.

Sidney appeared at the doorway with Adriana's boyfriend, Joaquin Alexander. "Ade's here. She wants to know where the quartet should set up." He rubbed the back of his neck. "Reaghan, can you come help with the kids? The boys want to go one direction and the girls another."

From the corner of my eye, I watched Cassie hurry out the door Clay had come in. She might refer to the wedding as a hoopla and a shindig, but I was tickled to note she wanted to adhere to the tradition of the bride keeping a low profile until the service.

I scooted around the counter to hug Joaquin. "You're finally here! Welcome to *Crossings*."

"This place is amazing," he said, returning the hug and shaking Clay's hand. "Is it really more than a hundred and fifty years old? Looks like it should be in a magazine."

Clay and I exchanged a smile. "Yes, it's really that old," Clay confirmed.

Joaquin thumbed toward the side of the house. "The single-story part, that's Michael's apartment? Where he lives when he's in the States?"

"Right again. He's due back from South Africa at Christmas. Come on." I put my arm through his. "I want to say hi to Ade before this gets underway. We haven't seen you two in a month." I began to turn but looked back and said, "Oh, and, Clay?"

He waved a dismissive hand but focused on the finger sandwiches. "You two go ahead. I'll make sure Tramps and Chubbs leave the hors d'oeuvres alone."

I cocked my head. "That's not who I was concerned about."

He tossed a sheepish grin. "Go."

As Joaquin and I strolled out the kitchen, through the dining room, and into the expanse of hallway, I explained that the exterior, the grounds, and most of the first floor had undergone extensive renovation in the past several months, but that the second floor remained to be tackled.

"It's perfect, just perfect," Joaquin said, admiration lacing his tone. "The rugs, the furniture, the design, fit for a king, yet still warm and homey. And that woodwork," he whistled under his breath as he pointed at the thick crown molding, "they don't make that anymore."

I studied this man at my side. He was tall, handsome, and perfect for Ade. Yet he was not someone with whom I would have thought she'd grow serious. She was an optimistic, bubbly musician. He was a pragmatic, stoical cartographer. But they were perfect together. They had met ten months earlier at the Rock of Gibraltar when she toured the Iberian Peninsula with the National Symphony Orchestra, and he served as a chaperone for his nephew's touring high school band. They'd dated steadily ever since, and each get-together Clay and I had with them involved meeting in the District. I enjoyed finally showing Joaquin my home.

As we passed a set of closed French doors to our right, he pointed at them, eyebrows raised. Before he could ask, I explained, "That's the drawing room. It's unfinished."

He tilted his head as though the explanation didn't make sense given the grandeur he saw throughout the rest of the first floor. But he didn't ask, and I wasn't about to explain that as long as Will resided here, the room would remain as it was. During the past year, Will repeatedly said he was leaving later, but for whatever reason he hadn't. "Later" became "after you heal," then it turned into "after you are older." Following my latest birthday, "later" morphed into "once you get married."

I didn't question him about it, and I sometimes wondered if I had become his unfinished business. Truth is, we barely saw one another what with my schedule and the size of the house. I was careful not to seek advice or turn to him with any concerns. I'd learned to place my focus on the living and the future. Instead, I talked *to*—not *with*—him in the same manner that I spoke to Jack, Mom, and Julie on occasion. I was certain their memories and their spirits were with me as well. The only difference was that I could see Will.

Clay never mentioned my houseguest, and when he visited, Will made himself scarce. I sometimes wondered if Clay secretly found comfort in knowing Will and his strength were in the house. Twice he had commented on the power he'd witnessed at the bluff, although he hadn't really seen anything and remembered very little.

In the foyer, Joaquin stopped and pointed at a painting hanging over the lower half of the grand staircase. "What a nice piece," he said, admiration lacing his voice.

"I had an artist do it. From an old daguerreotype I found in the house. The original picture was taken a year before the Civil War began."

"Who are they?"

"That's William Alan Kavanaugh in the middle, an ancestor of my stepfather Jack, and once-owner of this estate. With him," I pointed one by one, "are his best friends, Asa Garrett, Jubal McClain, and Braxton Lowe."

Joaquin cocked his head, studying the picture. "That blank spot. Seems odd. You would think the photographer would have posed them differently."

"There was a fifth person in the original. His name was Fergus Lowe. When the artist turned it into a painting, I had her remove him."

Joaquin furrowed his brow in confusion.

"He didn't fit the group," I said.

He nodded slowly, as though this answer, too, made no sense. No matter, because all the explanation in the world could never help people understand my peace at Fergus's removal.

He shrugged. "The artist did an incredible job."

"Her name is Colinda Montagne. She's the friend of a dear friend of ours, Seth Rendale. You might remember us talking about him?"

"Yes, he's studying medicine at West Virginia University, right?"

"Yes, that's him. They'll be arriving soon."

He stepped closer to the stairway and stared at a shadow box hanging below the painting. "A coin, a key, and a cuff link. Interesting grouping. But I know you're a history buff."

Best that I not share the story behind the origin of the objects with him ... yet ... so I smiled and nodded. "Come on, I'm anxious to see Ade."

Joaquin didn't move. I tracked his gaze back to the painting.

"Odd," he said, tilting his head right, then left. "It's like that guy in the middle ... what was his name, William? It's like he's watching us."

"Indeed, he is." Will's voice came from beside me.

He'd materialized when Joaquin said his name. I'd felt his cool aura, but I knew Joaquin couldn't see or hear him, so I stifled a chuckle and said, "That's a nice thought."

If Joaquin wondered about my comment, he didn't voice it. Instead, as we continued on, he said, "Civil War? A terrible time. I wonder how many of those four survived?"

"Only one." *But they each live in my memory.*

"One? So tragic," he said with a sad shake of his head. "Boy, if these walls could talk, eh?"

They have, and their stories are printed on my heart. "Yes, wouldn't that be something."

Joaquin and I exited onto the front porch, Will following behind. The sky was cloudless, and the sound of honking geese rode on rushes of gentle air to reach us, racing along with the sun's rays spreading toward the west.

As we descended the steps, I looked around, soaking in the beauty of the lush lawns that ran to the river and the wedding activity scattered across them. A huge white van sat in the driveway, "Sybil's Special Event Rentals" emblazoned in blue across its side. Sybil's employees were busy finalizing their work: straightening seventy folding chairs, unrolling the silk fabric for the bride's promenade, placing rose centerpieces on tableclothed tables, and scattering sprays of potted flowers in strategic locations. Caterers buzzed around them, preparing the buffet tables as uniformed waitstaff distributed my hors d'oeuvres to guests.

Beyond the buffet tables perched a stylish makeshift stand topped with dozens of presents. Standing at one end, beside an antique urn—unwrapped but adorned with a glittery silver bow— stood a semi-translucent figure. A soul! She was dressed like a Gibson girl from the 1890s, in a lacy white blouse and skirt that reached down to cover her lace-up boots. Her hair was perfectly coiffed and piled on top her head. Rather than menacing, she looked confused and demure, as though she were afraid to tarry far from the urn, which I surmised to be her center.

My breath hitched, and I looked over my shoulder at Will, who stood several paces behind me.

"On it," he announced as he walked toward her. He didn't seem alarmed either, so I relaxed and wondered about meeting our unexpected guest later.

A roar of laughter came from the right, near the arch where the couple would stand soon to become husband and wife. Joy surged through me as I soaked in the members of that happy group. Sheriff Barnes stood with his wife, Nidhi, and I heard him say, "No, really, that's the difference. In the city when there's a problem, everyone goes rushing out looking for help. In a small town, they all go rushing in with solutions." Heads bobbed in agreement from the group: Hilda, her son, Ted, Ade's mother and father, Jamaar Palmer and his date, Katarina, and Pastor Dale and his wife, Clarisa.

"Grace!"

Ade's voice caught my attention, and I watched her approach, sheet music in hand.

After we hugged and exchanged pleasantries, I assured her the quartet was setting up in a perfect spot. But I could tell she wasn't listening. Her eyes kept darting to Joaquin. Between this man, career with the orchestra, and part-time gig with the quartet, I knew her life was full.

Joaquin draped an arm around Ade but spoke to me. "The house, the grounds, I can see why you're so happy here. I'd like to join Clay in a little fishing and camping sometime. Where is that boat launch, anyway?"

I turned and pointed northwest, where Chocton Bluff and Devil's Cove used to be. "Angel Landing is straight down that trail. Just follow over a couple hills, past a small cemetery, and you'll reach the rocky landing in two minutes by four-wheeler."

"Sounds perfect," Joaquin said like he meant it. He yanked at the knot in his necktie. "Maybe later we can get out of these monkey suits and go see it."

"Ms. MacKenna! Got a minute?"

The voice came from behind me, and I turned to see Sheriff Barnes headed my direction. I excused myself and met him halfway.

"Sheriff, I'm so glad you could make it. I understand congratulations are in order."

"What? You mean Nidhi and me ... yeah, yeah. Thanks." He tugged at his bright yellow Jerry Garcia tie, looking as though he had something uncomfortable to discuss. "You may not be so glad I'm here in a minute or two."

"Why?" I raised my eyebrows, waiting for his explanation.

"Well, ya see, I have a colleague. In Gettysburg. He's got this case of a missing person he's been working on. And, well, blast it, he just can't make any headway on it. All leads bring him back to the same spot. Little Roundtop. Family has a house on the edge of the battlefield. Well, anyway, ma'am, he sure could use your help ... talking to possible witnesses."

I rubbed my forehead. "But I'm not a detective."

He shifted his weight, as though uncomfortable. "Ya see, it's on the battlefield." He exaggerated that last word. "Folks have reported seeing unusual things there through the years. Witnesses may not be of the *living* kind."

My heart gave an unexpected flutter. I took a deep breath. "Sheriff, I don't think—"

He pressed his palms at me. "Now, don't say no yet. Just think about it? Will ya? Just think about it."

I hesitated then nodded. "Alright, I guess I can think about it."

"Good deal," he said. "Good deal. Thanks."

He turned to go, but stopped and looked back at me. "Did I mention that missing person is a little five-year-old boy? Cute as the dickens in his picture. Imagine how scared that little tyke must be." He gestured goodbye for now by cocking an invisible hat.

I huffed a sigh as I watched him head back to Nidhi. "You fight dirty, Sheriff!" I yelled to his back. I pushed aside a whisper of remorse and added, "I said I'd think about it. That's all."

Without breaking his stride or looking back, he lifted his right arm to his side and pumped a thumbs-up.

"Wise guy," I muttered under my breath.

"Oh my, is this a bad time, dear?"

I knew that voice came from Hilda. I circled around to see her approaching, one hand thumping her cane and the other draped over the arm of her son, Ted. I'd met Ted and his brother, Dean, and their wives a few months earlier when they'd journeyed in from Florida and Texas, respectively, to visit Hilda.

"No, this is always a good time to see you two!" I responded.

Following hugs, Hilda said, "We were wondering if you could stop by the apartment tomorrow, dear. Around three? We'd like to discuss some paperwork with you."

"Paperwork?"

Ted nodded with a smile. "We want to talk about you working with Mom as more of a partner than an employee."

"Me? A partner?" My hand flew to my chest. "I don't know

what to say."

"First," Ted said, "I guess we should ask if you'd have any interest in running the business with Mom. With the goal, of course, of taking over one day."

"Are you kidding? I'd love it. But I'm still in school. I'm determined to earn my PhD so that means at least five years before I could take command of anything."

Hilda shook her head and poked her cane into the ground. "Well, glory be, I'm not checking out for several years, dear. I've always said I intend to beat Grandma Moses, and she lived to be—"

"A hundred and one," Ted and I chorused together.

"That's right," Hilda confirmed. She sighed with deep satisfaction and folded both hands atop her cane. "I was thinking about calling the new company Hildagrace."

A tear of happiness surfaced, so I kept my mouth shut and said nothing, in case the tears began to multiply.

Ted added, "Neither Dean or I are interested in running the company. We'd rather someone Mom loved … a relative, however distant … take over the reins." His gaze flicked to Hilda and back. "When the time comes, that is."

"I'll be there tomorrow," I said. "Thank you."

Hilda reached for my hand and squeezed it. "You've made an old lady happy, dear."

Less than an hour later, I, as a bridesmaid, stood beside the matron of honor—Reaghan—as we watched Cassie and Whit pledge to love, honor, and cherish one another for the rest of their lives.

I glanced from them to peek at the crowd, my gaze falling first on Seth. He looked tired and frazzled, but happier than I'd ever seen him. He and Colinda exchanged a private smile as the pastor read the vows to Whit and Cassie. Fortunately, as I suspected, Gwendolyn Crinshaw Bealle's will had stipulated that if Benny were no longer alive to need her home and money, it would all go to Seth. He'd sold the house and closed the accounts, enabling him to attend college with only minor debt. As for Holland Greer, I'd been wrong. He hadn't had anything to do with the evil at the bluff. However, he served six months in prison for stealing historical artifacts before being released for good behavior. Within the month, he secured permission from his parole agent and the courts to move away.

I veered my focus to the other side of the arch, where Clay stood, wiping a lone tear as he witnessed his mother's happiness. Love washed over me. He had recently begun his third and final year of law school, after which he planned to move back to Williamsport, hang a shingle, and secure several clients in the District. Most of his time, however, would be spent managing a nonprofit we hoped to found together to help wounded warriors. The gold buried in the tunnels at *Crossings*—and which took more than two months to unearth—was not stolen from the Dahlonaga mint all those years ago. Federal investigators could not determine who had originally acquired it, but the court decided it was stolen from that recipient by Thaddeus Fleming Calhoun. After several months, the courts finally awarded it to me with the provision that it be used for charitable work. We planned to name the nonprofit the Fletcher Foundation, after Kate's father who was killed in Iraq fighting terror.

As for me, I couldn't be happier. The house, school, and now Hilda's offer filled me with hope. And, Clay and I talked about getting engaged after he was done with law school.

Thanks to my ability, I know departed loved ones are still with me—Jack, Mom, Julie, Kate, Will, Mason, the others. They're all with me, wherever I go.

I gripped my flower bouquet tighter to wrap my fingers around the cross tucked within its cavities. Cassie wanted Reaghan and me to wear matching necklaces, so I had removed Grandma Sadie's cross but didn't have the heart to leave it in a drawer. Sure, I know now it harbors no spiritual or magical power. It was a symbol, nothing more. A reminder of love and trust.

I'm still not sure what all happened to me in *Crossings*, on the battlefield, or at Chocton Bluff. What was real? What wasn't? Except for Clay, the others were left with nothing more than recollections of a violent storm and a raging fire, both of which time has softened and distorted in their memories.

Most of what happened could have been avoided, and looking back, I see I put many people I loved in jeopardy. However, Pastor Dale eased my mind when, at the right time, right place, he quoted this passage from the Bible: "Forget the former things; do not dwell on the past."

When I think about the forces at play in the unseen world beside and around us—demons waiting to pounce, evil struggling to gain hold, battles carried out like those on Chocton Bluff—I begin to shake with realization that the realm of the demonic exists. I had been privy to that world, had seen how it disrupts and attacks the oneness and the holiness that we are supposed to live out in our daily lives. It's a dimension of evil that, for the most part, is incomprehensible. But I now know I am protected from those rulers and cosmic powers over this present darkness, and from the spiritual forces of evil in the heavenly places.

I do not have all the answers, but I do believe I could have addressed it all with trust, as Will had encouraged me to do many times. It wasn't until after Chocton Bluff crumbled, Josiah Sawyer was eradicated and Mason moved on, that the message finally made sense: Trusting is more important than seeing and verifying.

I wept a tear of happiness as Whit kissed his bride.

The past, the wrongs, have been dissolved, left behind in the mystic.

The End

We are pleased to present an excerpt from another Brimstone Fiction Book, *The Healer's Rune,* by Lauricia Matuska.

THE HEALER'S RUNE

by Lauricia Matuska

CHAPTER ONE

Sabine huddled in a window niche, her knees pulled up to her chin and her teary gaze not quite focused on the dark ruins around her. She knew it was time to go—lingering would certainly mean capture—but she could not force herself to rush to her friend's death.

A stone's throw in front of her, a shower of brick dust rained onto the floor. Sabine started, her muscles tensing as her thoughts ratcheted from mourning to high alert.

Straining to hear beyond the thump of her pulse, she concentrated on identifying the sounds that surrounded her. Crickets and frogs chirped in the grass ... an occasional bird chittered drowsily overhead ... a breeze rustled leaves nearby ... all normal sounds, characteristic of the forest just before dawn.

She pulled her cloak closed around her.

Probably a mouse, she reasoned as she scanned the shadows for a safe explanation. Or a night-cat stalking one last meal. Still ...

The air felt heavier, as if another presence stood close by.

But that was silly. The Dryht castle was long abandoned and was not haunted by its former inhabitants. Sabine stood to leave. Whatever had just happened, she didn't appear to be in immediate danger. That would change, however, if she were late to the execution.

Before she took a step, a quiet noise scraped the darkness across from her.

She peered into what was left of the ancient Dryht temple. The moon was still high enough to illuminate small patches between the oak and cedar saplings that grew among the grass-lined floor stones, but it wasn't full enough to show what moved among their needles and leaves.

Sabine tried to swallow, her mouth suddenly dry, and to reason through her fear. Although it was possible she had been discovered breaking curfew, it was not likely. All of the Rüddan stationed in her village were busy preparing for the execution.

Sabine shifted her weight, angling for a better view. An explosion of snapping twigs and flapping wings made her jump, a surprised shout catching in her throat. She flinched as a raven the size of a large cat landed nearby.

Sabine relaxed.

Just a bird.

Still … why did she feel as if she was not alone?

Cocking its head, the raven focused on Sabine. Intelligence gleamed in the blue depths of its eye. The directness of its avian inspection felt sinister, somehow, as if confirming local rumors that the birds were used as Dryht spies.

Stop it! Sabine chided herself. Just because her neighbors mistrusted the birds, that did not make the rumors true. The villagers of Khapor told many stories of hauntings in the woods, but Sabine had yet to experience one.

The raven stared, showing no signs of moving.

"Whoever you are looking for," Sabine said to the bird, "is not here. No one has been here for a few years, since the plague that wiped out most of the Dryht race. Well, no one except me."

As if pondering her inconceivable flaunting of the law, the bird cocked its head to the other side, leveling a green eye at her this time.

This difference in eye color unsettled her.

"I am pleased to have met you, I'm sure," she stammered, attempting to mask a growing sense of trepidation with a show of wit and bravado. "However, the sun is rising, and I am expected in the village."

A sudden vision of ravens feasting on her friend's body after the execution silenced her. Turning away from the bird, she hurried out of the temple.

More unnerved than she cared to admit, she picked her way carefully through the dead Dryht castle, the crumbled ruins of their city, and their memory-haunted wood. Outside the forest, she passed her house and continued along the road to the point where it dropped down the side of a hill that overlooked the village of Khapor.

She paused to remove her cloak before descending. The sun had risen and the air was warming quickly. Draping the cloak over one arm, she squinted through the white glare of the autumn sun, surveyed the narrow smudge of ocean on the distant horizon, then focused, with a complicated mixture of pity and disgust, on the village below.

Typical Human village. Sabine pursed her mouth. From this vantage point, Khapor did not look so bad. She could hardly see the slump of ramshackle hovels squished together as if huddling for protection. She could not yet discern the stench of salt and mold eating at wet, rotting wood, either. But even from this distance, she could see the Tower.

The Tower of the Rüddan rose above the village, its black stone bulk hovering over the enfeebled huts like a vulture waiting for something to die, patient and at ease, certain of the outcome. Sabine shivered, chilled by the view despite the morning's warmth. Most humans looked upon the Towers in their villages as symbols of peace and protection, but she knew them to be links in the chain of human enslavement. And people wondered why she lived so far away.

Sabine sighed. Directing reluctant steps down the steep hill, she plodded on, to the village of Khapor and to the execution of her friend.

Humans hurried along dirt roads, radiating a hushed sense of urgency. Clustered in groups of twos and threes, they kept their heads bowed in the proper gesture of humility, avoiding the attention of pale-skinned Rüddan guards posted at every other corner.

Sabine slowed to avoid one such group—an unchaperoned trio of sisters gossiping in a loud undertone. She was in no mood to deal with people right then. Especially not those three. Even so, a moist breeze reeking of dead fish blew their words to her ears.

"They say Mariel can read," the oldest murmured. "The Rüddan found scrolls covered with writing in her father's house."

Sabine tensed slightly. It was not hard to hide the ability to read; she had been doing it for years. But to actually possess anything with writing on it? Why would Mariel take such a foolish risk?

"What was she thinking?" Danelle, the village dairywoman, exclaimed in a tone too light to be genuinely surprised. "I don't know what could have possessed her."

Although she hated to admit it, Sabine had to agree. The ban on reading was the Rüddan's most strictly enforced law. If Mariel was truly guilty of breaking it, she risked exposing Humanity to the one thing that could destroy their alliance with the Rüddan. As much as she despised the Rüddan for enslaving her people, the alliance was the only reason Humankind still existed.

Danelle's younger sister gasped. "Oh, do you think that's it? Could she be possessed? Maybe she learned to read so she could practice magic? What if she was trying to summon a Dryht? Or, worse yet, an Aethel?"

"Idiot," the oldest sister sneered. "The Aethel are extinct."

"I know that," the younger girl snapped. "But she could summon their spirits. That's why they're called daemons."

Danelle nodded. "Could be. In that case, it's a good thing they caught her. If you ask me, they will end her torture too swiftly. If she was trying to summon an Aethel, they should make it last for years."

An image of her friend languishing through years of pain ambushed Sabine's imagination. Tears rose in her eyes.

Sabine blinked the tears away. She had already spent the night crying at the temple in the forest. There would be more tears later, to be sure, but now was not the time to indulge. Her grief would only draw attention.

"I wonder if her friend Sabine knows magic, too." Danelle's younger sister shivered, her tone of scandalized delight carrying clearly to Sabine's ears. "Elise says she talks to daemons."

She says what?

"Elise says she does more than that," Danelle said. "She told me her sister goes into the haunted wood almost every night. Mark my words: it is Sabine's execution we will be attending next."

Sabine's pulse quickened. If her sister was already spreading this idea, then it wouldn't be so easy for her to hide the fact that she could read, after all. Seething silently, Sabine resolved to be extra cautious for a while lest Danelle's prediction come true.

The prevailing breeze stilled for a moment, allowing a miasma of sewage and mold to collect between the small, crowded houses. Breathing in measured gasps, Sabine could not decide which was more unpleasant, the smell or the conversation, but she was ready to be rid of both.

Danelle pressed her hands to her hips and arched her spine, as if to stretch her lower back, then twisted from side to side. Using the motion of her twists to look behind her, she noticed Sabine. Her expression changed to one of facetious delight as, touching an arm of each sister, she brought the group to a halt. Since avoiding them would raise suspicion, Sabine was forced to join them.

"Welcome, Healer," Danelle said when Sabine reached them.

"Dairywoman." Sabine returned the greeting but did not stop walking.

Danelle and her sisters separated to let Sabine pass, then flanked her.

"Beautiful day for an execution," Danelle remarked casually, matching her steps to Sabine's.

Sabine glanced sideways. A faint glimmer of challenge sparked like green fire in the dairywoman's eyes.

"What's it like to be the only remaining healer of Khapor?" Danelle stared at Sabine as if watching for a reaction. "Think you can keep up with it?"

Sabine set her lips in a line, trying to control her expression. "I am not the only one."

"You will be in a few hours."

"There is still Auda."

Danelle snorted. "Ha! That old invalid? She can't even stand straight. Auda may be a master suited for teaching, but her healing days are over."

Sabine stiffened, stung by the deliberate jab at her friend. "Even if that were true, you need not worry." Sabine slowly dropped her gaze to Danelle's distended belly. "I'll be by to check on you and the baby next week, just like I said."

Danelle covered her abdomen with both hands as if to protect the unborn child. Her eyes narrowed. "We'll see."

Resisting the urge to spite her patient, Sabine quickened her stride, forcing Danelle and her sisters to scramble to keep up. Matching their steps to hers, they rushed between two corner shops and into the village square.

A large tract of land at the heart of Khapor, the square was outlined by Human shops on all four sides and pierced at its core by the Tower of the Rüddan. Fey soldiers stood at attention everywhere, spaced evenly in front of the shops and upon the battlements of the Tower. A small crowd of Humans already gathered on three of the four dirt roads that edged the Tower, separating it from the other buildings.

Sabine grimaced. She had planned to stand beside the window of the weaver's shop, where she would not be able to see what was about to happen, but that was no longer an option since the fourth road was blocked off by guards.

Unwilling to witness more of her friend's execution than she had to, Sabine claimed a position near the potter's shop—as far away from the gallows platform as she could go without attracting attention.

The Tower soared before her, a thick column of obsidian shrouded in a dull finish that absorbed the light. It cast a pall over all that surrounded it. A solid gallows built from oak perched like a skeletal bird of prey upon a raised platform to the immediate left of the Tower's entrance. Danelle and her sisters scurried across the square to claim a spot at its base.

Sabine scowled at their backs. What's the use of saving life when the Rüddan can take it away so easily? *Am I the only one who can see this is wrong?*

Overhead, a circling gull keened mournfully.

"You look like you're in need of company."

Sabine turned toward the familiar voice. "Tayte."

The old potter smiled, his lined face folding in small wrinkles that threatened to hide his eyes. "You seem to have found the best spot in the square. May I join you?"

"Of course, but I don't think we'll be able to see much once everyone arrives."

"Perfect." Tayte shifted his weight, positioning himself beside her with a sigh. They stood together in silence, watching the crowd expand.

"Lelia could never tolerate public executions," Tayte commented as he scrutinized the growing mass of Humans. The square was almost full. "They made her sick for days."

"Your wife was an exceptional woman." Sabine watched Danelle laugh with her sisters, wishing they could at least show some reverence for the life about to be sacrificed. "She saw the truth of things in a way most of us cannot."

"That she did." Something about the tone of Tayte's voice captured Sabine's attention. "It is a burdensome gift, really. What do you do with the truth once you find it?"

Sabine glanced at the potter to find him studying her with a sideways look. Did he expect an answer?

Regarding the crowd once more, Tayte shook his head. "Some

people see the truth but choose to ignore it. Others spend their lives fighting for it. Lelia was one of these. You remind me of her."

Sabine nodded. She knew she should thank the potter for his compliment, but she was not sure she could trust herself to speak. She did not even have the courage to watch her friend's impending death—how could she dream of fighting for truth?

Unwilling to follow that thought any further, Sabine returned to watching the crowd. Her attention was caught by her former betrothed and her sister, who pressed through the crowd until they stood in front of her and to the right. They gave no indication of having seen her, for which she was glad. The one thing she did not need was a public confrontation with Elise and Kenrick.

Sabine studied the two of them for a moment, frowning. Although it still hurt to think about how Kenrick had given her up and gone after Elise, that wasn't what bothered her. Something else was wrong.

"Mother."

"What?" Tayte glanced at her.

"I was told this is a mandatory execution." Sabine kept her voice low.

"It is. Why?"

The village blacksmith pushed against Sabine, jostling his way through the throng until he could go no further. Stopping directly in front of her, he blocked her view of the gallows.

Sabine shuffled a step closer to Tayte. "Ever since my father's death, my mother has been very careful to observe every aspect of Rüddan law. She even moved in with my sister and Kenrick before my father was buried, instead of using the sennight of grace given for finding a chaperone. I see Elise and Kenrick in front of us, but I cannot find my mother."

"No time to worry about that now." Tayte inclined his head toward the gallows.

Two large doors at the base of the Tower swung open, revealing a dozen Rüddan guards clad in black chain mail and burgundy surcoats, each emblazoned across the chest with a silver griffin clutching a boar. They moved forward in unison, a living box.

Instantly, the crowd fell silent, hushed by a sense of eager anticipation. As a single entity, it drew back, the front rows pressing together as if to let the soldiers pass, unhindered, to the gallows. More guards took up positions around the square, blocking all the roads to the village.

Sabine stood on tiptoe to peer over the blacksmith. What she saw drew an involuntary groan from her soul.

Bound at the wrists, gagged, and wearing only a soiled, ragged shift, Mariel was hardly recognizable. Her face was a swollen mass of bruises and blood. One cheek sagged in as if the bone beneath it were broken. Blue-black splotches covered her arms, crisscrossed by scabbed or bleeding welts. Her legs trembled as she approached the platform, but she held her back straight. Despite her mangled state, she drew near the platform with dignity.

The Rüddan guards guided her up the steps to the stage in front of the gallows. She collapsed at the top of the stairs, as if what little strength she possessed had been spent on the climb. Sabine started forward, wanting to rush to her aid, but stopped when Tayte placed a hand on her arm.

The soldier nearest Mariel grabbed her by the hair, pulling her upright as she scrambled weakly to regain her footing. She stood, wobbly and unsure, but on her own. As regally as her disfigured body would allow, she crossed the platform in front of the gallows.

The squad of soldiers was dismissed by another Rüddan, this one bearing the three silver caltraps of a captain on his surcoat and a long sword on his hip.

Sabine held her breath.

The Rüddan captain spoke clearly, his heavily accented words projecting throughout the square. "Mariel, daughter of Brock, you stand accused of treason against the crown and kingdoms of the Empress of all Ceryn Roh. Confess your crimes here, before your people, and death will find you quickly."

Silence fell upon the square, the entire village stilling to hear Mariel's reply. She stood for a moment, as if in contemplation, then rose as tall and straight as her tortured form would allow and spit her defiance into the Rüddan captain's face.

The crowd gasped. Shouts of indignation spread throughout the mob.

The captain struck Mariel in the mouth, snapping her head to the side with the strength of his blow. Blood erupted from her split lip, but she did not cry out.

Sabine closed her eyes and sank back onto her heels, using the blacksmith to obscure her view once more.

A few moments later, Mariel did scream, signaling that the torture had begun. Sabine squeezed her eyes shut, determined not to witness the atrocity. Somehow, though, her action felt like a betrayal, as if by not watching, she was forsaking Mariel.

Suddenly, Sabine regretted her decision to hide from the execution. She might not be able to help her friend, but she would not abandon her.

Wiping a tear from her cheek, Sabine stood on tiptoe again. Three guards surrounded Mariel now, shearing away jagged clumps of her long black hair while the captain moved to the front of the dais. "Mariel Brockselle has been tried and found guilty of magic use and conspiring with the Dryht. For these treasons, she is hereby sentenced to death by the Empress of all Ceryn Roh. Let this be an example to any who would emulate her."

"Treason and magic use are easy to claim," Sabine muttered, "and almost impossible to disprove. I wonder what she really did."

Tayte shot Sabine a warning glance. "Be careful. The ears surrounding us are not all friendly."

Sabine clamped her mouth closed. His chastisement stung, but he was right. Chagrined, she stared at the platform again, but her toes were getting tired. Glancing around the blacksmith, she noticed an empty space beside him where she would just fit.

"Excuse me for a minute," she whispered to Tayte as she darted into the empty spot.

"Sabine!" Tayte hissed as she passed. "What are you doing?"

Now that she had a clear view, Sabine saw two of the Rüddan tying Mariel to one of the posts that supported the gallows. But Mariel could not see her, and she needed to. How else would she know she was not in this alone?

"I'll be back," Sabine whispered over her shoulder to Tayte. Something gleamed in the potter's eyes—some emotion she could not identify, but it made no difference.

One of the soldiers turned away from Mariel, just beyond Sabine's field of vision, then turned back to her, holding something that looked like a smooth stick about the length of a Human's arm and the width of three fingers. He swung it, making a slashing motion across Mariel's upper arm, but it did not seem to touch her. Even so, Mariel flinched, her face contorting with the effort of hiding the pain as several rips slashed the fabric of her sleeve, revealing pink, torn skin.

Magic!

The soldier swiped the stick at her again. This time Mariel screamed.

Somehow, Sabine had to get closer.

The next few moments were a confusion of pressing bodies and heart-wrenching sounds of pain as Sabine slid between people, working her way forward. She tried to catch her friend's gaze whenever Mariel looked into the crowd, but she was still too far away.

Each time Sabine found a new opening to move into, her movement was accompanied by a new sound proclaiming Mariel's pain. It became like a dance, almost. A sickening, terrifying funeral dance beating to the time of her heart. Scan the crowd (one, two) … fill the space (one, two) … Cue the groans (one, two) … and repeat.

Sabine had no choice but to participate.

She hesitated only once, when her next step would have placed her right in front of her former betrothed and her sister. Instead of that, she chose to wait, missing the next few thumping beats as she waited for the crowd to part in the other direction. As she did, she stared at Mariel, willing her friend to notice her, to look into the Human crowd and notice that she was there.

As if in response, Mariel looked up, the desperation in her eyes clear. She glanced in Sabine's direction for a moment but gave no indication that she saw her.

The crowd shifted, as if agitated by the focus of Mariel's gaze, and fell unnaturally still. Noticing the resentment on the faces of those she passed, Sabine flinched. Rather than growing silent out of respect for Mariel, they were snubbing her, divorcing themselves from her so as to not be guilty of any part of her death.

And she had very nearly done the same thing.

Chagrined, Sabine fought even harder to get close to the stage.

Another cry of pain splintered the silence of the crowd. Sabine jumped. Trying to not gag on the cloying scent of blood that now saturated the air, she looked to the sky. She found a group of swans flying overhead and began to count the birds in an effort to ignore the bile building in her stomach. She counted thirty-four before the next scream reverberated off the shops.

She was close to the stage now—so close that she could hear the ragged gasping of Mariel's breath, could count the small, whimpering sounds that escaped her lips with each exhale.

I am here, my friend. Sabine stared hard at Mariel, thinking the thought so strongly that she felt it as a scream. Mariel did not look at her, she did not respond in any way, but Sabine kept thinking, *I am here, and you're not alone.*

The Rüddan captain stepped up to Mariel once more, signaling to the guards to step back.

"As you are convicted of two crimes against the Empress," he began, projecting his voice all of the way back to the shops, "you will be given two chances to repent. Do you have anything to confess?"

Ever so slowly, Mariel lifted her head. She studied the captain through swollen eyes, as if trying to focus through her pain, then shifted her gaze out over the crowd. At last, she looked directly at Sabine.

Sabine returned the look, staring hard at her friend and wishing that, by doing so, she could share some of her strength.

"It's all a lie," Mariel croaked as if speaking only to Sabine. The expression on her face grew stronger, more determined.

The Rüddan captain struck his hand across her mouth again. Once again her head snapped to the side, propelled by the force of his fist. Once again Mariel bled, and once again she screamed. Only this time, her screams were words.

"Everything you think you know is a lie!"

The captain hit her harder this time, aiming for her temple. She moved just enough for his fist to catch her cheekbone instead.

All around Sabine, people in the crowd started to grumble.

"Question them," Mariel screamed, staring directly at Sabine again. "Question everything."

The ring of a sword being drawn sliced the air, resounding over the growing mumbles of the crowd. Mariel's words were upsetting the people. Was that because she dared to speak against the Rüddan or because the Humans believed her?

"Search for the truth!" Mariel screamed as the Rüddan captain raised his sword over his head. "Don't believe everything they tell you."

Bringing his sword down, the Rüddan swung at Mariel's head. The swift motion looked gracefully languid, like a feinting motion meant only to scare, and at first it appeared to Sabine that nothing had happened. A moment later, though, Mariel's head toppled to the ground and her body slumped in the ropes that strapped her to the leg of the gallows.

Instantly, the crowd stilled.

Sabine gasped. Unable to look away, she gazed miserably upon the bleeding, shattered form of her friend. Why was it suddenly so hard to breathe?

The captain signaled and, in a flurry of burgundy activity, Rüddan guards surged across the stage to attend to the remains of Mariel. Rather than watch them, Sabine looked down, inspecting the pebbles sprinkled upon the ground. The stones blurred and wavered as she choked on the sobs she tried to hide. *Goodbye, my friend. May the Morning Star welcome you with open arms.*

Two soldiers hung Mariel's limp body upon the gallows, stretching the noose to fit under her arms while the Rüddan officer stepped forward once more. He glared over the Human crowd from the center of the platform. "The body of Mariel Brockselle shall hang on display for a sennight. Anyone attempting to remove it will be raised beside her."

He scanned the group before him, as if seeking dissension, then nodded. The guards that blocked the roads moved aside, allowing the crowd to exit the square. People pushed past Sabine, sauntering like gorged wolves into the streets of Khapor.

Sabine watched them go, too heartsick to bother getting out of their way until Tayte was suddenly there, taking her arm.

"Mariel fought well." Tayte spoke in an undertone, his tenor voice deep with reverence. "Her death was noble, despite their efforts."

Sabine nodded. Powerful fists of nausea assailed her, accompanied by fury and the helpless hate she harbored for the Rüddan. At that moment, she could not decide whom she despised more, the Rüddan who butchered her friend or the Humans who allowed it, but one thing she knew for sure.

She had to learn the truth.

www.ingramcontent.com/pod-product-compliance
Lightning Source LLC
Chambersburg PA
CBHW022151170626
46807CB00005B/2162